This is my Song

By Miranda Shisler

ISBN- 9798387203244
Cover art copyright © 2017 Kathleen Kirtland Photography
kathleenkirtlandphotography.wordpress.com

Published in the United States of America by Miranda Shisler

Miranda Shisler
mirandashisler.blogspot.com

For Erin, since every tortured artist needs a friend who loves intentionally.

 *Chicago, Illinois*

Prologue

That fated day, she'd worn new shoes, though it would have been more practical to wear comfortable shoes for walking in downtown Chicago. Since her fiancé would be there, she decided to go against her better judgment. She hadn't seen him in weeks. Wouldn't he be pleased to glance down and see the fashionable leather clinging to her ankles? Proud she was to be his wife?

Now her reasoning seemed silly. Costly.

The faces of dying children haunted her thoughts. One didn't soon forget the innocent despair in their vulnerable expressions. Nobody knew this better than Beatrice.

Maybe if she'd been more prudent, one of the children would have lived to see the dawn of the next day. Maybe she would have had the footing in the mass panic to grab hold of the boy.

Her vanity had come at a much higher price than she could have known.

Smoke lingered against the ceiling of the makeshift hospital, which was set up in the restaurant next door to the ruined theater. She couldn't move. She could barely breathe as she lay on the cold table. Her chest constricted with an impossible pain, warning her of the inevitable. She would die, just like all those helpless children.

It was just as well, for the ache in her soul wanted nothing more.

One

December 25, 1903

Beatrice hadn't been to a theater in all her nineteen years. For Christmas, her parents had given her and her ten-year-old brother, James, tickets to the downtown Chicago production of *Mr. Bluebeard*. She'd been thrilled. Especially when she realized they had bought a ticket for her fiancé, Edward, as well.

"He will be home in time, won't he, dear?" her mother had asked that quiet Christmas morning as they exclaimed over the gift.

"Oh, yes! These are for the Wednesday matinee. He promised he would be stepping off the train and into my arms Tuesday evening," Beatrice said happily.

"Good," Mother answered, smiling her easy grin that always made Beatrice feel calm. Not that she had anything to feel uneasy about. Little had ever gone wrong in her life. She had everything she could possibly need or want.

"I know it will be quite a haul, heading downtown from the Pullman Row station, but I told your mother it was worth it to see your happiness." Father winked at them. "I know you both love your music and dance."

"We sure do!" Jamie danced around the parlor to prove it.

"And not only that, you both have the determination and focus required to excel at musical pursuits," their mother reminded them in her best teacher's voice.

"Thank you for thinking of us," Beatrice stood to hug her father tightly, breathing in the familiar scent of his hair tonic as he held her.

"Hopefully it will inspire your own music," he said next to her ear. He pulled back and squeezed her hands. "Do play us a Christmas song. Both of you. Something from *The Messiah*, maybe?"

Beatrice nodded and went to the piano with Jamie. She pulled out several dog-eared pages of music, though neither of them needed them. They shared a conspiratorial smile and began in unison at exactly the same point within their favorite piece.

Their fingers flew the length of the piano in a rousing homage to their craft. Their parents watched proudly as Beatrice once again felt appreciation for her mother's patient and expert instruction. And what of her father, setting aside hard-earned dollars as a factory supervisor to take them to an amusing play downtown? Could she be any happier?

And life would only become more exciting in four days when Edward returned and they began to plan their wedding.

♫

Wednesday, December 30, 1903, dawned cold and dreary. Beatrice felt a twinge of annoyance when she glanced out her window. She had expected the weather to match their excitement with plenty of sunshine and a milder temperature. Instead, the dreary clouds seemed to carry an innate warning.

She fumed at the gray sky as she dressed in her nicest for-good dress, a burgundy broadcloth skirt paired with a white silk shirtwaist. The skirt clung to her figure perfectly, as if she was a model in an advertisement. Mother was a whiz with a sewing machine – no one would ever suspect they were penny-pinchers. The painstaking lace edges of Beatrice's collar and sleeves rivaled the most expensive Paris fashions.

She eyed her boots and felt a thrill. The fashionable shoes pinched her toes something fierce, but she would sacrifice for the chance to look as good as any other young lady attending the theater with her beau.

She styled her hair and adjusted her wide-brimmed straw hat adorned with white silk flowers. She couldn't help her smile, bordering on smug as she stared at her reflection with approval. It was to be a grand day no matter what the weather might want her to believe.

"Time to go, Beatrice!" Her father called up the stairs. "We don't want to miss the first acts."

She hurried down the stairs even as she winced at the stiffness of her new boots. Her feet would be aching by the time they met Edward at the train station, but she didn't care.

"Oh my dear, you are beautiful," her mother said, hugging her as she reached the bottom of the staircase. Jamie whistled his approval.

"Edward will scarcely be able to breathe," her father said as he helped her into her corduroy velvet coat.

They marched out of their house toward the train station two blocks away. Their train ride into the city would take an hour, but Beatrice didn't mind at all. Edward would be there.

She'd only seen him for a few moments the night before when he'd arrived home. He'd been whisked home by his family, so they'd only been allowed a moment for greetings. Today, she would have him to herself, and she couldn't wait.

She saw his face as they were purchasing their train fares. She forgot her uncomfortable shoes and ran to him. He picked her up and swung her around, paying no mind to a few disgruntled women who disapproved of the public display.

"My love!" Edward laughed and tweaked her nose as he set her down. "We are finally together again."

She smiled and took his hand, whirling in a circle so he could see her outfit. His mild-mannered expression took on an extra hint of shine, and his voice was a bit enraptured when he spoke.

"You are a vision."

She took his arm as they went to join her family in line. "I'm so glad you're home. Summer and fall were dreadfully dull without you."

"Believe me, I agree," he said. He sneaked a brief kiss as her father turned the other direction, watching the train approach the station. "Nobody in the army is as pretty as you."

Her cheeks went hot. He'd kissed her properly only once, when he'd proposed, as he was leaving for Camp Lincoln that June. She'd been dreaming about that kiss ever since.

"Are you excited about the theater?" Edward asked in a breathless voice, as if he was trying to find a safer topic. They stepped forward as the train heaved into the station, and she felt a blast of cold air against her face.

"Ever so excited," she answered, meeting his gaze directly to let him know he need not be embarrassed. "I've never been to the theater before."

"I just know you'll love it," he said as he helped her into the train car.

"So are you glad to be home?" Beatrice settled in the seat opposite Edward and next to her brother while her parents took the window seats.

"After six months of waking up every day resigned to the possibility of dying, I woke up this morning knowing death wasn't on the schedule. Only you."

Beatrice reached and grasped his hand. "I'm glad you're home safely." She didn't mention her doubt that he was truly in danger much of the time. Edward had the tendency to dabble in the dramatic from time to time.

The ride was pleasant and seemed to pass in no time. Before any of them realized it, they were coming into Randolph Street station. The train stopped with a great production of noise and steam while Beatrice and her family made their way to the nearest exit.

Space on the train was tight. Beatrice wondered if there must be quite a few headed to the Iroquois Theatre that Wednesday afternoon. She tried to stay close to Edward, but bodies were packed together so closely she lost hold of him. She had a moment of panic before she found her way to the door and spotted Edward just ahead, looking for her.

"Okay?" He grasped her hand firmly, pulled her through the door and out of the press of people. He traced her jaw in concern.

She nodded and blew out a long breath. "Thought I might be flattened into a pancake for a moment."

He chuckled and tucked her hand under his arm. They turned to find the rest of the family. "Don't worry. That won't happen while I'm alive to protect you."

It seemed a strange way to word his easy promise, but she shook off the peculiar feeling that creeped over her.

Immediately as they turned down Randolph Street, Beatrice regretted her shoes, which Edward had not noticed as she'd hoped. The new leather was unforgiving on her feet, and they quickly began to ache. She held Edward's arm tightly and tried to paste a smile on her face.

It was only a five-minute walk to the theater from the train station, though it felt much longer in the shoes. They had to wait in line in the cold as patrons filed through the entrance to the Iroquois.

Beatrice gasped, unprepared for the splendor. The size and grandeur of the lobby made her feel dizzy.

"Are you going to faint?" Her mother squeezed her hand.

Beatrice scoffed. "I never faint."

Her father jabbed Edward with his elbow. "Remember, Ed, this lady doesn't faint, and don't ever dare suggest she does."

They all laughed as Beatrice held her nose in the air. She hid her own smile out of principle.

"Laugh if you must, but Beatrice has never been ill a day in her life," her mother said with a proud smile.

"Let's not tempt fate." Beatrice quipped as she turned in a circle to comprehend the opulent surroundings.

"Where do we go from here?" Beatrice's mother held Jamie's hand as if she were afraid she'd lose him in the throng of people passing them.

"I believe we take the stairs up to the dress circle. The second floor," Edward said confidently. They followed him up the cool marble staircase. Beatrice's new shoes tapped on each step.

They found their seats on the far side of the dress circle, near the back. The seats weren't the best view, but they were the most her father could afford, so Beatrice exclaimed over the view they had of the orchestra seats and the stage. "No balcony for us! We're regular theater-going folk, sitting in the dress circle with all the fancy ladies and gents."

Her father smiled in appreciation, his eyes shining. Edward stared at her adoringly and squeezed her hand as she sat down.

Mrs. Walsh set her arm on the back of Jamie's chair and sighed with relief. "I'm just glad not to be pressed into that crowd any longer."

"It's quite full," Beatrice agreed. She watched the people continue to pour into the theater – mostly women and children, she noted. The matinee must be a popular time for city mothers or nannies to bring their children to the theater. Beatrice's eyes caught on a baby fussing several rows up in front of them.

"I hope the baby is quiet during the show," Jamie said in a quiet voice.

Soon the thick curtain glided back, and the lights went down. The doors to the dress circle closed with a strong click, as if they'd been locked, as the light from the Grand Stairway disappeared. Beatrice frowned. The sound had a finality she didn't like. She shook off the feeling and sat up, determined to act like a regular attendee who knew what she was doing.

Music sprang up from the orchestra below, frenzied and cheerful. The crowd quieted as the performers entered the stage. Beatrice felt a thrill when Edward's hand sneaked over the armrest between them and his fingers intertwined with hers. She leaned toward him, so their shoulders pressed together. She had trouble focusing on the performers after that.

The acts moved quickly. The crowd frequently erupted into

laughter or applause. Beatrice could see why the show was good for children. Jamie jumped out of his seat several times, clapping his hands in delight, especially when Eddie Foy, the comedian, came out as *Sister Anne* with his *pet elephant.*

A mellow group followed the riotous act. Eight couples stood in their places waiting to perform their song and dance. The lights changed, making the actors seem like they were swathed in shafts of moonlight.

Suddenly something caught Beatrice's attention to the left of the stage.

"Did you see that?" she asked Edward. He craned his neck to see what she meant. She leaned closer to him, sure she had seen a flash of light and a scurry of motion just inside the heavy curtain.

She didn't realize it at that moment, but the next ten minutes would change forever the lives of every one of the thousands of people in the theater that afternoon.

When it became clear that something was happening behind the curtain, the singers tried to calm the crowd. Eddie Foy came back to the stage and assured them nothing was wrong; they should stay seated. Beatrice felt a chill at the advice. She stared at the darkness where the closed door would be and had a sinking feeling they should leave immediately. She smelled smoke.

"Don't worry," her father leaned over Edward to assure them. "The curtain is made of special material. In the event of a fire, it will be closed and the flames will not spread."

"They say this theater is fire-proof, in fact." Edward nodded in agreement. "I'm sure they'll get it under control without incident."

Beatrice forced a smile, but she held his hand tighter. She could sense a growing unease in the sea of patrons.

Everything began to happen so quickly that no one had a chance to think rationally. First, people started moving toward the doors.

"The doors are locked!" A woman yelled as a man pulled at the door handles and tried to open them. "Someone locked us in!

Why would they do that?"

Panic ensued.

Beatrice glanced at her family members. Father eyed the people frantically trying to open the heavy doors that separated them from the staircase leading down to the exit. "Perhaps we should make our way outside, everyone," he said with forced cheerfulness. Beatrice knew he was trying not to worry them or scare Jamie. They stood and moved with the rest of the crowd until they were part of the mass of humanity pressed against the doors, waiting for someone to open them.

People grew more panicked by the second. Out of nowhere, an intense boom and what looked like a wall of fire shot forth from the stage. Beatrice stared in disbelief as it hit the people still sitting in the first rows and whooshed back through the theater.

"Get down!" her father commanded sternly and they all dropped to the ground. The blaze went over their heads, bringing with it bodies of those who had instantly died as they were swept up by the fireball.

There was no time to gather their wits. The entire mass of people remaining in the theater burst into crazed desperation. Screaming and pushing, the people became a wall, pushing toward another exit that someone had managed to pry open, only to have it close and lock again.

"Where do we go?" A woman cried out. Beatrice saw she was the mother of the baby who had been fussing before the performance. "How will we get out?"

The mother held her little one so tightly he cried breathlessly. In fact, they all began to cough from the smoke and fumes traveling up into the balcony. Beatrice's lungs felt like they were on fire.

Beatrice has never been sick a day in her life. Her mother's words, spoken so innocently, haunted her.

"We're all going to die!" Another woman screamed, clawing at the wall of people as she tried to get through. Beatrice frantically searched for signs above the many doors covered in heavy draperies and ornate décor. But there were no visible marked exits. No ushers remained behind to direct them safely out of the theater.

There was only madness.

Someone finally pried open the door, but the people pressed toward it too forcefully, creating a terrible tangle of bodies. People became wedged together in the small opening. The doors had been designed to open inward instead of outward.

Beatrice tried to hold on to Edward's hand, but the sheer power of the crowd tore them apart. She screamed as he disappeared into the sea of people. She turned in time to see the rest of her family pushed back toward the balcony.

"Jamie!" she screamed as she watched in horror. Too light to hold his footing, he lost his balance and fell over the side of the balcony into an equally crazed mob below.

Her parents tried to stay together as they leaned over the balcony and searched for any sign that their son had survived the fall. Her mother was heaving great sobs that broke Beatrice's heart at the same time she felt a surge of righteous anger. If the people would just be calm and consider others around them, there would be no need for anyone else to die.

She tried to swim through the crowd toward her parents, but instead she found herself lifted off the ground. At the same moment, she saw a man's body fall from the uppermost balcony and land on her mother. She fell and did not rise again, trampled by the rushing mob. Her father, sobbing as he tried to reach for another woman's hand to pull her up, was pushed beneath scrambling feet and disappeared.

Beatrice was helpless, carried up and away by the crowd. Tears fell down her cheeks as she called for Edward, desperate to find him. She screamed until her parched throat would no longer utter a sound. It was useless. No one heard her in the insanity.

Finally, her feet found footing near the door, and she grabbed on to the end chair of the row. She was about to dive toward the opening in the door when the cries of a young child stopped her.

She searched for the child and saw him standing alone, pressed to the wall, his wide blue eyes full of terror.

"Help me! Please, someone help me!" He caught her gaze and reached toward her with small white hands.

She tried. She held the chair and attempted to take a step, but he was pushed under a second before she could grasp his hand.

Once again, she was at the mercy of the crowd as her feet left the ground and she traveled over the bodies, the trampled mass of humanity under their feet. Behind them, she saw a pair of little girls near the balcony, holding hands and crying. They were knocked over the side by a big man running for the exit. Beatrice would never forget the haunted surprise in their eyes as they fell. How could this happen? How could so many little ones be lost? Tossed aside as if they were garbage not worth saving? Where were the gentlemen willing to valiantly give their lives for women and children? Where was justice in this tragedy?

The last thing she saw before she blacked out was the baby. He'd been abandoned on the floor, his clothes ripped from his body under the feet of the mob. His little face was barely recognizable as human.

He was quiet. Deathly still.

Two

Dempsey, Ohio
August, 1916

"Step up, folks, and see what is coming to your town by this fall! You'll be just like city folk with your own theater with genuine performers straight from New York City! All it takes from you is a trifle donation."

Evan glanced at the small crowd that had gathered in front of the hardware store to hear the salesman's pitch. He sidestepped the scene and made his way across the street to the railroad and telegraph office.

The bell at the top of the door rang as he opened it. He hung his hat on the stand, as he had a thousand other mornings exactly like this one.

"Morning, Evan," Isaiah murmured from his desk where he studied a ledger. The older man had a pencil behind his ear and a frown on his face.

"Morning." Evan went to the small kitchen off the main room where he was glad to find coffee freshly made. He filled a mug and inhaled the scent of the strong brew. Sipping, he went to his desk in front of the telegraph machine.

"So, it sounds like another business is coming to Dempsey," he said, looking back at the growing group around the salesman.

13

"So I've been hearing for the past half-hour." Isaiah sounded as impressed as Evan felt.

"Dempsey's grown so much in the past decade," Evan mused. "Makes you wonder how much longer it will feel like a small town."

Isaiah grunted a response. Evan knew he agreed. They'd had a few conversations about how Dempsey had changed, and neither was sure it was all for the best. Once upon a time, their biggest worry had been the one saloon's influence on the town. Though they had won that battle and the owner, Rita Dolsen, had closed her brothel and left town, others had sprung up in its place. Now there were three saloons just on Main Street alone.

"Times change whether we like it or not," Isaiah murmured.

The office lapsed into silence. Evan would have preferred to keep the conversation going, but Isaiah had recently sat him down and kindly asked that Evan keep his jabbering to a minimum or Isaiah wouldn't be able to balance his figures.

Evan took a few telegraph messages and spent some time on the telephone talking to Columbus about the railway expansion project. It baffled him how he'd ended up in this office instead of working on the railroad, leading his men. When he'd been offered the office employment, it had been a promotion for a job well done. He was moving up in the world. Going places. Truth was, though, he'd just resigned himself to solitary confinement.

He looked at the clock in frustration at noon, wondering how it wasn't nearly five yet. A firm whistling met his ears and he heard a familiar stride on the boardwalk outside.

Joshua Whitley threw open the door, frowning. "Evan."

"Josh! Glad to see you. Since you got married and started having kids you never leave your farm. What brings you into town?"

Evan's best friend, Joshua, had been married to Kathleen for ten years. They had twin boys and a thriving farm, on which they regularly sheltered saloon girls desiring to safely leave their jobs. They only came to town for wagonloads of groceries and church.

"Kathleen's due any day. She wants to send a telegram to her folks in Little Sicily."

Evan nodded and turned to the telegraph machine. "Why doesn't she just use the telephone?"

Joshua nodded with a terse expression. "That was my question. Apparently, she can't hear a blessed thing on that apparatus with the boys yelling. And apparently it was insensitive of me to suggest otherwise."

Evan smiled. "What's the message? I assume it's for Amy Able and Amelia Morehouse?"

"The very same." Joshua pulled a crinkled scrap of paper from his jeans pocket. "She says: *Dear Mama and Aunt Amelia, stop. Babies due any day, stop. Come as soon as you can, stop. Joshua says he thinks these are girls. Stop. Please advise as I only know boys.*"

Evan chuckled as he tapped out the words. "She knows this is a public wire, right?"

Joshua glared. "You don't question a woman expecting any day with her second set of twins in four years."

Evan snorted. "Good point."

Joshua slammed several coins on the counter. "I'm off to the grocery. Apparently, our unborn children need pickled eggs, and the ones on our cellar shelf aren't good enough."

Evan and Isaiah laughed and bid Joshua a good day. As Evan stood to go to the other room and see if there was any more coffee, his eyes caught on a bittersweet sight.

"Ah, Beatrice," he whispered, unable to look away. The woman stepped cautiously from the back door of her apartment above the parsonage. She cast a wary eye in both directions before she hurried down the stairs and next door to the church, piano books clutched in her arms. She disappeared inside the building.

Isaiah joined him at the window. "You been pining over that girl for twelve years, Evan. Don't you want to find a good woman to share the rest of your days?"

Evan knew Isaiah only said the words out of concern for his

well-being. And if Evan was being honest, he knew his friend was right. It was well past time to let go of the dream of marrying Beatrice Walsh. She was completely uninterested. She'd turned him down so many times he'd lost count. Something wouldn't let him give up hope, no matter how many times he was disappointed.

"I think by now it's safe to say I can't let go," he answered quietly, still watching the door of the church, wishing to see her familiar form again.

He felt Isaiah's eyes on him for a long moment. Finally, the older man clapped him on the shoulder in understanding before he returned to his desk and his figures.

Five o'clock eventually arrived, as it somehow did every day, and Evan packed up his papers. He headed to the hotel next door for supper. The building was a well-maintained and cheerful house that had been converted to a hotel twenty years before by Samuel and Martha Hays. A sprawling porch surrounded the entire first floor, accented by large containers of summer flowers and comfortable rockers.

Inside, he found his usual table by the window. Martha came over with a pitcher of iced tea. "Good afternoon, Mr. Masters. How was your day?"

Evan pasted on a smile for her sake. "Not bad at all, Mrs. Hays. And how is that new grandson of yours?"

She beamed. "He's just fine. Has the proudest granddad this side of the Mississippi."

"I bet."

"And I assume you'll want the special? Chop Suey tonight." Mrs. Hays filled his glass.

"That's fine. Thanks." Evan stared out the window, trying to feel grateful. Just once, he'd like to go home and have a meal waiting for him on the stove. The stove he'd barely used in the eight years he'd been living alone in his yellow bungalow on Vine Street.

He ate his meal in silence, watching the families around him. Some came from the train that had pulled in at four for a two-hour stop. Some were Dempsey folk having a special meal out. Others were like him. Loners and singletons without family.

He watched the door as a matter of habit. Once in a great while, Beatrice came in. He knew she liked Chop Suey because he'd seen her get it twice in the past couple years. Both times she had entered the hotel while he was there, he'd asked her to sit and eat with him. Both times, she neither looked him in the eye nor accepted his invitation.

He debated taking her a helping and knocking on her door. But the other times he'd tried it, she hadn't answered.

He had peach ice cream for dessert. When he resigned himself to the fact she wasn't coming in, he headed home.

It took him ten minutes to walk the several blocks to his house. When he climbed the steps and opened the door, it was dark and stale inside. He fumbled for the light. When the room suddenly illuminated, he stood in the center of the room and fumed at the simple furnishings and absolute quiet.

Evan hated living alone. Hated it with every part of his being, yet he'd been doing it since he was twelve years old.

Three

Beatrice entered her dark apartment and closed the door behind her. She leaned against it, thankful to live alone.

She carefully lit a small lamp and set it on the table. Mrs. Merchant, the pastor's wife, had asked her why she didn't use the gas lighting the church had installed in the parsonage years before. Beatrice hadn't told her it was because she feared the gas causing a fire. A single flame seemed much easier to control.

She was as careful with finances as she was with fire. She wanted the inheritance she'd received from her father's small estate to last.

Once or twice, she'd gone to the hotel when her food stores were very low. She wondered what they were serving tonight. She liked the oriental dish. What was it called?

She decided to make do with canned beans and a bit of beef from the icebox she shared with the Merchants. She went to the back porch and opened the door.

She frowned when she saw that items had been added to her shelf. No doubt, Mrs. Merchant had felt Beatrice's stores were too low. Part of her was thankful the older woman wanted to help her. But a larger part resisted the charity. She didn't want to have to depend on anyone. No interactions. No entanglements.

It didn't matter to her that she was known as the odd and reclusive spinster. It was her intention to avoid social situations no matter what people thought. She would stick to the promise she'd made herself thirteen years before, when she'd woke in a Chicago hospital with lungs and a heart mangled by the riot of the dying mob in the theater. She'd been told if she survived the night, she'd surely not survive another ten years.

So she'd resolved to wait for death. She'd not put herself in a place to love or be loved ever again. Beatrice would simply wait for death to claim her so she could rejoin her loved ones.

Until then, she would play the piano and read to pass the time. There was nothing else for her. No one else for her.

Evan pushed open the screen door of the Whitley farmhouse and called out a greeting. He realized it was getting dark and toddlers were being bathed and put to bed, but he also knew the Whitley door was always open to him. At worst, he'd be put to work scrubbing babies. He'd take that over loneliness any day.

Sure enough, Kathleen was standing at the sink – or rather leaning on it – pouring water over a squirmy little boy. "Hello, Evan," she said with labored breath as she dumped more water over the sputtering child.

"Hello," he answered, reaching for the towel on the butcher's block and throwing it around the shoulders of the child before he lifted him down and dried him off.

"Go find your pa and tell him to dress you," Kathleen gave the toddler a swat on the bottom in the right direction. She grabbed the other boy and proceeded to undress him and put him in the sink.

"I think you've got this motherhood thing down," Evan chuckled as the second twin howled in protest.

"There isn't much to it," Kathleen huffed, grabbing underneath her large belly and trying to take a couple deep breaths.

"What's the matter?" Evan stood up, uneasy. He prepared to call for Joshua. "Is it time?"

"No," she scoffed. "My lungs are squeezed into a tiny corner and I can't seem to ever catch my breath anymore."

Evan wasn't sure how to answer, so he was relieved to see Joshua enter the kitchen with the half-dressed first twin.

"Hey, Evan. I thought I heard you come in. Sorry, you caught us at washing time."

"I like watching the commotion," Evan said with a grin.

Kathleen looked at him as if he was crazy before she grabbed both twins and waddled for the stairs.

"Shouldn't you help her?" Evan asked Joshua.

Joshua sighed and put his hands on his hips. "Probably should."

"I can clean up here while you get them in bed." Evan moved for the sink, smiling at Joshua's reticence.

"Thanks. Here I go." Joshua started to move for the stairs, but turned back in the doorway. "Pray for me."

Evan laughed and turned to mop up the wet mess around the sink. By the time he was finishing up, Joshua returned.

Evan followed his friend out to the porch and sat down on the bench, stretching his long legs to rest on the railing while Joshua sat on the steps and sighed deeply.

"Where's Kathleen?"

"She's off to bed. Says my children have driven her to exhaustion and she doesn't intend to do any more living today that involves having her eyes open."

Evan smirked. "You look a little past done yourself, Josh."

Joshua nodded. "I am. But there's nothing more precious than after-bedtime quiet. I aim to enjoy it a spell."

Evan felt morose at his words. "Don't take it for granted – all that noise. It means you have folks to love."

Joshua eyed him silently for a long moment. "You're right, of course. I'm thankful for my family, no matter how crazy they drive me."

"Sorry. It just rubs me the wrong way when I hear folks complain about blessings I missed out on."

"You don't have to apologize," Joshua said with a shrug. "But neither do you need to miss out on it. There are widows and unmarried women in our church who would make fine wives. Why don't you just set your cap for one of them?"

Evan sighed and stared out across the recently harvested field. "You know it isn't that simple. I don't think any of those women would want me settling for them when my heart belongs to someone else."

Joshua shook his head. "Even if that someone else has made it clear she has no intention of ever feeling the same as you?" He sat up, clearing his throat. Evan prepared for the familiar lecture. "I have no earthly idea why Beatrice Walsh is so dead set against you. The woman isn't even interested in holding polite conversation in the churchyard, let alone having a family. She's a recluse, Evan. I know she's every bit as pretty as a princess, but you've been putting your life on hold for more than ten years over a hermit."

Evan frowned. A barn cat came along and rubbed against his chair, so he picked it up and ran a hand over the soft gray fur. "I can't explain it."

"Then just stop it," Joshua urged him. "Kathleen and I want to see you get all the things you've worked hard for. We want to see you with that family you deserve."

Evan knew they worried about him. They knew as well as he did that he wasn't made for the bachelor life. But it wasn't his fault he loved a girl who would never love him back. Was God testing him, teaching him to rely on reason rather than emotion? Had he failed for so many years because he was clinging to an ideal that didn't matter?

"I should head back," he said, clearing his throat and standing. He reached for Joshua's hand. They shook firmly and Joshua reached for Evan's arm to stop him from moving away.

"I'm here for you, brother. Never forget it."

"I know," Evan said. "Thanks."

They said goodnight, and Evan headed through the woods, his head so full of thoughts the long walk back to town didn't seem very long at all.

"Is this ever going to make sense, Lord?" he whispered, kicking at rocks in the graveled path. "Are you ever going to fill me in on why you seem so determined to keep me all alone? I'd much rather you change this. Change my feelings or give me a reason. But you're God and I'm not. I trust you for the answer in your own good time."

No answer spoke through the mild wind stirring the trees that gently gave up the last of their brittle leaves.

Evan headed home.

Four

Beatrice woke with a sick feeling in the pit of her stomach. It was Thursday. The day she must make her rounds of errands. She had no food left, which meant she would also need to visit the bank to have money to pay for the food. She would need to stop at the library as well. The ten books she had dragged home the week before were read, and she was aching for new words.

The dread lay in the prospect of interacting with her fellow townspeople in order to accomplish her tasks.

She set out to do the hardest first. The bank opened at nine in the morning, so she was waiting in front of the doors when they were unlocked, eager to be done with the distasteful task. She pulled open the heavy doors ornately decorated and approached the nearest teller in the echoing room.

"Good day," she mumbled without looking at the man. "I wish to make a withdrawal."

"Very good," the teller said in a business-like tone. Beatrice requested five dollars. It was all she would need for the next two weeks. She didn't like having too much cash in her home. The last thing she wanted was a thief to steal any of the precious income she had stored away.

After the fire, she had depended on the kindness of a family friend who was a lawyer in Chicago. Their family had rented the row house in Pullman, so she was evicted as soon as the landlord discovered she had no money. The lawyer had invited her to stay with his own family until he was able to pull together a small inheritance with what was left of her father's bank account and the sale of their possessions. She had received what seemed at the time an enormous amount of money and gone east, hoping to find a quiet town where she could stow her money in the local bank and live off the funds until she succumbed to her weak lungs and heart.

The teller frowned as he stamped the book and sent back the cash and passbook. "Do you realize your account is very low?"

Beatrice stared at him, stunned. She tried to speak but nothing came from her throat. Two weeks ago, she'd had five hundred dollars in her account.

"How... how much is left?"

The teller opened her book as it faced her and pointed to the bottom line. "You have forty dollars and sixteen cents remaining."

Beatrice stared at the man. "I should have much more than that."

"Are you saying I'm lying to you?"

Beatrice shook her head. Her hand went to her forehead as she fought off a wave of dizziness. This was no time to lose her head. She refused to be one of those ninnies who swooned at the slightest upset, so she leaned against the counter and steeled herself. "I think I should speak to someone in charge."

The man eyed her suspiciously before he walked around to the heavy iron gates and motioned her back.

He knocked on the solid wood door of the office in the back, still staring at her with disapproval. "Mr. Johnston, there is a woman here who claims her account is missing money."

Beatrice was summoned inside, and she passed through the doorway into a large office. A short man with a thick mustache and large spectacles ogled her openly. He leaned back and smiled in appreciation of her appearance, which only served to irritate her.

"Two weeks ago I had five hundred dollars in my account.

Would you like to explain why I now have forty?"

Mr. Johnston stood and adjusted his lapels. "Now, now, let's see what's happened." He held out a hand for her passbook and she handed it to him unwillingly.

He peered through his spectacles and grunted as he searched the record. "You've been making withdrawals of five dollars every two weeks for the past ten years, with very little variation," he commented. "Yet this Monday past, you withdrew four-hundred and sixty dollars."

Beatrice scoffed. "Impossible. I didn't leave my house Monday, except to practice piano."

Mr. Johnston showed her the book. She saw the withdrawal printed neatly on the second line from the bottom.

She shook her head. "Someone must have stolen my book and returned it without me knowing."

Mr. Johnston handed her the book and considered her with the same suspicious expression his teller had. "Or you are trying to swindle the bank."

"Why in the world would I do that? Do you not check to see that the person making the withdrawal is the owner of the account?"

Mr. Johnston shrugged. "How would you propose we do that? Dempsey is a growing town. It would be nearly impossible for my staff to remember every person with an account. We've never had such a need before, anyway. Plenty of husbands and wives share accounts. If someone stole your book, he probably claimed he was your husband. This is why you were warned to protect your passbook with your very life."

"So nothing can be done?" Beatrice stammered in disbelief.

"Ma'am, why don't we call your husband? There's no need to distress you with such matters."

"I am not a hysterical woman," Beatrice countered hotly. "My funds have been stolen, and I demand that someone tell me what I must do to get them back."

"My dear, nothing can be done," he shrugged, as if he was

helpless in the matter. "I suggest you go home and calm yourself. These things happen, after all."

The man actually dared to put his hand on her back and direct her to the door. She stood her ground. "I am not leaving until I get my money back in my account."

"Then I'm afraid I'll have to call the sheriff's office." Mr. Johnston answered delicately, as if he were addressing an emotional child.

Beatrice raged. "This is not the end of this matter," she said as she pushed past the arrogant little man and stomped out of the office and through the gate, not stopping to bid the teller good day.

She stepped into the sunlight, her eyes blurred by tears she refused to allow. She turned, her face hot with anger, and ran straight into a veritable wall of man. At first, she was frightened by the sheer size of the person she had collided with. But then she realized who it was.

"Miss Walsh?" Evan stared down at her in concern, his hands reaching for her shoulders. "What's wrong?"

She didn't want to tell him. Him, of all people. Her pride burned just at the thought of it. But what if he could help her get her money back?

"Come, sit." He directed her to a public bench and sat down next to her, leaving plenty of room between them, she noticed. And appreciated.

She didn't look him in the eye as she spoke. "Someone stole my bank book and took most of the money I had in my account. The bank manager says nothing can be done."

Evan frowned. He pointed at the book. "May I?"

She hesitated, but sighed and held it out without looking his way. She watched his fingers flip through the pages of the little book that seemed miniscule is his oversized hands. She breathed in and noticed the pleasant, masculine scent of the pomade he must use to smooth back his long locks. Aware of every movement he made, she closed her eyes at the overwhelming sensation of being close to a man again after so many years. Being near him made her think of Edward. Dear, sweet Edward who had died so long ago she could barely recall his features. She hadn't forgotten his love, though. She'd never forget that. Or recover from it.

"Have you been living on five dollars every two weeks?" Evan's deep voice caught her off guard. "What do you eat?"

She frowned. "I don't see how that's your business."

She stood, reaching for the book, but he held it back and patted the seat.

"Sit down and tell me about it, Miss Walsh. I want to help."

"I don't need a man to figure out my problems for me," she said disdainfully, crossing her arms over her chest.

"I didn't say you did. I want to help because I care."

She met his eyes for the first time in the conversation. She was irritated that she found herself tongue-tied. She didn't understand this man who cared so much for her, for so long, when she had ignored him so completely. Why couldn't he just leave her alone? Hadn't she made her wishes plain? Why did he always persist?

She took in the sight of him, trying to deny how he affected her. She considered the unruly hair that touched his shoulders, paired with neat sideburns and just the shadow of a beard covering his strong jaw. His eyes drew her in. They were intense, filled with concern and the open heart he'd worn on his sleeve for all the years she'd known him. His unending arms and legs seemed ill-fitted for the suit he wore, as if his body obviously preferred a more casual form of attire. His bowler hat didn't fit his personality, either. She worked hard to ignore the curiosity she suddenly felt. Why did he work at the rail office and not farm or ranch, which seemed better suited for him? Why was he so friendly and kind, yet perpetually alone? He must be at least thirty, perhaps even older than her thirty-two years. Why didn't he have a wife? Children?

She'd never allowed herself to wonder anything about anybody in Dempsey before that moment, and it scared her that she was unable to avoid the questions now.

"May I have my book, please?" She held out her hand, intent to leave and pretend this discomfiting conversation had never occurred. He met her eyes and held out the book.

Her fingers brushed against his as she took it, and his breath caught in his throat. Beatrice's heart began to beat recklessly, unsettled by the accidental contact.

She turned and fled.

Out o

Five

Evan hadn't fully recovered from touching Beatrice's hand by noon the next day. He made his way to the church parsonage to eat lunch with Pastor Merchant and his wife as he continued to think about how soft her fingers had been. How long and graceful. Perfect for piano playing, as he'd noticed on many occasions.

He was worried about her. He doubted she could have enough to eat on so little an allowance. He wanted to go to the bank and give Johnston a piece of his mind, but what could the man really do for her? And how could someone have sneaked into her apartment and stole her book without her knowing?

"Evan!" Rebecca Merchant met him at the door and enveloped him in a motherly hug. He had to bend down pretty low to hug her back.

"Hello, Mama Merchant." He used the name he'd called her since he met her as a youngster.

"My boy," she said proudly, leading him in by the hand into the dining room where Pastor Merchant stood by his chair, smiling a greeting.

"It's good to see you, Evan."

Evan nodded. "Always good to be here."

They sat down and prayed. Mrs. Merchant piled Evan's plate with egg salad sandwiches and peaches.

"These peaches from the Whitley farm?" He took a bite of the perfectly ripe fruit.

"Of course. Best in the county." Mrs. Merchant smiled. "Kathleen's been out picking the last of them before the weather turns. I keep telling that girl to rest, but she seems set on getting every duck in a row before those twins come."

"I'll go out and help with the rest of the harvest this weekend," Evan promised. "I know she's beside herself and Joshua has plenty of work to do, too."

"You're good to them," Pastor said, pausing with his sandwich mid-air to consider Evan.

"They're the closest thing I have to family besides the two of you," Evan said with a shrug. "What else would I do?"

"You do it because you're a good boy," Mrs. Merchant argued in a gentle tone.

"Something's bothering you, son." Pastor set the sandwich back on his plate and folded his hands in his lap. "It might help to talk about it."

Evan chuckled. "Always the mind-reader, Pastor."

Pastor Merchant nodded. "I care about you. I have ever since you were a headstrong boy convinced he could make it on his own. And I know when something's troubling you and you're trying to hide it."

Evan tossed his napkin on the table. He sighed. "It's just that I talked to Beatrice today."

He had the Merchants' full attention.

"You spoke with her?" Mrs. Merchant said in awe.

"I ran into her coming out of the bank. She's was awful spun up with tears in her eyes."

"What happened?" Pastor frowned in concern.

"Someone stole her money."

"They stole it out of the bank? Heavens!" Mrs. Merchant touched her husband's arm in concern. "Does she have anything left?"

"She has forty dollars to her name. But the amount she had wouldn't have lasted her more than three years, even with her careful spending. I worry she doesn't have enough to eat."

Mrs. Merchant nodded in concern as Pastor spoke. "She came to Dempsey with all the money her father's estate was worth when he died."

Evan considered the new information. He hadn't known her father had died. "Didn't she figure the money would eventually run out? What was she going to do then?"

"I don't know what to tell you, Evan." Mrs. Merchant sighed helplessly. "She doesn't talk to us, either. We had no idea she was surviving on so little."

Evan stood up, frustrated. He walked to the window and peered out. "I don't understand why she won't let anyone help her. Why is she all-fired determined to make sure no one comes within ten feet of her? It's one thing not to feel the same way about a man who's sweet on you, but a body isn't meant to be alone. What in the world made her so afraid of connections?"

"All I know for sure is that her parents died. She mentioned having their inheritance and a bit of life insurance when she came to Dempsey. She asked us for a place close to the church where it might be convenient for her to practice the piano daily. She was determined to pay rent until we insisted she take the apartment in exchange for playing piano for services. She's never said anything about finding a position."

"It doesn't make sense to me," Evan said.

Pastor Merchant joined him at the window. "I know you care about her very much, son, but I'd hate for you to get your heart broken. I worry about your longstanding interest in Miss Walsh."

"Nonsense," Mrs. Merchant chimed in. "His heart was broken long ago. That girl needs someone to love her, and it's all of God that Evan's feelings haven't changed after so many years."

She took Evan's hands and turned him to face her. "Don't give up on that sweet girl until the Lord Jesus himself tells you to let her go. You keep loving her and taking care of her as best she'll allow you. God is going to see you both through this. I've seen his miracles. You just hold on and wait for your miracle. Do you hear me, Evan Masters?"

Evan hesitated, but he finally nodded. "I don't know what else to do, anyway."

"I'm going to pray, down on my old knees, every day," she promised. "Every day. Until this whole matter between you and Beatrice Walsh is settled."

Evan didn't doubt she would. "Thank you." He kissed her cheek and shook the pastor's hand. "I better get back to work. Thank you for lunch and the talk."

Beatrice didn't sleep well. She couldn't afford any extra light, so she lay in the dark most of the night staring at the ceiling.

What would she do about her bank account? How would she buy food and necessities?

It would be easier if she'd just died as the doctor had all but promised her thirteen years before.

When the sun finally cast the sky in the blush of sunrise, she got out of bed. She hadn't gone to the grocery or library after what had happened the day before at the bank, so she had nothing to eat for breakfast and nothing to read as she waited for businesses to open. She reread a favorite Shakespeare play, *Hamlet*, as the sun made a slow journey over the eastern horizon.

She took her five-dollar bill and went first to the grocery as soon as old Dickinson was opening up the doors and sweeping out the entrance. He smiled cordially without speaking to her. Little did he know she preferred his store to the others in town because of the fact he never spoke to her any more than he must, and he kept his ogling to a minimum as well.

"May I have two cans of salmon, six eggs, a pound of butter, a pound of rice, a canister of tea and a loaf of bread?" She set the money on the counter.

"No produce this week?" Dickinson totaled up the prices on his cash register.

"No, thank you," she said primly.

"That'll be $1.52. You have $3.48 in change." He dropped the bills and coins into her hand before he went about gathering her items.

"You hear this?" Walt, who was in his eighties and known to spend his mornings in the grocery reading the paper and hobnobbing, shook the newspaper in agitation and called to Dickinson. "They say John D. Rockefeller over in New York City is going to be the world's first bona fide billionaire. Can you imagine having that much money?"

No one person should have that much money to spend on themselves. Beatrice thought, annoyed. Why did some have so much and others, such as herself, have so little?

"I could think of a few things to spend that kind of money on," Dickinson answered. "See you next week," he said to Beatrice.

Her next stop was the library, but it wasn't opened yet, so she waited on the bench outside the doors until Mrs. Reynolds made her way down the sidewalk and unlocked the door.

"Hello, dear," the older woman said kindly as Beatrice hurried inside and headed for her favorite aisles of books. "I missed you yesterday."

Beatrice nodded and left the woman at the counter. Ten minutes later she had overloaded her arms with so many books she could not possibly carry another one. She'd selected two novels, four books about learning Greek and Latin, one about South American travel and three dealing with the sciences.

"My goodness, but you are a reader, aren't you?" Mrs. Reynolds said as she checked the books out, writing Beatrice's name neatly on the next available line. "I wouldn't doubt you've read every book in this library at least once."

Beatrice smiled politely and left as quickly as she could with her added burdens.

When she arrived back home, she straightened, dusted and swept her apartment. She had a lunch of tea with bread and butter, though she was hungry for more. She hadn't eaten since the morning before.

With an armload of piano books, she left the apartment,

locking the door behind her and tucking her bank book into the pocket of her navy skirt.

She went next door to the church, expecting the usual quiet, empty room. What she found instead was an auditorium full of women.

They sat informally in the pews while Kathleen Whitley, quite large with child, leaned on the podium where the pastor usually stood to preach.

Beatrice quickly tried to back out of the room, but it was too late. Kathleen caught sight of her and motioned her in.

"Oh, Beatrice, do join us. We're almost done. We had to move our Ladies' Aid Meeting to the sanctuary since Evan is working on the plumbing in the basement, but we'll be out of your way soon."

Beatrice sat in the back of the room. She stared at her books in her lap and listened as Kathleen addressed the group.

"We have rehabilitated four girls at the farm, so far," she said in a defensive tone. "I believe we are doing a good thing. These girls would still be in brothels if it weren't for our ministry."

"I know you have personal interest in the saloons, and we all agree that we should do everything to see the saloons are closed for good," Mrs. Dawes said in a lofty tone. "But we cannot invest our money in women with no moral capacity."

Kathleen gave a harsh laugh of disbelief. "Mrs. Dawes, if you had any idea what these women go through... most of them feel they have nowhere else to go. They're looking for a way out, and it is our privilege to provide that for them."

"Let's not let our emotions get out of hand," Mrs. MacGregor stood and held up her hands as if the gesture would inspire calm.

"We don't need permission to keep helping these girls," Kathleen said in a more measured tone. "I don't need your money. The girls come to me, I put them up in our bunkhouse and they help with farm chores and the harvest. In exchange, they have shelter and food until they can figure out what to do next. I welcome your support if you feel compelled, but I don't want your money if you don't believe in what I'm doing."

"To have those harlots out there with your little boys," Mrs. Dawes continued as if Kathleen had not spoken. "I don't know how you can justify it."

"It's called grace," Kathleen said in a darker tone. "And without it, *none* of us would stand a chance."

Beatrice watched the women exchange uncomfortable glances. She supposed none of them had forgotten that Kathleen Whitley herself had lived in the saloon. It only proved to Beatrice that she had made the right choice by removing herself from society. No one even saw her anymore, and she was glad. She wanted nothing to do with judgmental fools. Obviously, the very pregnant Mrs. Whitley was a different person now, but none of these women cared. Their pride was more important.

She rolled her eyes in disgust.

Kathleen sighed. "I guess this meeting is over."

The women abandoned the church quickly, caught up in their hushed conversation. Beatrice silently bid them good riddance.

Kathleen was still leaning on the podium watching them leave as Beatrice came forward, headed to the piano. Apparently, she felt she owed Beatrice an explanation. "I think I'm well past my time to be moving around with two nearly done babies inside me."

Kathleen gingerly stepped down. Suddenly, she inhaled sharply and put her hands on the sides of her swollen abdomen.

Beatrice hated to have to speak to her, but she could see no way around it. "Is anything the matter?"

Kathleen lowered her awkward form into the front pew. "Miss Walsh, please get Evan. I need his help to get to my wagon."

Beatrice shifted uncomfortably. "Perhaps the pastor could help."

"Evan's much stronger, and it's going to take a giant to lug me into that wagon," Kathleen said ruefully.

Beatrice unwillingly set down her books and went to the stairs that led down to the Sunday School rooms and kitchen. She found Evan under the sink, completely absorbed in whatever he was fixing.

He was dressed more like himself. She noticed the jeans, the white cotton shirt that seemed rather small over his large arms, the suspenders he didn't need, seeing how well his clothing fit...

Her face heated. She cleared her throat.

"Miss Walsh?" Evan came out from under the sink so quickly his head hit one of the pipes. "Ow!" He rubbed the sore spot.

Beatrice probably should have asked if he was okay, but she just watched him, stepping back as he stood up.

"You surprised me," he said with an embarrassed chuckle.

"I'm sorry. Mrs. Whitley requires your help."

"Why mine?"

"She is in need of a large person," she said before she thought better of it. "I mean strong. I mean…"

He tried not to smile. "She needs someone to heave her into her wagon, I take it. Josh keeps telling her just to stay home, but she's going stir crazy."

They walked toward the stairs together. She folded her hands in front of her and stared at the ground.

"It's not often I get to speak to you two days in a row," he said softly. She could feel his eyes on her face, and had seen the expression he'd be wearing enough to know how tenderly he was watching her.

She walked faster.

"Wait! I didn't mean to scare you off." He caught up to her and offered his arm to escort her up the stairs.

His bare, noticeably muscular arm …

She shook her head and went up without his assistance. She was conscious of the fact that he followed her closely.

They went into the auditorium where Kathleen was still in the front pew.

"Need some help?" Evan went to Kathleen, who was trying in vain to stand up.

"Just get me to the wagon, if you please, Evan," Kathleen held up her hands so Evan could pull her up. He took them and when she was in a standing position, he offered his arm as he had done for Beatrice. Kathleen accepted it and tried to take a few steps.

"Don't tell Joshua I admitted it, but I shouldn't have come out today. These babies are getting so heavy."

Before Beatrice could prepare for the sight, Evan swung Kathleen up into his arms. Beatrice almost gasped aloud at his display of strength.

"Oh, my! Well, I suppose this is one way to get it done," Kathleen laughed. "Good day, Miss Walsh."

Beatrice gave a small wave as she watched Evan effortlessly carry the bulky woman down the stairs and out the front door where her wagon and horse waited. When Beatrice could tear her eyes away, she headed for the piano.

Scales, she told herself. *Focus on the scales. Forget the arms.*

She played the first scale loudly and with as much force as she could muster. The thoughts of Evan's physique inevitably led her to remember Edward's arms, pressed against her in the theater.

She played the second scale more insistently than the first. Her eyes closed and suddenly all she could think of were Edward's lips against hers. His fingers threaded between hers.

She gave in and surrendered to the memory. But as it always had before, the memory led to the cries of terror. The smell of smoke.

Children dying.

"Beatrice?" Pastor Merchant peeked out of his office. "Is something wrong?"

She stared at him, wide-eyed. *Everything is wrong.*

She swallowed back the truth. "I'm sorry. I'll be quieter."

Six

Evan got Kathleen safely home where Joshua insisted she go to bed and demanded she stay there. Evan listened to them argue for a few minutes, but Joshua didn't seem worse for the wear when he came back down the stairs.

"She's not thrilled about staying in bed," Joshua explained. "But I didn't give her a choice."

Evan smiled. "Guess that means you're on father duty."

"Nope. Kathleen left the boys at Mary's for the night."

"How much longer until you're a father of four?"

"Doc says they'll come any time now. It's early, but that's normal for twins," Joshua said. "So, did you talk to the lovely Miss Walsh today?" Josh poked Evan in the ribs.

"She's the one who came and got me when Kathleen needed help. She seemed a little... surprised when she saw me."

"At what?" Joshua grinned. "Your rugged good looks? Your prowess with a wrench?"

Evan rolled his eyes at the teasing. "I think she might have been offended by my clothes." He looked down at his dirty jeans and faded shirt.

"Well, did she expect you to wear your bowler hat to do the plumbing?" Joshua went to the icebox and got the milk, which he poured into a pan on the stove and stirred.

"You making the wifey a glass of warm milk?" Evan teased

back in a high-pitched, mocking tone.

"Dry up, Evan," Joshua snarled.

"I think it's adorable," Evan said, dodging Joshua's swinging fist. He made a quick exit and slammed the door in Joshua's face. "Night!"

"You better watch yourself or I might accidently tell Miss Walsh a few things about Evan Masters that will offend her way more than your clothes!" Joshua called as Evan made for the woods.

♫

Sunday morning at church, Evan tried to focus on the pastor's words. He made a valiant effort, but Beatrice was in rare form on the piano. He'd never seen her so passionate about her music before. Her hands flew up and down the keyboard with a crescendo he'd only noticed a few times when he was working somewhere in the church and she thought she was alone.

Her brow furrowed with thoughtful intent and her dark eyes watched the music. He could imagine she thought of nothing but the notes on the page. How did they translate from her brain to her fingertips with such speed?

Her thick brown hair flowed over her back as a dark waterfall, contrasting the pure white blouse she wore. She was a vision. He'd never seen anything as beautiful as Beatrice Walsh. She put girls ten years younger than her to shame. And it wasn't something Evan could put his finger on, such as a finely formed nose or even features or a tiny waist. There was a light that started somewhere within herself and shone through every part of her like a sort of sunbeam. Intelligence, thoughtfulness, a keen intuition – he liked to think these were her attributes, possessed in abundance.

"Close your mouth," Joshua whispered loudly beside him. Evan frowned as he snickered.

"You're an open book," Joshua continued. A squirmy twin climbed on the pew between them. "I can see the sunbeams and rainbows shooting out of your eyes."

"Quiet. You're worse than your boys. Who are pretty bad, by

the way."

Evan watched Beatrice step away from the piano and sit in the front pew on the side, alone as always. When the service was over, she would leave without speaking to anyone. For all the years she'd been a resident of Dempsey, she could have showed up the day before for as much as anyone knew anything about her.

Pastor Merchant preached about charity. He admonished them to focus on the needs of others around them rather than on their own plans and desires. Just like Jesus.

Evan stole several glances at Beatrice. She stared at her folded hands, apparently unaffected by the sermon. Her expression was a hard stare.

You're a stubborn one, he thought, wishing he could say it to her. *No one is going to deter you from this path you've chosen. You've decided it's for the best, and no one is allowed to disagree.*

But why did she feel that way? He yearned to have the question answered. Why did she shun society, community and family? What could make being completely alone for over ten years preferable? If he could understand, at least on some basic level, he thought it would be easier to accept it. If she loved someone else, he would find the strength to let her go. If she had dedicated herself to God's service and had no place for love, he would find that pursuit noble.

She'd never said she didn't feel anything for him. She'd blushed when their hands touched in front of the bank. He had a suspicion lack of attraction was not the problem.

But what *was* the problem? Not knowing was driving him crazy.

By the time the service ended, he was ready to have another conversation, whether she wanted it or not. He jumped up as soon as the service was over and followed her all the way to the stairway leading to her apartment.

He stepped in front of her so she couldn't escape him. "I'm getting better at cornering you," he teased, smiling and keeping his distance so he wouldn't spook her.

"Please let me by," she said without looking at him. She hugged her ever-present piano books to her chest and stepped back.

He gathered his courage. "I will. But first I need to talk to you. Can you just look at me and answer my question? This once? If you give me five minutes, I'll never bother you again. I just need to understand something."

Her eyebrows drew together in alarm. She took another step back. "I do not owe you a thing. Please let me by."

He felt concern as he considered her. She was pale. A thin sheen of sweat covered her forehead though the November air possessed more than a little chill. "Are you okay?"

She gulped and took another step back, but she faltered and started to fall. He caught her before she hit her head and swung her up into his arms before he remembered how she'd feel about it.

"Put me down!" She was gasping, her breathing labored. "Please put me down!"

Before he'd decided if it was possible to put her down without her crumpling to the ground, her eyes lolled back and she fainted.

"Pastor! Mrs. Merchant! Please get Doc!"

Doctor Luke Thomas and the Merchants came within seconds. Luke instructed him to take her up to her apartment and lay her on the bed. Evan did so as gently as he could and sat down beside her, pushing the locks of hair from her face.

Luke held his stethoscope to her chest. "Her heart is racing. Did something happen?"

Evan shook his head. "I was talking to her and she just fainted."

"Her corset isn't tight," Luke mused, then caught Evan's embarrassed expression. "Sorry. Sometimes women faint because their stays are too tight and restrict their lungs. Hers is loose, as if she knew something like this could happen. Maybe she knows what's wrong with her."

Evan held her hand tightly as he considered the news.

"Why don't you and Pastor wait downstairs? Mrs. Merchant and I will see to her care."

Evan didn't want to leave, but he knew he had no choice. Beatrice wasn't his wife. She wasn't even his beau. He had no right to stay by her side, and it frustrated him as he followed Pastor Merchant down the stairs.

"I think lunch is in order." Pastor went into the kitchen and came back a few minutes later with roast beef sandwiches and tea.

Evan ate, but he hardly tasted the food. All he thought about was Beatrice. What could possibly be wrong with her?

"Evan, I know you're worried, but Luke is an excellent doctor and my wife is a pretty good nurse, as we both know. They'll know what to do. I'm sure she'll be fine."

"It bothers me we don't know anything about her. She has told us nothing. Has this happened before? Would she ask for help if she needed it?"

Pastor nodded. "It bothers Mama and me as well, and we have tried to reach her. But we can't force her to do anything."

Evan shook his head, but he didn't argue. It seemed like an eternity later, but Luke eventually came through the door.

"She's resting," he said as he sat down and accepted a sandwich.

Evan watched him. "What's wrong with her?"

Luke shook his head. "That girl hasn't told us everything."

"What do you mean?" Evan dreaded the answer.

"I'm telling you this only because I believe it's in her best interests to have people aware of her condition. Her heart and lungs are both very weak. Damaged, somehow."

Evan's throat felt as thick as molasses in December. "Is she going to die?"

"I'm sorry, Evan." Luke's expression softened. "I know you don't want to hear this. And honestly, I don't know. She's not in immediate danger. I think whatever injured her happened a long time ago."

The room was quiet as the doctor paused. Finally, he

continued. "I don't think she's been eating enough. That's the main reason she collapsed today. Her kitchen is almost empty, and she didn't have any fruit or vegetables. I'm concerned at how thin she is for her height and build. Obviously, the three of you care about her or you wouldn't be here. I'd ask you to make sure she gets enough healthy meals and that she takes a walk outside every day. We all know days can go by when she doesn't even come out of her apartment."

"Maybe she just needed to go to the grocery." Pastor clamped his hand on Evan's shoulder. "We'll have a talk with her and make sure she has enough food –"

"She's out of money," Evan reminded him. "Someone stole her money from her account. She's trying to make her remaining few dollars last as long as possible."

"That's terrible news," Luke said, setting down his teacup. "Who would do such a thing?"

"This town is growing so fast it's hard to keep track of everyone," Pastor said.

Luke nodded. "There are two other doctors besides me now. Businesses pop up all the time with new faces everywhere you turn. A thief could have been watching her habits."

Evan heaved a sigh. "I aim to have a conversation with her. She can't keep hiding from life. Nobody can live like they're on a deserted island."

Evan could feel Pastor Merchant's watchful gaze. He realized he was probably speaking out of turn, and it may very well not be his business. But if Beatrice had no money, no food and a previous injury serious enough to threaten her life, Evan wasn't going to let her get away with pushing him out this time.

He didn't wait for permission to return to her apartment. He climbed the stairs two at a time and knocked briefly before he entered.

Mama Merchant looked up. "Evan," she said, seeming surprised to see him return. "Did Dr. Thomas speak to you?"

He nodded, flexing his jaw. "And I'm worried."

She stood and held her wrinkled hand to his cheek, her palm still as soft and warm as he remembered. "I know you are, dear. Just you remember Jesus loves this little girl much more than you do, and he knows how to take care of what belongs to him. You trust him, my son."

"Thanks," Evan answered.

"Sit with her. I'm going to get some lunch and make some broth for Beatrice. I'll return within the hour."

"Of course."

Evan sat beside her and stared at her face, enthralled. He'd never had the opportunity to look at her for so long and up so close. Her skin held an almost porcelain quality. Her frame seemed swallowed up by the bed. He wanted to ask her all the questions that had not been answered.

To distract his mind, he surveyed her apartment. It was really just a room with a small kitchenette and a bed, chair, table and bookshelf.

Beatrice had little to nothing in the way of sentimental décor or homey touches, though the bookshelf was crammed with books and piano music. He got up and went to her closet, peeking in the door that stood slightly ajar. She owned two other dresses. He walked to the kitchen cupboards and found them nearly empty. She had a bit of rice, some butter and bread.

"Who lives like this?" His throat constricted. She was living only enough to survive. But why?

He heard a groan from the bed and quickly turned back to her. "Miss Walsh?"

She saw him and her eyes grew wide. He quickly made his way back to her side and crouched down beside her, hoping to seem less intimidating that way.

"What are you doing in my apartment?" She shrank from his hand reaching for her shoulder to calm her.

"I'm watching you until Mrs. Merchant comes back with your broth. You collapsed this morning after church. The Merchants, Doc Luke and I have been looking after you."

"No!" She sat up, horrified. "You must leave!"

He shook his head. "If you're worried about propriety, Mrs. Merchant left the door ajar. She has the window open downstairs as well since it's a warm day. She can probably hear every word we're saying."

"I can, at that," Mrs. Merchant answered merrily from below the floorboards. Evan smiled at Beatrice.

"I wish you would leave now." Beatrice seemed like an animal caught in a trap. Her eyes were wide and her skin and lips so pale he was afraid she might faint again, or try to bolt.

"I'll stand outside on the stair landing if you prefer," he said as he moved toward the door. "But I can't leave you alone. And I think we're going to need to have a conversation when you are stronger."

"No," she refused, pulling the thin blanket around her chin and looking in the other direction. "Please go."

He backed up and stood just outside the door. "I understand you feel that way. But here's the choice you have: You can have the conversation with me, you can have it with the Merchants, or we can have the doc come back and talk to you. So, what's your pleasure?"

In order to lessen the sting of his words, he gave her a friendly grin.

Seven

Beatrice wished for a gun. Maybe, if she started shooting at the overgrown man, he'd leave. She had no intention of answering questions from him, the Merchants or the doctor. She owed them nothing. She'd been careful not to owe anyone anything.

"What I do in my own house is none of your concern." She stood up from her bed and met his gaze to convince him she was not weak. But when she looked at him, the intense concern in his features gave her pause. She'd done nothing to encourage this man, ever, in the twelve years she'd resided in his town. She had flatly rejected every overture he had made. She'd treated him as trash, even curling her lip in disgust when he spoke to her. He didn't know the truth she was hiding. She found him quite the opposite of disgusting.

In fact, it only took a glance into his warm brown eyes to make her insides feel like they'd melted into jelly. He had no idea how much he affected her.

"I don't know if I agree that it's none of my concern," Evan said, sticking his hands in his pockets and speaking slowly, as if he was sorry to argue with her. "You're a God-fearing woman, are you not?"

"Of course," she said, indignant that he would ask.

"Well, if you don't mind me asking, how do you interpret the verse Pastor mentioned just this morning in his sermon? I think it was Ephesians. *Speak every man truth with his neighbor: for we are members one of another*."

At first Beatrice was going to argue she was not a man, but she knew it would make her look foolish. She chose not to answer at all. She had managed to avoid such passages of Scripture for years. She did not intend to have it brought to light now. She believed her situation was a special case.

"Well, at least you're not arguing," he said with a small smile and shrug. "So tell me. Why haven't you been eating? It is because you don't feel well? Or because your money was stolen?"

She'd have to be crazy to answer that question. It was a trap. "What I eat and how much money I have are not your business."

"Maybe," he said. "But God clearly said to *bear one another's burdens*. So tell me who to follow. You – or God?"

He had rendered her speechless. He stepped closer. "Why don't you have any food?"

She fumed, but gave him the easiest answer. "You know why. Someone stole my money."

He took another step, his hands still in his pockets. "See, Doc says you haven't been eating enough for some time. Your money was stolen a few days ago. Why weren't you eating enough to keep yourself healthy?"

She felt anger like a cord wrapped around her neck. "It's *my* body. How dare you –"

"Just answer the question, Beatrice."

She stared at him in surprise. She'd never given him permission to call her by her first name. But it rolled off his tongue as easily as if he'd said it for the past ten years.

Her voice was little more than a deadly whisper. "I had a certain amount of funds that was supposed to last a specific amount of time. That time has come and gone, so I am trying to make it last as long as possible."

"The time for what?" Evan's voice faltered as if he didn't want to hear the answer. She clamped her mouth shut and stared at the floor.

He shook his head. "I get you were running low on funds. But it's 1916. Why didn't you go the library, one of the dry goods stores, the school or any other business in Dempsey and ask for a job? At the least, you could have offered to teach piano lessons at the church. It's just money, Beatrice. It's easy enough for a young woman to make enough to live on."

She clenched her hands at her sides. "I do not require your approval."

He shuffled his feet, hesitating before he spoke. "You won't get a job because you don't want to interact with any of the townsfolk? That doesn't make a bit of sense."

There was a long silence. She debated what she might say to get rid of him. She was not about to stand in her own apartment and argue with the man.

Mrs. Merchant came through the door before she could say anything else. She was carrying a tray of steaming broth and fresh buttered bread and tea. "Time to get back in bed, Beatrice. You eat up every bit of this, sweetie. Get some rest and we'll talk more later."

Beatrice hesitantly complied as Mrs. Merchant turned and reached up to lay her hand on Evan's chest. "Evan, be a dear and knock on Dickinson's door. See if he'll let you pick up a few emergency groceries and put them on our account."

"No need," he said, squeezing her hand. "I don't mind picking up the tab."

"No," Beatrice said as he turned to follow Mrs. Merchant out the door. She felt her face grow hot. "I won't accept them."

He sighed as he reached for the door handle. "I wasn't asking permission."

He was gone before she said another word.

Beatrice was winded by the time she arrived in front of the little yellow house on Vine Street. She set down her burden and leaned against the porch railing to catch her breath and allow her heart a few moments to stop racing.

She glanced at the house in curiosity. Evan Masters seemed far too rugged a man to own such a quaint little home. The sight of it immediately made her wistful. She had grown up in a row house, but it had been as homey as this one. She remembered the sound of children playing in the street and birds singing in the tops of the old spindly oak trees. She had listened for the cheerful whistling of the postman each afternoon as he made his way down the street.

The memories were threatening. She would not be undone, especially in the middle of town at this man's house. She pushed the emotions away and thought of nothing.

She did not expect Mr. Masters to be home, but she didn't knock. She had no interest in seeing him. She heaved the box of groceries up into her arms and made a precarious trip up the stairs. She set the box in front of the door where he would be sure to see it. Her eyes fell on a sleepy white and orange cat, relaxing in a rocking chair on the cozy sun porch.

She closed her eyes and surrendered to the sweetness of a memory ruined by grief. She saw her father tenderly caring for the tabby cat who had come out the loser in a street fight. The cat had possessed an indomitable spirit and had pulled through. He became her father's constant shadow. He spent many an evening sitting on the front porch with the orange cat in his lap, absently running his hand over the cat's back, as if he was releasing his worries with each stroke.

She turned to leave with a muffled cry, not wishing anyone to see the evidence of her tears. *Anyone* being Mr. Masters, of course. She sincerely hoped he was where he should be – at the train and telegraph office for another two hours.

She walked the two blocks from Vine Street to the public library. The block-shaped library had been built the year before. It wasn't the most ornate building in town but Beatrice appreciated its simplicity. The double white doors stood open since the fall day was unusually warm.

Beatrice knew the library would be fairly empty this time of day. She was counting on it. She had no interest in mingling with a crowd, only in finding books. She walked through the doors and into the front hall where a large fireplace graced the left wall, surrounded by reading tables and chairs. The front desk stood directly ahead as her one obstacle before she would be able to access the shelves of books beyond.

The desk was empty. The usual librarian, Mrs. Reynolds, was nowhere to be seen. Beatrice felt relief as she headed for her favorite section: architecture and the history of buildings.

She'd read through all the library's copies, but she always hoped a new selection may have been added. If not, she settled for rereading the ones there. She would have liked to become an architect, if she had lived a different life. The ability to take a shelter and wrap it in grace and ingenuity fascinated her. She thrilled at the way lines and spaces worked together in a compelling dance.

To her delight, she found a new commentary on medieval castle design. She clutched it to her chest as she headed for the fiction aisle. She found a few favorites and a new novel called *The Oakleyites*.

When she had loaded all the books she could carry, she made her way to the desk and set them on the counter with a loud thump. From behind the stack, a new face peeked around to smile at her.

"Hello," the woman said as she took the books and stamped them. Though she said no more, she kept looking up at Beatrice as if she was waiting for her to say something. The woman was in her forties with a pleasant appearance and demeanor. Beatrice fought a sense of curiosity.

"Good day." Beatrice forced herself to break the eye contact. The woman seemed to sense her hesitation to engage in conversation and went silent. Beatrice was grateful. The usual librarian liked to give her opinion on every title Beatrice checked out.

"I'm Amelia Morehouse," the woman explained. "I'm Kathleen Whitley's aunt. I'm here until the twins are born. Mrs.

Reynolds had an unexpected death in the family and had to leave town for several weeks. I have a little experience, so I agreed to help out."

Beatrice gave a short nod. She turned to leave, laboring under the heavy stack of books, but she turned back.

"I've read an author named A.J. Morehouse. Are you a relation?"

The woman's face turned pink. She gave an embarrassed chuckle as she stumbled over her words. "I'm A.J. Morehouse, actually."

Beatrice was shocked. So much that she forgot her reservations. "I read your time travel story just last month."

Amelia smiled awkwardly. "Oh, good. Did you enjoy it?"

Beatrice nodded. "The story was obviously inspired by *The Time Machine* by H.G. Wells. I found the contrast between present and future quite plausible. I wondered about the question of –" She stopped abruptly, swallowing.

Amelia's smile seemed awkward. "Perhaps we can discuss it another time when you aren't in a rush."

Beatrice nodded once more and left, heading directly toward her apartment. As she turned the corner, she saw a crowd had gathered in front of the old billiard hall, listening to someone speak from the boardwalk. She endeavored to move around them without drawing attention to herself until she heard the subject of their speech.

"The citizens of Dempsey deserve to have their own theater right here on this very spot. Just imagine your pride as you bring your families to the traveling shows, musicals and dramatic presentations. You'll have the theater for graduations or important religious speakers. All it takes from you, folks, is your generous one-time investment. In return, you'll get to see this work of art built here in your town, and you will have the added value of tourism, not to mention a brand of entertainment found only in New York City or Chicago!"

Beatrice nearly dropped the books in the muddy street. Her

breathing increased, and dizziness came on her so suddenly it was as if one of the automobiles ambling by had hit her. She stumbled backward and fell onto the bench outside the barbershop. Her books tumbled to the ground around her.

The speaker went silent. He made his way through the crowd until he stood before Beatrice. He knelt and picked up her books. "A lovely lady with such a diverse interest in literature must surely be overwhelmed with excitement at the prospect of a town theater."

He handed her the books with a winning smile. He was well-groomed, with a fashionable suit, vest and bowler hat. His face was clean-shaven, revealing eyes bright with intelligence.

"No," she said in a whisper, horrified at the suggestion. "No, Dempsey does *not* need a theater!"

The man's smile wavered. He glanced at the crowd. She stood and grabbed her books before she fled. She could feel him watching her.

Huffing and puffing, she finally climbed the stairs to the safety of her apartment, closing the door behind her and sinking to the floor.

Eight

Beatrice thrust her hand into the hot, soapy water and rinsed her sponge. She returned to the task of scrubbing the old tile floor. The sight of her red, raw hands satisfied the ache of her heart, even if just a bit. She scrubbed until she was gasping for air, until her eyes stopped watering and her throat stopped constricting and her brain stopped thinking.

But her brain never stopped thinking.

She had asked God several times why he chose to make her the way she was if he knew she would experience so great a loss. Now the weight of her doubt crippled her. She dropped the brush and covered her face with her hands, her eyes aching with tears she refused to allow.

"God," she gasped as the memories flooded her mind. She could see nothing but the children – their terrified expressions and innocent anguish. "You took my family and the only man I wanted to love for the rest of my life. You took so many who didn't deserve to die. So why didn't you just take me, too?"

She slammed her fist on the floor, finding a measure of relief in the pain. "*Why can't you just take me?*"

The doctor in Chicago had promised she wouldn't live to see her thirtieth birthday. Yet here she was at thirty-two. Why? Why did God have to be so unfair? Why couldn't he just end her suffering and let her be with her family and her beloved? Thoughts she usually tempered raged through her mind like wildfire. Doubts about God's love. The kind of thoughts she must always keep hidden.

"It's not fair," Beatrice whispered. "I don't see the point of living. I'm not accomplishing anything. I don't have anyone. I don't *want* anyone."

Suddenly, the image of Evan Master's face filled her mind. His kind eyes. His gentle touch. His unassuming, friendly nature. For the first time in the many years she'd known him, she considered how different her life might be if she hadn't pushed him away.

If she'd accepted his invitation to the dance the first time he'd had the courage to ask, over ten years ago, how would her life be different? Would they be married now, living in the yellow bungalow on Vine Street? Would she be rocking Evan's babies and cooking his meals, welcoming her hard-working husband home each afternoon? Lying next to him at night, feeling his strong arms around her?

"I'd be dead." She shook her head stubbornly. Being married and having children would surely have caused her death. Hadn't the doctor said so?

But she was unprepared for Evan's persistence. She wouldn't have guessed he'd still be pursuing her after so many years. She had figured he would get tired of her rejection and move on to find a girl that could make all his dreams come true. Yet a year had passed, then two, then five, then ten. Evan never looked in another woman's direction, even once. He had stayed true, no matter how many times she ignored him or pretended disgust at his offers of friendship.

She leaned back against the wall. Her hand rested on her chest and she felt the steady rhythm of a heart that should have long since stopped beating, and often struggled to keep up. She felt her lungs pull in air and thought of the times when she could only gasp and wait for the moment her body would stop functioning for the lack of oxygen.

No matter how she tried not to think of her weaknesses, she was always aware of them, every waking moment.

I'm broken, she admonished herself. *I'll never be like anyone else. It's not fair for me to try to live as though I'm one of them. I'd only cause them pain.*

And she knew that sort of heartbreak well enough that she'd never wish it on another soul.

The candle on the table sputtered and reached the end of its life as the flame went out. Darkness claimed the room, as heavy and menacing as the thoughts within her. She stood and blindly made her way down the wall. Her fingers fell across the switch for the gas lights.

I could turn it. I could use the lights everyone else uses at night.

She put pressure on the ends of her fingers, enough that the switch moved slightly. If she turned it on, would she turn to a new chapter of her life?

I wouldn't have to go to bed at sunset. I could read all night if I wanted.

But she knew she'd never press that switch. Not in a thousand lifetimes. She was too broken for second chances.

Her hand fell from the switch and she stumbled through the darkness to her closet. She pulled on her nightgown and climbed into bed, pulling the thin blanket up to her chin. She stared at the ceiling without moving until she fell asleep.

It had taken many nights of tossing and turning before she'd discovered the trick. If she didn't allow herself a single movement, not even to adjust a hair that tickled her cheek or an itch that begged to be scratched, she would fall asleep within minutes.

If nothing else, Beatrice could retain control of this one thing. She had no control over her life or her fears, but there were little things she could control. She held fast to them. Doggedly. No one would break her resolve to stick to the choices she had made. They were *her* choices no matter how irrational they might seem to someone else. She wouldn't apologize.

Some things were better left unsaid, anyway.

♫

Evan woke up with the sun on his face.

He stared up at the same white ceiling he'd woken up to every other morning. Every morning of every day for the past ten years.

The white ceiling was a precursor, a foreshadowing of sorts, to what he could expect the rest of the day. The same breakfast alone, except for his snooty cat. The dumb animal seemed intent on reminding Evan every day that life as a barn cat on the Whitley farm had been far more interesting than living in a house in town with Evan.

"When did this become my life?" Evan asked the cat before he shooed him off the kitchen table.

After breakfast, he walked the same route to work, where he greeted the same five people on the same endless routine. He faked a broad smile when Mrs. O'Malley waved to him. She adjusted her window display of hats with piles of toile, painted fruit ornaments and fake birds atop straw bases. He had the same thought he had every other day. She seemed to find her job as important as if she were saving children from the streets. Never mind she'd charge a customer four dollars for the privilege of weighing down her head with such a monstrosity.

Yet he couldn't deny he felt a bit of envy at her passion.

He sighed as he turned the corner and again ran into the man who'd been there for several days trying to convince folks they needed a theater in Dempsey.

"We've moved on from the days of saloons and bawdy houses where men's entertainment fed into wanton desire and the evil intent of their affections," the man proclaimed to the nodding throng. "Now we can enjoy entertainment together as a family. Just imagine it, citizens of Dempsey. Laughing, crying and singing along as you are carried away by the amusements of shows never before seen outside of New York City!"

Evan shook his head in irritation as he passed. He'd never been much for salespeople and their lofty promises that never seemed to come true.

Unfortunately, the man was perceptive enough to notice. "Good sir, do you doubt what I'm saying?"

Evan stopped and sighed. "You're here for one reason. To take our money. Why don't you just tell them the truth instead of promising things you can't make good on?"

The man narrowed his eyes slightly, but worked to suppress his reaction. He smiled at the crowd. "I intend to fulfill every promise I've made you. I invite you all to step forward and make your donations. You will see what I will be able to do to put Dempsey on the map and bring in folks from everywhere ready to spend their money in your shops. This theater will make your town strong and vibrant for the coming years of growth in America."

Evan scoffed as he turned back toward the building with the *Train and Telegraph* sign.

♫

Beatrice pounded the notes until her frustration was satisfied. Playing the classical piece with expert precision reinforced her resolve to remain in control of her life. She turned the page without missing a note and continued the piece with mastered skill.

She had a twinge of disappointment that no one heard her play, but she was also glad she was alone. Pastor Merchant was on his Thursday visitation circuit.

She built the dynamics of the song in perfect increments, controlling each sound with the practiced ear of a perfectionist. She knew the result was astounding, even if she was the only one to witness it.

"I'm sure I've never heard that piece played so perfectly," a voice said from the back of the church.

Beatrice abruptly stopped.

"Please don't stop!" Amelia Morehouse from the library came down the aisle with several books tucked within the crook of her elbow. "I don't think the composer could have played it that well."

It was either keep playing or talk to the woman, so Beatrice chose to continue playing.

To Beatrice's chagrin, Mrs. Morehouse sat down next to her on the piano bench. As Beatrice reached the final crescendo, Amelia closed her eyes and hummed along.

When the song ended, Beatrice scrambled for another song so she wouldn't have to find something to say. She pulled the hymnbook forward and began to play the first song she saw.

Mrs. Morehouse began to sing in a clear, quiet voice.

> *This is my story,*
> *This is my song,*
> *Praising my Savior,*
> *All the day long.*

Amelia's fingers reached for the keys, and she played an accompanying melody. They finished the chorus with equal, but different, flair.

"Wasn't that fun?" Amelia asked with a chuckle.

Beatrice was not about to admit it. "May I help you with something?"

Amelia's grin faded but did not completely disappear. "Pastor Merchant asked me to drop off several titles he needed for reference in his sermon."

"I'm sure you could leave them on his desk. The office door is just there."

Mrs. Morehouse nodded and did as Beatrice suggested. When she returned, Beatrice was leafing through pages of music.

"You know, *Blessed Assurance* is one of my favorite hymns."

"The words seem rather like the author has never seen a day of trouble. I don't find that realistic." Beatrice regretted her words immediately. She did not intend to begin a discussion.

Amelia nodded. "It might sound that way at first, until you understand what the author had been through. What she dealt with on a daily basis."

Beatrice shrugged. "Fanny Crosby was blind. I know. But

she'd been that way since she was an infant. She was accustomed to it."

"You're right. She chose not to let her blindness keep her from knowing joy. But that was only part of her story."

Beatrice didn't want to discuss it further. She changed the topic. "You were playing from memory, then?"

"Oh, goodness, no." Amelia laughed. "I was playing what I felt."

Beatrice frowned. "You played what you felt?"

"Yes. I noted your key, closed my eyes and felt something that might intertwine with your notes and be pleasing company."

Beatrice shifted on the bench. "That is an odd way to play the piano."

Amelia shrugged. "I never claimed I wasn't odd. But isn't music simply creative expression? And in such a state, should we not use our knowledge to create something new, originating in our heart?"

"I play the notes. I play them correctly. That's what it means to play the piano," Beatrice contradicted.

Amelia considered her thoughtfully. "If that was really the way you are, I wouldn't say another word. But I see something in your eyes. You have an understanding of what I'm saying, Beatrice. An intuition. But something has made you afraid of using it."

Beatrice was horrified at the woman's insight. She felt white heat spread across her face. She stood up and grabbed her books, leaving Amelia to stand alone next to the piano.

She raced to the door and across the yard to the parsonage. How had she let the other woman see what was within her? Why had she engaged in conversation at all? If one woman could so easily break down her defenses, what might happen with another lapse in judgment?

Beatrice needed to be more careful. She needed to stay home when it was possible to run into anyone. She must not let people ask questions or look too deeply. What she had stored away was off limits. No one could open it, for she had locked it up and thrown away the key. She could not afford to have anyone trying to break open that lock.

She would die first.

She should have died already.

Nine

The telephone rang insistently, vibrating on its stand.

Evan looked up in surprise. He didn't get many calls at the office on Friday afternoon. He stood up and took up the receiver.

"Hullo?" he said loudly, knowing the lines could sometimes crackle and make it hard to hear.

"Evan! Get over here and bring the doc! The twins are coming!"

Evan forgot the customary phone etiquette of saying "goodbye" and slammed down the receiver. He grabbed his coat and hat from the stand and called back to Isaiah. "Kathleen's having the twins. I'm going for the doctor."

Isaiah came out of the back room and got his own coat. "I'll lock up and bring Mary out to the farm."

Evan made a beeline for the livery to rent a horse and carriage. He didn't see the salesman from that morning before he barreled into him and knocked him into the street.

"Sorry," he said, distracted. He reached out a hand to help the man up.

The man dusted off his suit. "May I ask where you're headed in such a rush?"

"A friend's wife is having her babies. I need to get the doctor out to their farm quickly. There could be complications."

The man replaced his hat. "Wouldn't an automobile be

faster?"

Evan breathed a laugh. "Maybe if I had one." He excused himself and started to turn away.

"I have one." The man's words stopped him. "Quite a nice one. You're welcome to borrow it, since this is an emergency."

Evan stopped, tempted by the easier solution. "You'd let a stranger who doesn't believe in your theater take your shiny new automobile?"

"The name's Jacob Wylie. Jake, if you like." Mr. Wylie held out a hand for Evan to shake. "I'm not one to hold a grudge. I mean to show the people of this town my goodwill."

Evan shook Jacob's hand. "Evan Masters."

"Do you know how to drive a car, Mr. Masters?"

Evan considered the question as he surveyed the vehicle. He was certain he could get it started. Beyond that, he'd just have to figure it out. "Sure. Starter button, brake, accelerator. Who doesn't know that?"

Jacob Wylie smiled and gestured into the street. "It's parked just there, by the grocery."

Evan waved his thanks and jogged across the street to the automobile. It was nice. Nicer than the Model T's some folks in Dempsey had sprung hard-earned cash to buy. This car was a luxury roadster. He couldn't even imagine the money Wylie must have at his disposal to be driving it.

He jumped over the door and landed on the shiny leather seat. For a moment, he looked at the unfamiliar controls and wondered if he could really drive it. Finally, he hit the starter button and heard the engine roar to life. He followed the procedure he could barely remember from the Ohio State Fair the previous summer during an auto demonstration.

He pushed his foot on the accelerator, and the car took off with a strong jerk. He compensated by pushing the brake, which made the wheels screech to a stop. He avoided anyone's gaze as he tried pressing the gas pedal a little more slowly. The car eased away from the curb and carried him down the street toward the clinic.

He managed to stop the car without too much of a jolt, remembering to put it into park before he hopped out. He ran through the open door, calling for Luke.

"Kathleen's having the babies. We gotta go!"

Luke appeared from the back room. "Let me gather a few things, and I'll be right there."

Evan went back and started the car again. He realized a group had gathered around the car, including several pretty women who were sending smiles in his direction.

He couldn't help the grin that spread across his face. He pushed the hair out of his face and laid an arm along the side.

"Evan?"

Luke stood on the walk with his bag in hand, searching for the expected horse and cart.

"Right here, Doc," Evan called.

Luke stared at the automobile in surprise. "Where in the world did you get that?"

Evan shrugged. "The theater guy loaned it to me. I didn't argue. This thing will get us to the farm much faster than a horse and cart will."

Luke seemed reticent. "Have you driven one before?"

"I'm driving it now. Get in."

Luke frowned, but he opened the passenger door and slid in. He set his bag on his lap, holding the leather handles with white knuckles.

"You aren't going to die." Evan made a face at him as he started the car. It roared back to life. Evan pushed the accelerator. The car lurched forward and made a sputtering noise before the engine promptly died.

"Huh," Evan said, trying the starter button again. This time, he quickly pumped the accelerator. The automobile seemed to jump off the road in a takeoff that sent Luke's derby hat flying into the road. Luke waved him on with a perturbed expression.

As Evan laughed and turned to look back in the road, a figure came into the street in front of them.

Beatrice.
He slammed on the brake pedal as hard as he could.

Ten

Beatrice wasn't one to read while she was walking, but Mrs. Morehouse had saved her a book called *Anticipations of the Reaction of Mechanical and Scientific Progress upon Human Life and Thought* by H.G. Wells, and her curiosity had gotten the best of her. She was quickly swept away by the imagination of the author's attempt to predict what life might be like in the year 2000.

She looked up from the book as she stepped into the street across from the church, but only had time to hear the sound of the automobile's horn and look over to see the machine hurtling toward her, brakes squealing, on a certain collision course. It happened so fast she hardly had time to respond.

She jumped back toward the sidewalk and fell, books spilling in every direction.

Her heart raced and her vision grew dim. She closed her eyes, attempting to breathe deeply. She clung to consciousness as she felt large hands on her arms. Her eyes flew open to find Evan's face looming over her, panic written in every line of his expression.

"Beatrice! Tell me you're okay!"

It was the last thing she heard before everything faded to black.

♪♩

When she opened her eyes again, she was moving. On a

horse? In a cart?

She opened her eyes and gasped aloud. She was in the automobile, and it was moving.

"Lie still," she heard a familiar voice and felt something cold against the thin material of her blouse.

"Don't touch me!" She sat up and tried to push the hand away.

"I'm sorry, Miss Walsh. It's me, Doctor Thomas. I treated you when you collapsed a couple weeks ago. You've had a scare, and I'm concerned it may have affected your heart."

Beatrice felt the jostling motion and grabbed hold of the seat cushion. "Where are we going?"

She sat up and saw they were traveling through the woods on a dirt road. She glared at Evan as he gripped the steering wheel. He had an undeniable expression of guilt.

"Have I been kidnapped?" she seethed, indignant.

Evan met her eyes. "Is that really what you think of me?"

Dr. Thomas cleared his throat. "I'm afraid this is my fault. I'm needed at the Whitley farm to deliver twins, but we couldn't leave you unconscious on the boardwalk. I felt the best thing to do would be to bring you along."

"I want to go home," she said, searching for her books. "Please take me back."

"Can't do that." Evan shook his head. "Kathleen needs the doc *now*."

"Where are my books? I demand you stop this car and let me out!"

She tried to open the door, but the doctor stopped her. "Your books are right here on the floor, Miss Walsh. I'm afraid I must insist you accompany us so I can monitor your heart for a time. I'm worried about you."

"I didn't ask for your concern." Her voice sounded high-pitched and thick with emotion. She swallowed hard to contain it. "You are making my heart stressed by forcing me to accompany you in this contraption with that man."

She looked up in time to see Evan's eyes in the rear view

mirror. She didn't miss the hurt. The guilt she felt over wounding him only made her angrier.

"Just try to relax," Dr. Thomas said, patting her hand before he felt for her pulse.

"I just want to go home." Beatrice tried to avoid Evan's watchful gaze.

"You have some heavy reading here." The doctor picked up the Wells book. "Do you think we can imagine life in a hundred years with any accuracy?"

Beatrice suspected the doctor was more concerned with diffusing the tension than talking literature, but she reluctantly took the bait. "Why not? Perhaps if humanity has direction, they will find greater purpose."

"You say that as if you're on the outside looking in," Dr. Thomas observed. He seemed immediately sorry for saying it. "Forgive me; that was forward."

She shrugged and looked away.

The roar of the engine made any further conversation difficult, so they fell silent. Beatrice could not seem to keep her eyes away from the mirror. She met Evan's gaze once again.

Are you okay? He seemed to ask, though he spoke no words. Since his eyes were on her and not the road, he had to swerve to miss an unsuspecting skunk who had sauntered out into the path. Beatrice flew across the seat and landed in the doctor's lap. She hurried to push away from him and return to her own side, aware of the bright pink shade of the doctor's cheeks.

"You might think to take those corners a little more slowly, Evan," Dr. Thomas called, chuckling awkwardly.

Evan pulled the car into the barnyard and pushed the brake pedal so hard they skidded to a stop and nearly took out a row of indignant hens. The car bumped the wall of the feed shed and the rickety old walls promptly fell in. Evan swore.

Beatrice jumped out of the car as if it were on fire, clutching her books. The doctor followed her out and hurried down the path toward the farmhouse. Evan backed the car away from the shed and turned it off before he got out and examined the damage to the brand new vehicle.

"Is this yours?" Beatrice asked before she thought better of it. How could he afford such a luxury?

"Nope." He tried to smooth out a scratch with a spit and shine using his untucked shirttail. It didn't help much. He stood up and sighed, throwing his hat and jacket into the front seat and rolling his sleeves up to his elbow. "That theater salesman loaned it to me when he heard there was an emergency."

Her gaze rested on his muscular brown arms as he spoke. When he turned back to her, she quickly looked away.

"Do you think he'll notice the scratches?" Evan said with a hopeful voice.

She had the sudden urge to giggle. She tried to subdue it by walking over behind him and peering at the jagged scrapes along the new paint. "I think it's highly unlikely he'll miss these."

"He's probably going to make me pay for it," Evan said.

"Perhaps you shouldn't try to drive again until you learn how," she said smugly, still trying not to smile. He looked at her, a quizzical smile in place.

"You aren't flirting with me now, are you, Miss Walsh?" His face spread into a wide grin, the damaged car forgotten.

She huffed. "I'm simply suggesting you learn to operate dangerous vehicles before attempting to drive them."

Evan took a step closer to her, his hands on his hips. Beatrice smelled a tantalizing combination of coffee and hair tonic.

She took a step back.

"Come on now." He came toward her, beckoning. "I'll carry you up to the house."

"I beg your pardon!" She took several large steps backward and tripped on a log by the side of the path. He easily caught her arms and kept her and all her books from falling.

For one moment, she hesitated. She stared into his eyes, tempted to enjoy being in the circle of his embrace. But it became overwhelming. She shook herself free of his grasp and stepped over the log to safety.

"Thank you," she muttered. "But I will walk."

"Worth a shot." He smirked.

She twisted her mouth to keep that bothersome smile from appearing. They turned and headed toward the bridge that led up the hill to the house.

"Have you ever been to the Whitley farm before?" He stayed close to her side, his hands in his pockets. Beatrice was aware of him. More aware than she'd ever been before.

"Never."

"Josh inherited it from his grandpa quite a few years ago, before he married Kathleen. I don't mind telling you I've always been envious of it."

She didn't answer him, though she couldn't blame his feelings. The farm was the picture of the American dream, with every feature and amenity it could possibly hold. The farmhouse was picturesque against the blue sky and bright sun.

"You ever been around for a birthing?" Evan asked cheerfully.

Beatrice stopped walking when it dawned on her why they were there. "I want to go home." She had no desire to know anything about birth.

"Sorry, Doc says he has to check on you for a while yet." He stopped with her and smiled an apology as he spoke. Her stomach began to roll and her head felt dizzy.

"Careful or I'll have to carry you, after all." He caught her chin with his fingers. Her heart pounded and her lungs felt starved for air. He watched her reaction curiously as he let her go. "Why do you do that? Overreact, I mean. Women have been having babies since the good Lord made man and woman, and no one expects you to watch anyway. We'll just sit and wait in the kitchen. I'll be with you."

"I never asked for you to take care of me," she argued. "In fact, I'm here against my will."

"We all need folks to look out for us, and you don't have family."

She raised her chin slightly, glaring. "I'll wait in the car until you're ready to leave."

♫

Evan wondered what to do. Should he push or let her be for a few hours until he could take her home? He made up his mind to press his luck. "I insist you come inside, so Doc doesn't have to go looking for you to check your pulse. You could sit in the parlor and read your books, if you prefer."

She looked at the house as if she was considering complying. All at once the sight of her, small and yet strong, beautiful and yet stern, captured him. Audacity getting the best of him, he suddenly stepped closer to her – closer than one would stand in normal conversation. He reached a hand to hers and ran his finger gently along the length of her thumb before he took her stack of books.

Her face paled and then turned a pretty shade of pink as she quickly turned back to him. He liked the sense that he could affect her with the lightest touch. He wasn't exactly unaware that women found him attractive, and he knew what it felt like to connect on a physical level. There were definitely sparks between them that Beatrice wasn't keen on admitting to him –or to herself.

He turned and headed up to the porch, and to his amazement, she followed without argument. He looked back and saw her clenched jaw and frown. My, but the woman was downright adorable.

"You're short, aren't you?" he teased as he held the door for her, noticing her head only came up to the middle of his chest. If he were to have occasion to embrace her, that head of silky black hair would fit nicely against his torso.

She refused to look at him. "Perhaps I am normal-sized, and you are just gigantic."

He laughed at her words spoken so quietly he barely heard them. "You may be right."

They walked into the kitchen, immediately bombarded by toddlers who appeared to be on the loose.

"I should have thought to get in here a little quicker," Evan said as he gathered the boys up in his arms and carried them to the table, where he deposited them in seats and looked for snacks to keep them busy for a few minutes. They stared at the ceiling with wide eyes as the sounds of their mother's cries of pain, though muted, drifted through the floorboards. Beatrice seemed as nervous as the two-year-olds.

"Don't worry," he said to anyone who needed to hear it. "She'll be okay."

"Evan?" Joshua hollered down the stairs, his voice panicked.

Evan jogged to the stairs and waved up at him. "I'm here, Josh. Miss Walsh and I will take care of the kids. You focus on Kathleen."

Joshua nodded in relief and turned back to the bedroom. He stopped short and grinned. "Miss Walsh is here?" he asked in a suggestive tone.

"Don't start," Evan said, pointing at Joshua in warning. "Don't even start. Go be a husband."

The panic came back to his friend's expression. "Oh, yeah." He disappeared into the bedroom, Kathleen's wailing becoming louder for a moment as he opened and closed the door.

Evan watched after him, worried. "Lord, let her come through this okay. Let her and those babies be alive and well when all's said and done."

What did it feel like to be a nervous father waiting to meet his children? What if it was Beatrice moaning in pain? The thought gave him new respect for Joshua.

He returned to the kitchen. Beatrice had found two tin cups on the counter and poured milk from the icebox for the twins. "Now, don't cry," she said awkwardly, though her tone was soothing.

The twins stared at her, their eyes glassy and their lower lips protruding as if they were about to erupt into tears.

"Hey, boys," he said cheerfully, stepping into the room. "Let's go visit the sheep."

♫

Beatrice watched warily as Evan followed the boys to the

sheep pasture. She wasn't sure what to do, so she walked after them. The sight of the large man walking behind the tiny brothers tried to warm the edges of the heart she intended to remain icy.

Evan started running after a particularly disgruntled sheep, and the boys toddled after him with screams of laughter. He pretended to fall and let them jump on his chest.

"You got me!" he cried in mock dismay, feigning powerlessness. He grabbed them suddenly, growling and capturing them in large hands.

They laughed and tried to get away. He let them go and chased them, pretending he couldn't run fast enough to catch them. After Beatrice had watched them play for several minutes, Evan finally stopped, out of breath, and watched the two run away after the sheep.

The memory found her before she could shake it off. She saw Edward's friendly eyes crinkled at the sides as he played baseball with her little brother in the park across the street from her family's row house in Pullman.

"Jamie Walsh knocks it out of the park and the crowd goes wild!" Edward yelled as Jamie hit the ball. "No one has seen this kind of hitting since Davy Jones of the Chicago Cubs! This kid's going to go far, I tell you!"

Jamie laughed and ran the bases as Edward made a show of running after the ball that had gone into the street. He timed his return perfectly so Jamie had just crossed home plate as he was reaching out with the ball to tag him.

"I made it!" Jamie shrieked, jumping up and down on the plate. "I'm safe!"

Edward grabbed him around the chest and ruffled his hair. "When did you get so doggone good at this, kid? Seems like just last week you could only toddle. Couldn't even lift the bat."

"Guess I went and grew up," Jamie laughed.

"I guess so," Edward caught Beatrice's eyes and smiled. "Your sister grew up, too."

"Whew!" Evan interrupted the memory, for which she was grateful as much as she was sorry. She leaned against an apple tree and tried to appear disinterested.

Evan watched her until she wanted to squirm under the scrutiny. "I don't know where those kids get all their energy. Too bad we can't bottle it up and sell it like medicine. You know?"

She met his gaze briefly. "I suppose I have energy enough."

"That ain't the truth and we both know it, Beatrice," he said, standing and crossing his arms over his wide chest. "I'm not trying to pry, but this is the second time in the space of a month you've given us a scare. There's something wrong with your heart."

She wanted to be angry for his intrusion, but she recognized the deliberate tenderness in his tone. He was opening the door. Allowing her an opportunity to tell him the truth.

It was not surprising that Evan was trying to reach her. It was nothing new. But what did catch her off guard was her sudden desire to tell him the truth. He must be wearing down her defenses. She'd need to fight harder. It jarred her that he could affect her so much. This wasn't supposed to happen.

"I'm fine," she murmured, though both of them knew she was lying.

He watched her for a long moment before he had to run after the boys. She turned abruptly and walked back to the house alone.

Eleven

Two hours after they arrived, Dr. Thomas came back downstairs. Evan had put the twins down for a nap in the parlor and was sitting at the kitchen table sipping coffee while Beatrice looked out the window in silence.

"Just made a fresh pot." Evan motioned to the stove. Dr. Thomas nodded and reached for an empty cup. He took several gulps, wincing at the heat.

"How is it going up there?" Evan asked.

Dr. Thomas sighed. "The first twin is in the wrong position. It's slowing the process considerably. I'm considering sending someone to get the midwife. I've seen her save enough lives."

"Just say the word and I'll go fetch her. Are you going to check on Beatrice?" Evan looked at her.

"That's why I came down," the doctor said, giving Beatrice a cordial smile before he came to her and held up his stethoscope.

She took an unconscious step backward as he reached for her, but he took her arm gently and placed the instrument on her chest. "I know this makes you uncomfortable, but if you panic, it will be harder for me to see that your heart is functioning well. Please try to relax."

She tried to will her heart to beat normally, realizing she would never get home if she didn't pass his inspection.

The doctor shook his head with a frown. "I'm not sure you're well enough to send you home. It's rather erratic, actually. Do you feel the pauses and extra beats?"

She nodded. "It's the way I am. It's been like that for years."

"Were you injured?"

She avoided his eyes. "Please let me go home."

"I can't advise that right now."

She chafed. The stillness of the room left as a clamor of people appeared in the doorway.

Mrs. Morehouse and Mary McAllister appeared. "Kathleen?"

Luke turned to them, his attention taken. "She's having a rough time. I'm sure your presence would be a comfort. She keeps asking for you both."

Amelia squeezed Beatrice's arm with a small smile before they followed the doctor to the stairs. Neither woman asked why Beatrice was there, for which she was thankful. Once again, she was alone with Evan.

"Beatrice," he spoke quietly.

She stared at her half-filled cup of coffee. "What do you want me to say? I don't owe you an explanation."

He didn't argue. He folded his hands under his chin and watched her with eyes she suspected could see her soul's secrets.

The deep tone of his voice filled the quiet kitchen with warmth not unlike the cup she was holding. "You aren't surprised. You know what's wrong with you."

Beatrice fingered the handle of her mug. "Yes."

"So you're at peace with whatever it is?"

"I am." She nodded.

He took a deep breath, and his expression took on a measure of uncertainty. "Will it kill you?"

She considered her response. Would it help matters to be honest? Would it make him pursue her more or give him closure to walk away and live his life? She made herself meet his gaze and was unprepared for the vulnerability in his eyes. What she said would deeply affect him, whether she liked it or not.

She attempted to hide her emotion. "Yes, it will kill me."

♫

Evan thought he was prepared to hear the worst. But an avalanche of devastation crashed down on him. He felt pressure behind his eyes and reached to massage his temples.

Beatrice didn't give any explanation. He wanted to know the details but didn't have the courage to ask. How long did she have? Years? Months? Weeks? He felt her watching him with a kind of detached fascination, as if he was a bug she'd smashed that still flailed around in a desperate attempt to cling to life.

"How soon?" He heard his voice tremble as he asked the necessary question.

She shrugged. The woman actually sat there and shrugged at him, as if her very breath was a trivial matter. As if losing her life and breaking his heart meant little. Her face betrayed no recognizable emotion.

"I should have already died." She gave the prognosis as if annoyed she had outlived it. Was that why she lived as she did? She was simply waiting for death to come and steal her beautiful soul away from him?

His mind swarmed with questions. *Are you sure? Who told you? Could they be wrong? Why didn't you tell me? Is this why you reject me? If it weren't true, would there be hope for us?*

He sat for so many long moments he could track the late afternoon sun's movement across the room.

They heard the desperate screams above them, growing in intensity. Suddenly, everything was quiet, and a baby's cry pierced the air with the promise spoken of new life. A fresh beginning. Hope.

Evan smiled in spite of his grief. He glanced at Beatrice, but she kept her expression neutral. She did not speak or meet his eyes.

It wasn't long before Kathleen began to labor again, but this time, it was only a few minutes before another baby wailed along with the first. Evan sighed in relief. Kathleen would be okay. The babies would be okay. Death wasn't going to come knocking at

Joshua's door that night.

"They're here," he said. "Safe and sound."

She met his eyes, her features impassive. "I suppose that's something. When do you think the doctor might be able to leave?"

He didn't answer her. He finished the last of his coffee and after a few minutes, he went to check on the boys. They were awake, settling onto the sofa with their Aunt Mary, reading a picture book. Mary smiled at him. "Go up and see them, Evan. They're beautiful little ladies." Her smile slipped when she saw the look on his face. "What's wrong?"

He shook his head. "Nothing I feel like talking about."

She nodded, the concern still present in her expression. "Go see the babies. Maybe they'll give you a measure of peace."

He climbed the stairs with heavy steps and went to knock on the bedroom door. A moment later Joshua answered with a squirming bit of life in his arms. He grinned at Evan.

"I got myself two daughters, Evan. Ruth and Ellen Whitley. This here is little Ruthie. What do you think of that?"

"I think they're fortunate little girls."

Joshua paused as if he had noticed something in Evan's features, but he didn't comment. He came out of the bedroom and handed the baby to Evan.

"I thought she looked itty bitty in *my* arms," Joshua said with a chuckle.

Evan smiled and stared at the wrinkled little face, as beautiful a promise as he'd seen in quite some time. A lump settled in his throat, and an incredible yearning made him feel short of breath.

"I want this," he said, not realizing at first he'd spoken aloud. He looked up at Joshua. "I want a family so much, Josh."

Joshua clamped a hand on Evan's shoulder. "I know you do."

"God knows best."

Joshua sighed and watched his daughter squirm and bat an awkward fist in the air. "I don't know if it's his plan to keep you from a family. He put that desire in you for a reason."

"I've been alone since I was twelve. I'm tired of it."

Joshua nodded. "Tell the Lord. I will, too."

Evan forced a smile, not wanting Joshua to think he wasn't grateful. But how could he just let it go and trust God? He'd just found out the only woman he'd ever wanted was dying. His dream was dying with her, and there was no way around it.

Joshua eyed him. "Something happened."

Evan nodded, staring at the baby. "Beatrice told me she has a heart condition."

"But you knew that," Joshua reminded him. "Did she say something else?"

Evan couldn't look at his best friend. "She says it should have killed her already. She's living on borrowed time."

Joshua sighed again, walking to the small window on the landing and looking out over the creek and barnyard. "Seems to me borrowed time could be the best days of your life."

Twelve

Beatrice lay awake for hours after Evan brought her home. She couldn't forget the flushed faces and happy babbling of toddlers and the mewling cries of infants. When she closed her eyes, she saw the features of an overjoyed grandmother and relieved father. Everything that might have gone wrong washed away in a wave of blessing. Love had conquered the night, and life had stolen the possibility of death claiming their joy.

But it wasn't what kept her awake. Evan's silence during the ride home bothered her. She had hurt him. She hadn't meant to, in fact, she'd thought she was being kind by telling him the truth. She had hoped he would let go of his dreams of their future together.

She had come to terms with her secret years before. To her mind, it was commonplace. Waiting for death was her normal. But she hadn't given Evan a chance to become used to the idea. She'd just hammered him with her truth.

She'd never known Evan to lack for words, and it troubled her that she had caused his silence. She hated that it bothered her, though, because it felt like an entanglement. The very condition she'd hoped to avoid at all costs.

Evan spoke only once, when he came around to help her out of the automobile. "Beatrice, I'd appreciate your honesty from this point on. I know you don't think you are answerable to anyone, but I believe God would disagree with you."

Beatrice could not escape his words. Did God disagree? She had to admit she had never considered God's opinion. If it was true, she wasn't prepared to consider the repercussions of going against him.

The next morning, as if to make her more uncomfortable, Amelia Morehouse appeared in the church auditorium while she was playing piano.

"Miss Walsh, I'm afraid I need to ask you a favor. I volunteered to care for the library until Mrs. Reynolds returns, but I have no time or motivation with those babies at the farm. Kathleen and Joshua need an extra pair of hands, anyway. Kathleen's mother, Amy, wanted to come straight away but she's been ill and can't travel. I would be indebted to you if you were to oversee the library. You know your way around, and it would come with a small salary."

Beatrice was as surprised as anyone else in Dempsey would be when she heard herself accept the position. She felt as if she were compromising something fundamental to her character. But what could she do? She needed money.

The first morning she worked in the library, she didn't see anyone for the first hour. She took the opportunity to organize her favorite sections to better suit her, then she improved on the haphazard filing system. She found a stack of books she'd been eyeing and sat down at the desk to read for the rest of the day.

Just when she thought she might escape her first day without having had to talk to anyone, the doors began to creak open and patrons stepped inside.

She nodded her only greeting, and said nothing while she checked out their books. She had started to feel a measure of confidence until she looked up and saw the fancy theater salesman standing in the doorway. He smiled at her and bowed, hat against his chest. She lost all her nerve.

He approached the desk with his walking stick tapping against the black and white checkered tile floor. "Good afternoon, Miss.

My name is Jacob Wylie, and I was hoping to entertain a moment of your time."

She glared at him, refusing to speak.

He wasn't put off by her response. "I get the sense you have strong feelings about my occupation and my reasons for being in Dempsey. I hope you will attempt to overlook your reservations so I might speak to you about another matter."

She still said nothing. She hugged her book to her chest.

"You're a quiet one, aren't you? Ah, but the quiet ones are the most lovely."

She frowned.

He smiled. "Especially a gem like you with your nose caught in a book." He touched the binding of her book.

She was angry that she couldn't argue with him because she quite agreed with him. "Don't attempt to manipulate me."

He chuckled. "Well, you don't mince words, do you? I apologize for any wrong impression I've given you. The matter I wish to speak to you about is of a personal nature. I believe I may have recovered some funds that belong to you."

Beatrice met his eyes, confused. "How did you know I was missing funds?"

"Forgive me, but I happened upon some thieves. I overheard their conversation of how they stole into your apartment while you were playing the piano at your church. They were going to ransack the place for valuables until they noticed your bankbook inside the crock on the kitchen window. The one made to look like a hummingbird. They said they decided not to leave anything amiss so you wouldn't suspect the book was gone, and agreed to return it to its place before you were finished practicing."

Beatrice stared at him with suspicion. "That's an awfully detailed accounting, Mr. Wylie."

"And you suppose I must be in on the scheme," he said with a nod. "However, I am not. I am proving it to you by returning your money to you."

"How did you get it?" Beatrice took the roll of bills the man held in front of her.

"I strong-armed the men and threatened to involve the police."

Beatrice counted the ten-dollar bills. "There is only ninety dollars here. Ninety of five hundred."

He nodded. "I suspected it wasn't the entire amount. I will investigate further, if I have your leave to do so."

She hesitated. She didn't like being dependent on anyone, especially a shifty salesman whose demeanor seemed a little too polished to be genuine, but she did need her money back. She shrugged. "If that's the way you want to spend your time."

"Is it too early to close the library, or shall I accompany you to your bank as your security while you return your funds to your account?"

She sniffed, but she nodded quickly and proceeded to organize the desk and lock up.

"I couldn't help but notice you the first day I arrived in town," Mr. Wylie said as he followed her out the double doors and waited as she locked them with the key she wore on a string around her neck.

Beatrice didn't ask what he meant. He kept a steady pace beside her, hands folded behind his back.

"It was in your church. I'd noticed your lovely features, if I may say so, upon first laying eyes on you as I walked into the sanctuary. But it was when you stepped to the piano that I knew you were special. Such heart! Such passion! I was simply spellbound."

She doubted it. "You are a music lover?" she said skeptically as they turned the corner. She was relieved to see the bank was in view.

Within herself, she struggled. She hated that his words had found a soft landing in her love-starved heart. She walked faster, clutching the envelope.

"I am more than just a music lover. I cannot put into words the joy I feel when I hear a well-played piece. That is why it is my life's mission to see that the stage, and all it can offer the human soul, is available to anyone. Anyone who will step away from the doldrums of this life and live in their imagination. Anyone who knows that indefinable urge to discover beauty."

Beatrice spared him a glance. The words seemed heartfelt, though they made her uncomfortable with their personal nature. "Are you sure it is pursuit of beauty and not profit?"

He must have noticed her sardonic tone, but he smiled easily. "I do not deny my labors have been rewarded. But it is only a testimony to the lure of the arts. They are as breath to our souls. Brilliant music like yours draws people. Talented performers are like magnets to world-weary spirits."

Beatrice regarded Jacob Wylie as he held the bank door for her. She might have swooned at his words in a different time of her life. But everything had changed. There was an obvious truth standing in the way of her accepting his occupation.

"Theaters are not safe," she said primly, attempting to hide the great emotion behind her statement. "They are prone to fire. Safety is overlooked in the name of profit and people die. You offer us a death trap and ask us to finance it for you."

He didn't answer, and she saw the surprise register in his features. She held up the envelope. "I thank you for returning this to me. Since you must hold a measure of integrity, I suggest you use it, along with your good sense, and leave our town alone. Good day, Mr. Wylie."

♫

Beatrice stared at the notes on her page of music, trying to filter out the voice from the platform.

Without warning, Pastor Merchant had changed things. Normally, she was to play one hymn while everyone dutifully sang along. No one was to sing too loudly; everyone was to stay in their seat and say nothing. This was the way they did things. Beatrice was comfortable with the routine.

But this morning, Pastor had invited anyone to come to the front during the song if something was on their mind. This was not exactly uncommon, but no one ever did so. It was rote; nobody responded except the occasional attention seeker.

"Our dear sister, Mrs. Morehouse, would like to say a few words," Pastor said, smiling his encouragement to Amelia, who stood by his side, her face pink.

"I don't usually speak in front of people," Amelia said, holding her Bible open in front of her. "Forgive me if I stammer. But I have been affected by your pastor's words this morning and I sense God would have me give an illustration of his point."

She looked at her Bible. "Pastor Merchant read from Second Corinthians, chapter four: *For the things which are seen are temporal, but the things which are not seen are eternal.*"

Beatrice wanted to disconnect from the woman's words, but the verse sparked her curiosity. She had wondered about it the entire sermon. How could something unseen and unknown be eternal, yet the tangible, which she trusted, be temporary and transient?

Amelia continued in a soft voice, her voice wavering slightly with emotion. "I do not wish to keep you from lunch. I will make this brief."

Beatrice sized up the older woman. She knew how to recognize a person's motivations by observing them. Amelia looked as if she'd rather be anywhere than standing in front of a roomful of people. Yet there was a contrasting peace in her expression. No doubt, this woman's testimony could be trusted, whether Beatrice liked what she had to say or not.

"I lost my husband ten years ago, right here in Dempsey," Amelia said. "He died saving his daughter from a man who meant to hurt her. I am proud of him for how he died. Looking back, I can honestly say I wouldn't change anything that happened, as strange as that may sound, because he wouldn't have been the man I loved if he hadn't protected his family with his life."

Amelia looked down at the Bible, her eyes full of unshed tears. "It is these kinds of experiences that make us realize how temporary life is. One moment my husband was here, the next he was not. His strength, kindness and protection are no longer a part of my daily existence. I rely on catching glimpses of him in our sons, and I rely on memory to hear his voice or see his face."

The image of Beatrice's fiancé suddenly filled her mind. She closed her eyes and remembered his strength, the warmth from his body as they sat close together in the theater. She heard the rumble of his voice as he spoke close to her ear. Her mind's eye peered around her, seeing her parents and her little brother. They had been real. They had existed, just as she lived at that moment, sitting at the piano. But now they were only a memory.

"I know we have all lost people. We understand how it feels. But we must take heart, because these loved ones who died in Christ are no longer part of the temporal. They are now eternal! The next time I see William, he will be a perfect part of eternity. We'll never be separated again. This verse promises those who have left us are no longer temporary."

Beatrice bit the corner of her lip to keep the ache of her tears at bay. Amelia had meant her words as a comfort, but years of fighting the memories made the encouragement feel like the edge of a knife on an old wound that had never healed correctly. She drew her hands into fists, accidentally bumping the keys of the piano in the process and producing a discordant sound.

A hundred pairs of eyes turned her way.

Pastor Merchant saved her. "Thank you, Mrs. Morehouse. We will remember what you have said with joy. You are all dismissed."

Beatrice sighed with relief as the room became busy with activity. She shrunk back behind the piano and slipped into the pastor's office. She pushed her forehead against the wall and tried to will away the unwanted emotions. They needed to return to their compartment, locked away where they couldn't hurt her.

But even as she tried to control them, a strong hand caught her arm. She could tell who it was before she looked at him.

She didn't offer an explanation, and he didn't ask. He stood next to her for many long moments. The building quieted as the church members left, until the only sound was her labored attempt to breathe.

"Take it slow. In. Out." Evan's gentle tone soothed her heart until her panic began to subside. He made no move to hold her or say anything else. Finally, she gave an exhausted sigh and opened her eyes.

She had expected him to be looking at her, but his gaze was fixed on the window, watching the comings and goings of the citizens of Dempsey. His hand was warm through the fabric of her sleeve. It covered her, from her shoulder to her elbow.

He must have noticed she was looking at him. Their eyes met, and a sympathetic smile appeared on his face. Her heart skipped a beat, this time for an entirely different reason.

"Feel better?"

She nodded. He watched her for another moment before he let her go and stepped away from her.

She felt the loss of him, disappointed. For the first time since the theater fire, she wanted to curse her conviction that she should remain alone.

Even more when he placed a hand at the back of her neck and pulled her forward, pressing a fleeting kiss against her forehead.

"See you later," he said, and was gone.

Thirteen

Evan walked away from Beatrice, trying to keep his wits about him, trying not to let her know how wildly his heart was beating. It was the first time she'd ever let him get that close. Not only that, but she'd trembled as he touched her soft skin with his lips. She'd leaned toward him as he moved away as if his absence made her cold.

Lord, could it be there's something there, after all these years of her saying there's not?

He wondered why she had responded to Mrs. Morehouse's speech in such a way. What was her story?

"Hold up there, Goliath," Joshua called, trying to catch up with Evan's long strides.

Evan glanced at his friend. "I thought you had already headed home."

"Mary invited us for lunch. She really just wants to *ooh* and *ahh* over baby dresses for an hour, but she calls it lunch and I get food out of the deal, so I'm not complaining."

"Baby dresses?"

"Don't ask me. I couldn't even tell you what the girls are wearing this morning." Joshua shoved his hands in his pockets as they walked. "What's wrong? Why are you just coming out of church?"

"Curiosity killed the cat, Josh," Evan said, unsure he wanted to share what he was thinking. He'd been dunked in Joshua's creek a few times already for pining over women. Or one woman, anyway.

"Let me guess. You had an encounter with Beatrice."

Evan shrugged. "Don't ask if you don't like the answer."

"I like the answer just fine. Means I can knock you around for not listening to me *twelve years ago* when I told you that woman wasn't interested in you."

"I'd like to see you try knocking me around," Evan said.

Joshua grabbed his arm and whirled him around, holding up his fists and jabbing Evan in the chest.

Evan pushed his hand away. "Come on, Josh. We gotta grow up sometime."

"Doesn't have to be today." Joshua took another swing, this time at Evan's chin. His fist made contact, a little harder than Joshua probably expected, and Evan grunted in irritation at the sting.

"Knock it off." Evan blocked Joshua's fist and pushed it away again.

Joshua dropped his hands at Evan's reaction. "What's wrong, Evan?"

"I don't feel like talking about it. You'll just tell me to get over it and forget about her, and I *can't*. So why don't you just leave me be and go with your family?"

"That's not how I treat friends." Joshua's expression became serious.

Evan sighed. "I'm sorry, Josh. I don't know what's wrong with me today." He was ashamed when he saw the concern in Joshua's features, so he looked down at the ground.

"Tell me what happened with Beatrice. You have to talk to someone, might as well be me."

"Why?"

"Because you know I'll give you an honest answer no matter what fool-brained ideas come out of that noggin of yours."

Evan shrugged. "There's not much to tell. Beatrice ran off

after Mrs. Morehouse spoke and I followed her."

Joshua nodded, his brow furrowing. "I remember watching Morehouse fall after he was shot. It was a bad day. Seems strange to consider it a blessing, but I know she does. That woman can't seem to help finding the upside to anything. She says loss makes us stronger and capable of seeing suffering in others. *Everything happens for a reason, to those who love God,* she says."

"The Bible does say to give thanks in everything."

"Did Beatrice say why she ran off?"

Evan shook his head. "She didn't say anything. But I could see it in her eyes, Josh – something in her past terrorized her. I can't help wondering if someone hurt her."

Joshua nodded. "That'd make sense. And it makes sense to me that you would notice. You've had your own share of sufferings."

Evan nodded slowly, memories of his past trying to bombard his brain. "I see that in her as well. But she won't talk. Won't tell me or anyone else. Makes me think the worst."

Joshua nodded. They had stopped walking and stood on the boardwalk across the street from Isaiah and Mary's home. The air around them felt heavy with the memories the discussion had brought to light.

Joshua punched his arm. "I take it you took full advantage of the situation, though? Put your arm around her? Kissed away her tears?"

Evan made a face. "You make it sound so romantic," he said in sarcasm.

"You *did* kiss her! I oughta dunk you in the pond," Joshua said with a straight face.

Evan chuckled. "I'm not telling you anything. I know better."

"Fair enough," Joshua saluted as he turned to cross the street. He turned back. "I know I give you a hard time, Evan, and I've spent plenty of time worrying you are putting off your life with this preoccupation of yours, but I can see as plain as anyone that you aren't just curfuddled by a pretty face. You care about her.

That says a lot about you."

"Curfuddled? Is that a word?" Evan smirked.

Joshua scoffed. "Is now." He slapped Evan hard on the back. "Are you going to be alright?"

Evan nodded. "Soon as I figure out what a man's supposed to do when he finds the only thing he wants is the one thing he can't have."

Joshua frowned. He twisted his mouth and looked skyward. "Seems to me that's when a man finds something new to want."

He walked away, leaving Evan to ponder his answer.

Beatrice wouldn't have opened the door if she'd known someone was on the other side. She'd been on her way to the church to practice. She stared blankly at the young doctor, wondering if she could get away with closing the door in his face.

"Good morning, Miss Walsh. I'm just checking on you, since I haven't seen you in the office... as I'd asked."

"I feel fine, Dr. Thomas. Thank you for your inquiry. Good day."

She tried to close the door, but he slipped past her. "I'm sorry to have to insist, but I take my patients' care seriously. I need to check your heart."

"There must be some law about invading a woman's privacy," Beatrice said, standing at the open door. She stood awkwardly for a long moment as he watched her. "I'm just leaving. Please close the door on your way out."

"I will follow you wherever you're headed and conduct my examination at whatever public place I must." He smiled to soften his threat. She sighed and reluctantly pushed the door closed.

"Please have a seat," Dr. Thomas gestured to the kitchen chair. "I promise I'll only take a few moments of your time."

She sat down and watched him as he pulled several instruments from his bag and neatly sat them on a handkerchief he'd set on the table. He reached for the stethoscope.

"Take several breaths," he instructed as he pressed the cold metal pad to her upper chest.

She breathed deeply, covertly observing the doctor. He'd barely been more than a teenager when he began an apprenticeship with the elderly Dr. Hale. When Dr. Hale died, it took the town time to trust Luke's medical judgment. He'd proven himself, though, as far as Beatrice could tell. He was as serious as the spectacles perched on the end of his nose.

Being so close to him, Beatrice did not miss the fact that he was an attractive man. He had fair hair and a reddish complexion with startling blue eyes that seemed more vibrant under the lenses of his spectacles. He smelled nice, as well, like shaving soap and cloves.

Edward's breath was clove-scented when he kissed me the first time, she thought. She tensed when Luke moved the stethoscope to her back.

"Your heart rate just increased," Luke mused. They made eye contact and his cheeks turned pink. "Or perhaps I imagined it?"

"You imagine things about your patients?"

He turned redder and didn't comment. Beatrice knew she shouldn't tease him. He was obviously attracted to her and the last thing she needed was another would-be suitor following her around town.

"How have you been feeling?" He made an admirable attempt to subdue his interest. She supposed that his primary concern was that of a doctor to a patient.

She forced her body to relax. "I've been no worse."

"You are eating?"

She glanced at the cupboards. "Yes."

He glanced around her kitchen as if he suspected she was lying, which she was. Evan had tried to return the box of groceries twice. Each time, she had carted them back to his front porch and left them in care of his lazy cat.

Dr. Thomas packed his things into his bag. He stood at the table with his bag in hand for several moments before he spoke. "Miss Walsh, I am concerned. I don't believe you are frail, but I have never seen someone so intent on refusing the help and care of others. God gives us people in our lives to help us. To watch out for things we can't see ourselves."

Beatrice folded her hands in her lap and stared at them.

"No one was meant to live like this. I'm worried to distraction for your safety."

Beatrice stood and walked to the door, opening it and standing beside it. "I appreciate your concern, but it's unnecessary. I've accepted my fate. You should as well."

"Everyone dies. But most people want to live first," he argued.

She waited silently at the door.

It took several awkward moments before Dr. Thomas heaved a troubled sigh and left.

Fourteen

"I'm sure he was just checking on her health," Joshua said as Evan watched Doctor Thomas descend the stairs from Beatrice's apartment. Joshua lifted crates of supplies into his wagon in front of the store. "Luke doesn't have the guts to be forward."

Evan chewed on the inside of his cheek and watched Luke make his way down the sidewalk toward his office. "Does he seem kinda sheepish to you?"

Joshua scoffed. "Sure. That was a tell-tale sheepish expression if I ever saw one." He made a sound of frustration. "You gotta let it go. Big strapping man with his heart bleeding out all over the place."

"I don't think that's how the expression goes."

Joshua shrugged. "Whatever. You know what I mean. I don't want to be forced into it, but there's an icy cold creek just yonder behind the church. It will do fine for a dunkin' if you need reminding you're a man."

"Don't you have diapers to change?" Evan complained.

"That's my business." Joshua heaved the last of his crates onto the back of the wagon and walked around to jump up to the buckboard. "Come over tonight. Kathleen's making those biscuits you like."

"Nah. It's meatloaf night at the hotel."

"And by that, you mean there's a chance you'll see Beatrice

93

walking by if you stay in town."

Evan took a moment to answer. "I hear what you're saying. But I have to find my own way through this."

Joshua eyed him for a moment as he held the reins. "I wouldn't care about you if I didn't knock you upside the head once in a while."

"Thanks, Joshua." Evan shook his head. "I can always count on you."

"You bet you can. See you tonight."

Evan waved his acquiescence. He waited until the wagon had reached the edge of the woods and disappeared from sight, then he turned and headed toward Luke's office.

Luke sat alone at his desk in the main room measuring some kind of powder into a glass jar. He barely spared Evan a glance, but Evan didn't miss the way his face turned red.

"Afternoon, Evan. Can I help with something?"

"Why were you at Beatrice's?" Evan blurted the words out before he could stop himself. He felt foolish, knowing full well he had no business bringing it up, but he needed to know the truth.

Luke sighed and pushed back from his desk as if he had anticipated the question. "I can't discuss my patients' business with you, Evan."

Evan felt a twinge of irritation at the evasive answer. "You trying to start something, Luke? Because if it's Beatrice we're talking about, I'm willing to go – all in."

Luke looked like he was certainly *not* willing to do the same. "Be reasonable, Evan. I was trying to help her, as a doctor. If you think about it, I'm trying to help both of you."

"How's that?"

"It's no secret you care for her –"

"How do you know anything about it?" Evan shot back.

Luke chuckled. "The whole town knows how you feel about her. You haven't made it a secret."

Evan huffed and leaned forward on the desk.

Luke continued in a softer tone. "I've been thinking about her since the day the twins were born. Since she collapsed after church, really. I've wondered if there might be something I can do."

"You say you're concerned about her, but you blush like a little girl just talking about her. If you're trying to find a way to win her, be honest with me, Luke." Evan felt ashamed of himself. He didn't wait for an answer, but headed for the door. "I think it's time I go."

Luke followed him, catching his shoulder before Evan walked out the door. "Wait, Evan. Yes. Yes, I find her to be a lovely woman with an intriguing personality, but that doesn't mean I'm trying to steal her from you, even if you had her to begin with. We're friends." He paused and his brow furrowed. "At least I thought we were."

Evan felt a stab of guilt and stopped in the doorway. He turned to face Luke. The doctor was a head shorter than he was and much smaller in bearing, but wisdom made him seem larger. Evan had let jealousy get the best of him, and it wasn't becoming. "Sorry, Luke. I don't know what came over me."

Luke nodded. "I understand." He hesitated, glancing out the window. "But I think we should have a conversation."

Evan shook his head. "If you're trying to talk me out of my feelings, you won't have been the first to try. It's not worth your time."

Luke nodded. "I understand. But I believe I can see a few things you're missing. I want you to look at the big picture."

Evan hesitated, but he finally sat in the chair across from Luke's desk and resigned himself to hear what the man had to say. "Go on."

Luke sat at his desk and adjusted his spectacles. "I probably shouldn't be telling you this. I'd appreciate it if you kept it to yourself." He cleared his throat. "Miss Walsh has a serious heart injury. After inquiring with the Merchants about her history, I tracked down her doctor in Chicago and wrote him a letter to get his opinion on how to treat her."

"You went to that much trouble on her behalf?"

Luke hesitated, and Evan shifted in his chair.

"We spoke on the telephone. He was surprised she was still alive. He told her she would die before she was thirty."

Evan stared across the room, his eyes blurry. He resisted the urge to ask for details about what had happened to her. He knew Luke wouldn't tell him, anyway. "I already know she's sick. It doesn't change anything."

"I know," Luke said with a nod. "But that's not my point. I wonder if you've objectively thought this through. Have you considered how having Miss Walsh as your wife would be different from a normal marriage?"

Evan felt pressure in his head. He hadn't considered it, and he didn't know what the doctor was trying to say.

"Evan, can I be blunt with you?"

Evan gave a short nod.

"When a person has the kind of heart ailment that Miss Walsh has – the facts of life that seem quite normal to the rest of us could have serious consequences for her."

"The facts of life?" Evan asked, unsure he wanted to hear more.

"Characteristics of the marital relationship. The physical ones, including pregnancy and birth."

Luke's tone was professional, but his face was as pink as a flamingo. Evan fidgeted with his hands in his lap. He hadn't considered it since he'd found out about her condition. Now that Luke brought it to his attention, he saw the past ten years in a different light.

"I believe, though I have no way to prove it," Luke continued, "that Beatrice has not put you off out of disinterest. Have you considered the possibility that she hoped to spare you the difficulties you might experience if you were to get married?"

Evan didn't answer.

"You want a family. You haven't made that a secret. And if I know it, I'm sure she knows it, too. Pursuing her to the ends of the earth won't get you what you want, and it may end tragically. Why not put your effort into searching for someone who can spend a lifetime with you and give you children?"

Evan felt a spark of irritation. "You mean let her go so you can have her."

Luke shook his head. "That's not what I'm saying, and you know it. I'm just giving you a bit of advice as your friend and her physician. Be there for her. She needs companionship. Be her friend until she succumbs to her disease, then go on with your life."

Evan stood abruptly. "Thanks for nothing, Luke."

He left the office before Luke could say another word, and he felt downright ashamed as he did.

♫

Evan watched Beatrice play as he had a thousand times before. With every delicate sweep of her fingers across the keys, she produced beauty. Her effortless gliding up and down the keyboard amazed him. He played the guitar, and he knew he played it well, but her skill was on another level. It hinted of genius.

Had he ever told her? Did she know she was a true artist? Had there ever been a time she'd been ambitious to profit from her talent? So many questions Beatrice refused to answer.

She reached a difficult transition and her teeth absently caught the end of her lip. Determination flashed in her dark eyes – deep pools he couldn't swim in. He ached for her. He ached to know what it was like to run his fingers along her cheek. He wanted to sift his hands through the thickness of her long dark hair, traveling in waves down the back of her simple white blouse. To hold her waist in his hands and pull her against his chest.

Lord, if you didn't think it was a good idea for me to want her so badly, why'd you have to make her so beautiful?

Mrs. Hammond waved the offering plate under his nose until he saw it, reminding him there were indeed people in the church other than Beatrice and himself. He took the plate and passed it on as she sniffed her disapproval of his wandering eyes.

To keep himself focused on the right things, he concentrated on the words of the song she was playing. Truth be told, it was a hymn that had brought him comfort in the earlier days of his life. He'd played it on his guitar over and over by the fire when he was trying not to be afraid of coyotes howling in the distance and who-knew-what rattling around nearby in the bushes.

"Let not your heart be troubled," His tender word I hear,
And resting on his goodness, I lose my doubts and fears;
Though by the path he leadeth, but one step I may see;
His eye is on the sparrow, and I know he watches me;
His eye is on the sparrow, and I know he watches me.

Evan felt peace in the midst of his questions and doubts. And when Pastor Merchant stood up to the podium with his Bible in hand, Evan realized God was speaking. Straight to him, right there in the back pew where he sat, twisting the edges of his bowler hat in his lap.

"Dear people, this morning I ask you to direct your attention to the forty-first chapter of Genesis. Remember, Joseph had asked the chief cupbearer to speak to Pharaoh on his behalf. He said he'd been forcibly carried off. He had done nothing to deserve the dungeon.

"Joseph is understandably ready for his circumstances to change. It isn't fair. He didn't bring it on himself. But what he doesn't understand is that God isn't finished remaking him yet. There is still work to be done. And while Joseph frets in prison, the cupbearer goes on his way and promptly forgets Joseph ever existed.

"Did God forget Joseph, too? Were these extra two years in the pit somehow a mistake on God's part? An oversight?"

Evan breathed a chuckle to himself, earning another glare from Mrs. Hammond. He understood Joseph's doubts. He knew what the pit was like, since he'd been in one form of it or another most of his life. He'd asked God countless times to set him free. What would it be like to wake up one morning and realize Beatrice was next to him in bed, right in that spot she'd always belonged? Or at least to be free of the attachment he felt to her? What if he could simply be the friend Luke suggested he be? Free of further expectations. Wouldn't that be something?

Had God forgotten him these past twelve years of living day-to-day, waiting for some impossible longing to be fulfilled?

The pastor interrupted his train of thought with strong words. "God did not forget. God has been there all along. He has been present. Not only present, but working. God works even when we don't hear him or see him actively engaged. If you understand nothing else, hear me on this: *God has a reason for the waiting.* He is creating something of immeasurable worth in you. He wants your complete satisfaction in him alone. From his perspective, this part of your journey – right now, in the waiting – is as precious as the final result."

Evan looked up and expected to see Pastor Merchant staring right at him. Was Pastor talking about him?

Hear my voice.

He clutched his Bible, recognizing that quiet voice of the Spirit.

"Beloved, if God is for you, who can be against you? God will answer the promises he has made to you. You can find joy in the waiting. But sometimes you must let a dream die to find the gift of satisfaction God wants for you."

Evan felt a lump as big as his throat and gasped softly for air. His head burned with pressure. He couldn't give Beatrice up. He *couldn't.* Just the idea hurt more than being punched in the gut.

Give her to me. I love her more than you do. I have a purpose in all of this.

Let her go.

Fifteen

After the service, people herded out behind the church to set out picnic blankets and put up a tent for food tables, taking advantage of the unseasonably warm day in late November. Evan had forgotten today was the Thanksgiving Day celebration. He felt a little guilty partaking of the feast without having contributed, but he was thankful for the distraction, since he continued to wrestle with the sermon.

He mounded large portions of casseroles and salads on his plate and balanced four of Kathleen's biscuits on the top.

"Don't be shy, Evan, we all know you're a growing boy," Joshua tossed another biscuit on Evan's plate with a smirk.

"We're going to have these biscuits in heaven," Evan said as he took a bite and groaned with satisfaction.

"I get it, believe me. Why do you think I've got this gut ever since I married that woman?"

Evan raised an eyebrow in doubt. "I haven't seen too many farmers with guts."

Joshua shrugged. "Guess it's a good thing I'm a farmer."

"How are the girls?"

Joshua grinned. "Downright cute as pumpkin pie. They have my heart wrapped around those tiny little fingers of theirs."

Evan smiled, trying to ignore the twinge of jealousy and regret. "That's great."

"One of them isn't growing as fast as the other. Luke's keeping an eye on her. Says she might just be having a slow start. Kathleen's giving her extra milk from the goat, trying to plump her up a bit."

"Hope that does the trick," Evan said as they made their way across the grass toward Kathleen's blanket.

"You're quiet today," Joshua said as he balanced his own plate of potluck goodness.

"Just thinking."

They reached Kathleen sitting on the blanket surrounded by babies and toddlers.

"Don't overdo the thinking, my friend," Joshua joked before they sat down to eat.

They sat down and Kathleen greeted Evan with a weary smile. She looked behind him and waved. "Miss Walsh! Sit with us."

Evan turned and saw Beatrice standing stiffly outside the food tent, eyeing the crowded grass. Evan was astounded she had come. He was even more surprised she was holding a plate of food. He scooted over and patted the blanket between himself and Kathleen.

Beatrice hesitated before she walked their way and sat down.

Her leg accidentally brushed against his, and he was sure he could never let go of his hope. His heart nearly stopped, beating for joy.

♫

Beatrice quickly pulled her leg under her so she wouldn't touch Evan. To her relief, it wasn't long before Joshua and Evan left to fill their plates a second time.

"Aren't you hungry?" Kathleen asked, staring at Beatrice's plate as if she couldn't fathom eating so little. Feeding twins must make one ravenous, Beatrice assumed.

Beatrice picked up her sandwich and took a bite. "I won't be staying long."

Kathleen nodded at the musicians setting up near the tent so the picnickers might dance. "They didn't lug out the piano for you?"

"I wish it had been possible," Beatrice answered. *I'd rather be playing piano.*

Beatrice watched Kathleen balance the two babies in her lap while she took another bite of her chicken salad sandwich. One of the babies fussed, so she bounced the leg under the unhappy twin.

The twins had hair the same straw color as their mother and wore matching white dresses that reached the ankles of their bare feet. She wondered how Kathleen managed to take care of two babies at once, especially with the toddlers. She didn't ask. She'd never need to know.

Kathleen didn't seem too troubled as she continued to eat over the babies in her lap. "Did you try these thin potatoes fried into a crisp?"

Beatrice shook her head and took the potato crisp Kathleen held out. "Mm," she murmured her approval.

One baby started to fuss when Kathleen accidentally dripped strawberry juice on her face. "Bother," Kathleen said, reaching for a napkin. Beatrice handed her one as the other baby started crying.

"Take this one," Kathleen held out one of the twins in Beatrice's direction.

Beatrice panicked.

She stared at the child's face as she cradled the back of the baby's downy soft head. Her heart began to race and her eyes filled with tears. She looked into the eyes of the quieting baby and could almost forget why she didn't want to have anything to do with it. What if it were her child? What would it be like to look at a baby and see not only hints of her own features, but those of... Evan's?

Her cheeks warmed. But immediately following the thought of Evan and her imaginary baby came the memory of the dead baby on the floor of the theater, cast at an awkward angle on the step of the second row aisle. Clothes torn off. Bloody and completely still.

"I can't." Beatrice abruptly put the baby back in Kathleen's lap, speaking in a strangled voice. "I can't hold her."

Kathleen adjusted the babies in her lap before she reached for Beatrice's arm and squeezed it. "I'm sorry. I didn't know."

Beatrice shrugged and pulled away.

Kathleen considered her. "You might not think it to look at me now, but I've had a hard road. If you need a listening ear, I'm here. It might lighten the load."

Beatrice frowned. What had Kathleen faced that could possibly compare to Beatrice's past? And yet, when she looked into Kathleen's eyes, she recognized a kind of wisdom that only came from knowing loss.

"There is a way through it. It's possible to recover," Kathleen said.

"What happened to you?" Beatrice surprised herself in asking the question, but she couldn't deny her curiosity.

Kathleen looked down at her babies. "I lost my father to a man I drove to insanity. That man stole my innocence in my husband's barn after he tricked Joshua into leaving me alone."

The air stuck in Beatrice's throat, making it hard to breathe. "I'm sorry."

She would never have guessed such a thing had happened. She remembered when Kathleen had first showed up in town. She'd been a saloon girl. Joshua Whitley had married her a few months later, but she had no idea there had been so much violence.

"That was back when the saloon was a big problem in Dempsey," Kathleen said. "My husband fought that evil. Ended up with me for his trouble." She smiled at Beatrice.

Beatrice forced a polite smile in response. "He doesn't appear to regret the choice."

"No, he doesn't. He's a good man who doesn't spend much time looking back. Always pressing on, that one. He still wants the saloons closed for good and he gets in tangles with the owners, but his priority is his family now. We try to help the girls from the saloons. We offer them shelter for doing chores – give them an alternative."

"That's good of you." Beatrice fidgeted with the hem of her dress. "I envy you."

The words came from her lips before she could stop them. She hadn't realized how true they were until she said them. She *was* envious of Joshua and Kathleen's home and family, and even their ministry. She wanted it, just as any other unmarried woman her age might want the same. But her past wouldn't allow it. She could never look at an infant without thinking of the dead baby in the Iroquois fire. And even if she could, how could she be close to a man without thinking of dear Edward who'd died without becoming her husband? She still smelled his scent. She still heard the frantic wail of that dying baby in the spaces between her dreams and consciousness. It was too much to consider – too difficult to manage.

And even if she somehow could, her lungs and heart would never stand it. She was envious of Kathleen, who could receive the embrace of her husband without worrying her heart might give out and cause her to die in his arms. And even should Beatrice survive that, bringing a child into the world would most certainly kill her and probably the baby, as well.

It wasn't fair. Not to her, and not to Evan. He deserved better.

She steeled herself once again. She needed to be careful. If she wasn't, Evan could be hurt badly. She must protect his heart.

"Here come the menfolk." Kathleen's voice brought Beatrice out of her thoughts.

She lifted her gaze and found Evan's. His expression was different, somehow. She had grown accustomed to his eagerness and the way his spirit seemed perpetually bent toward hers, but now his forehead furrowed and a shadow darkened his eyes.

Joshua sat down next to Kathleen and kissed her soundly on the cheek, which caused a pretty blush to spread over her features.

"Where are Mary and Isaiah today?" Evan asked as he sat down across from Beatrice.

"Lou and Fred are down with colds. Mary stayed home with them. Isaiah and the rest of the brood are here somewhere."

Joshua pointed to the teenaged twins, Jedidiah and Jeremiah, who headed for the outhouse with a handful of firecrackers. "If those boys ever become profitable members of society, it will be in spite of themselves."

"*Boys!*" Joshua stood up and glared at them until they gave up and headed toward home. Beatrice covertly observed Evan. He continued to eat with a hard stare. He didn't look her way, in fact, he didn't even look up. She'd never known him to be so quiet. What was wrong?

"That theater salesman is up to no good as well, I'd bet my farm on it." Joshua nodded at Jacob Wylie, who made his way through the crowd, shaking hands and spreading charm as thick as butter.

Beatrice stole a glance. Mr. Wylie had been kind to her, but she agreed he did not seem genuine. "I wish he would leave," she said quietly. "We do not need a theater."

"Whether we do or not, folks go for new and exciting ideas." Kathleen wiped the mouth of one of her boys and the nose of the other. "I suppose it would be a distraction from the saloons, if nothing else."

Beatrice shook her head, but she didn't argue.

"Evan Masters, I've never known you to take so long eating one of my biscuits," Kathleen said. "Why don't you be a gentleman and take Miss Walsh to the dance floor. This is a beautiful waltz that shouldn't be wasted and there's no way I'm going to be able to make use of it."

"As if I never dance with you," Joshua said. "Who would watch all these kids if we were dancing?"

"Go on, before you have to sit here and watch an old married couple get into a brawl," Kathleen said, slapping Joshua on the leg.

Beatrice should have turned and ran. But she was caught in the moment without an excuse. It would have been more awkward to try to avoid a dance with Evan. Besides, the hesitation she felt from him made her curious, and perhaps a little hurt. Since when did Evan avoid her?

He got up and led her to the dance floor. "Are you sure you're okay to do this?" he asked.

"As long as we don't go very fast," she said. She didn't want to make too much of her illness, though perhaps she should use the excuse to get away.

He didn't smile as she'd expected. His features didn't light up with hope and enthusiasm as usual. He only held out his hand with a serious expression on his face. "We'll go slowly."

He took her hand and held her waist. "I need to say something to you, anyway."

She focused on the sensation of his fingers threading through hers and the warmth of his hand on her waist. She felt lighthearted and had to take a moment to will her heart to beat at a normal rhythm. She still felt the pounding in her head as they began to move.

"Relax, Beatrice," he said quietly, taking slight steps for his oversized feet. "I don't want you getting sick on account of me."

"I'm fine," she said, hearing the stubborn edge of her tone. "What did you need to talk about?"

He sighed deeply and his features settled back into that unsettling frown. What could the man possibly have to say that troubled him so much?

"Beatrice, it's no secret I've cared for you for many years. And you've made it clear you don't feel the same. This morning during the sermon, it occurred to me I've been holding on to a dream everyone says I should let go. Including the good Lord."

Beatrice had to tilt her head back to look up at his face. He watched her intently, thoughtfully. The kind of thoughtful that caused a twinge of foreboding. Evan had been making his overtures for over a decade. Was he telling her he was over it? He was moving on?

She swallowed hard, surprised by the disappointment that swarmed her spirit. Wasn't it a good thing? Hadn't she thought all along he should find someone more suitable, settle down and have a family? She cared for him, after all. More than she'd realized if she was being honest. She wanted him to be happy, not pining away all alone in that house which should be full of people and warmth.

"I'm going to try letting you go, Beatrice. You can always consider me your friend, of course, but I will aim not to pursue you anymore."

She gulped. The closeness of his body to hers, the space where they shared heat and connection, seemed an irony to his distant words. She was closer to him in that moment than they'd ever been before, but he was putting her further away than she'd ever thought he would.

I don't want to lose him.

The thought stole her breath. She was unprepared for the weight of it. She closed her eyes and stopped moving. He stopped with her, and let go of her waist with a gentle squeeze.

When she opened her eyes, he was gone.

Sixteen

Beatrice stepped away from the dance floor, disoriented. Without Evan's strong presence, she was overwhelmed by the crowd. She backed away from the others, realizing Evan had been the only thing that made her feel a part. He was her tie. Without that link, she was completely out of place. But did she care that she was suddenly untethered by Evan's newfound lack of interest? Didn't she want separation?

She walked back toward the Whitleys. In the back of her mind, she was conscious of a mewling, strangled and anguished. She thought of the baby in the theater, living the last moments of his brief life.

Her eyes searched for the source of the sound and rested on Kathleen, who was standing and gently bouncing one of the twins on her shoulder. The boys were running in circles nearby while Joshua held the other twin and watched Kathleen with helpless concern.

When Beatrice laid eyes on the infant, her breath caught in her throat. How many times had she seen that same blue pallor in her own face when she looked in the mirror? How many times had the sound of her own strangled breathing been the only sound for hours?

"Kathleen," she said, walking faster. She came up next to them and leaned her ear against the baby's tiny back. She heard a faint, trembling heartbeat. It sped up as the baby tried again to cry and grew almost indecipherable as the child gave up and went silent.

"Get the doctor!" Beatrice demanded of Joshua. With wide eyes, he put the other twin in Mrs. Merchant's arms and ran, shouting for Luke.

"He's gone home!" Someone pointed in the direction of the clinic. A crowd gathered around Kathleen and watched in concerned silence.

Kathleen took the baby from her shoulder and eased her forward in her arms so she could look at her. "Oh, Lord Jesus!" Her voice trembled as she beheld the ghostly white face of the baby. "Please don't take her!"

Beatrice thought quickly, trying to remember what the doctors had done for her the day of the fire. She seemed to remember someone rubbing her chest and back, banging on her, really. They had held her arms out and turned them in circles. It had been excruciating in her condition, but her heart had kept beating.

"Rub her chest," Beatrice said.

Kathleen shook her head, tears freely falling down her cheeks. "Take her!" Her voice was the most heart-wrenching, desperate tone Beatrice had ever heard. "Do something! Please!"

Beatrice inhaled sharply as Kathleen put the baby in her arms. She did her best to ignore the panic and kneeled on the ground. She set the little girl on her back on top of the blanket. She gently but firmly applied pressure to the baby's chest, then turned her over and did the same to her back. She waved the baby's tiny arms in a circle over her head.

The baby seemed to struggle less.

"It's working!" Kathleen cried hopefully. "Please, God! Please let Ruthie live!"

It seemed several lifetimes before Luke arrived, but eventually he was there, pushing through the onlookers with his bag in hand. He fell on his knees beside Beatrice, giving her a glance of wonder.

"You did the right thing, Beatrice. Thank you."

Immediately, he picked up the child and ran for his clinic.

Evan had been halfway down the street, about to turn off for home, when he heard the commotion behind him. He turned and jogged back, praying as he ran.

A crowd surrounded the clinic. Someone must be injured or ill, enough that half the congregation sensed a need to stand vigil.

He caught sight of Joshua and noticed the panicked, wide-eyed expression on his face. Evan's stomach felt heavy, as if it had suddenly dropped all the way to his toes. *No, Lord. Not Kathleen. Not one of the kids.*

He eased through the crowd. When the townsfolk saw him, they stood back and let him through.

Kathleen's inconsolable cries greeted him before he stepped inside the door. Joshua was holding her, holding her up, really, and she was fiercely hanging on to one of the baby girls. Evan felt a little better when he saw that the baby seemed okay, sucking on her fist and fussing in protest of her mother's grip.

Then he remembered there were two of them.

His breath left him when he saw the bit of flesh lying so still on the table. She looked as if she was sleeping, except that he knew no baby should be that color. Luke looked up at him and shook his head slightly, indicating he had done all he could.

Evan moved behind them and put his hand on Joshua's shoulder. Nothing would be able to comfort them in that moment. There was only grief, unrelenting, suffocating.

He knew that feeling well.

Beatrice kept her eyes away from the little casket. She had no desire to see the peaceful little face. She looked at her music and played the gentle notes of *Safe in the Arms of Jesus* as the family filed past the coffin to say goodbye.

She felt a presence behind her and heard Amelia begin to sing the words as the rest of the congregation got up to pay their respects. Beatrice felt her heart twist within her as Amelia sang.

Safe in the arms of Jesus,
Safe on his gentle breast,
There by His love o'ershaded,
Sweetly my soul doth rest.

Hark! 'tis a song of heaven
Borne in the sweetest voice,
Echoed by saints in spirit,
Making my heart rejoice.

When the song was over, Amelia squeezed Beatrice's shoulders. "Thank you. That was the perfect song."

Beatrice turned to face her. "I'm sorry for your loss."

Amelia nodded, considering Beatrice. "I can see it in your eyes. You are sorry. You don't want me to know just how much."

Beatrice looked away, embarrassed. Her eyes fell to the coffin and she saw the still form of the baby girl. She fought the pressure gathering in her eyes.

"It's okay," Amelia said, patting her arm. "There's not a dry eye in the Lord's house today."

"That song is far too happy for a day like today," Beatrice said as she closed her music books and picked them up.

Amelia was thoughtful. "I suppose that depends on your perspective. Today is a happy day for Ruthie and Jesus."

Beatrice shook her head, rebelling against the idea of joy in the midst of such circumstances. She didn't want to think of Ruth's brief story having a happy ending. Not when everyone was in so much pain over it. It wasn't fair that innocents died.

Just like her Edward. Her parents. Her little brother. They hadn't deserved their fate, either.

All have sinned and come short of the glory of God. The verse, memorized long ago in a Sunday school class, occurred to her.

Beatrice had no interest in contemplating the divine nature of a God who felt so distant and unfair. He remained unrelenting in the sorrows he poured out on people who loved him and did their best to serve him.

Amelia's family was leaving the sanctuary, but she turned back to Beatrice once more. "I must go to the burial, but I want you to think about something. I see something in you, Beatrice. I can only describe it as a kind of light I don't notice in too many people. It's rare. But I also see you are trying to put this light out. God gives us unique gifts as blessings for others, just as your playing has comforted his children this day. If you hide his light, you will regret it, either now or in eternity. I'm not often wrong about these things, and I feel you *must* find out what God wants you to do. Don't let anything stand in your way."

She left Beatrice at the piano. Beatrice was only angrier at her words. Angrier with a God she didn't understand.

How could she shine for a God who did these kinds of things? Who had caused her to lose everything, including her own health and strength?

What could she possibly accomplish for him in her condition, anyway?

Seventeen

Evan climbed the stairs of the Whitley's back porch and reached out to knock on the screen door leading into the kitchen. He stopped short when he saw Kathleen sitting at the kitchen table with a baby in her limp arms. Two little boys played at her feet. Her free hand wound through her hair and pressed against her forehead.

Evan's hand fell back to his side. What did a person say to a mother after losing her baby? What words could possibly offer any consolation?

He turned back and headed for the fields. After hiking a ways out in the barren field, he found Joshua, shirtless though the weather was cool, attacking a stump that had broken the neat lines of his wheat field.

Joshua must have known Evan was walking toward him, but he didn't stop swinging with the ax. Chipped wood flew in every direction. A fierce expression mingled with the dirt on his face. Suddenly, he yelled in frustration and threw the ax.

"Talk to me," Evan said, standing still and pushing his hands into his pockets.

"I don't know what to say," Joshua answered in a growl. He squinted at the crisp, clear sky. "I failed, Evan. I failed my family."

Evan shook his head and took a step closer. "How in the world did you fail? Ruth had a heart defect. Luke explained it. He said sometimes babies have them and there's nothing you could have done to cause it."

Joshua snarled. "I don't care what Luke said. I was the pa that didn't protect his girl. I let Kathleen's heart get broken, and now I can't fix either one."

Evan sighed. "I can imagine it's normal to feel that way, Josh, but it isn't the truth. God allowed this for some reason. It will only make sense when we're on the other side with her."

Evan knew he was saying the right words, but he could see they weren't helping. He walked around Joshua and retrieved the ax. "Go be with Kathleen. I'll do this."

Joshua grabbed the ax out of his hands and took a few more ferocious swings. He stood still, his shoulders slumping in defeat. He handed the ax to Evan and walked away.

Evan watched him go. He knew how powerless his friend must feel. He didn't fault Joshua for his emotions one single bit.

He found solace in decimating the old stump. He hacked away at it until it was nothing but a pile of chips. He returned the ax to the barn and went home.

It seemed to Beatrice, looking in from the outside, that once something bad happened to the community, they were ripe for more problems. The theory held up in the days following Ruth Whitley's funeral.

A young railroad worker was shot outside one of the saloons. He lingered for a few days in the clinic before he succumbed to his injury. The temperance group quickly began picketing and shouting all day long about the evils of demon liquor to anyone who would listen.

Jacob Wylie used the opportunity to ally with the women. He said with a mighty dose of charm that Dempsey needed an outlet that didn't involve drinking, gambling and women. They needed a place they could go to relax and enjoy entertainment without trading their soul for it.

Beatrice stood at the window by the piano at the church and

fumed as she watched citizens give him cash. They were convinced he was the answer to the town's problems. Couldn't they see he was only interested in their money? Was she the only one who knew the truth?

She couldn't forget he had returned some of her stolen money. He didn't have to do that. He could have put it in his theater fund and she would have never known. For that act of kindness, he deserved a measure of respect. But that didn't mean she was going to fall for his sales pitch like all the foolish housewives of Dempsey.

Mr. Wylie had found excuses to meet her in the past days. He came to the piano to discuss the music she played. He asked her to look at the musical notation of songs he was writing for a stage production. He came to the library nearly every day, asking about books. He seemed fascinated by her intelligence, and she couldn't deny it was flattering.

"I've never met a woman as clever as you." He laughed with delight at her recollection of the aspects of the serial piece *The Golem*, published a couple years before.

She hesitated, frowning. "It's just that I believe the Golem is meant to represent the tendency of the human spirit to want to create, yet in the end not be able to control his creation. The Golem's path of destruction is a warning. We should be careful not to attempt to be God, or we will be sorry."

Beatrice clamped her mouth shut. She knew better than to unleash her thoughts to a man she hardly knew and didn't trust. She'd forgotten how good it felt to voice her opinions about the imagery in modern fiction that fascinated her. Yet if she must speak of them, it would better to discuss it with Amelia Morehouse.

"I think Golem would make a captivating stage play, don't you?" Mr. Wylie leaned further over the large library desk where Beatrice sat with a book in hand.

"Perhaps for an outdoor occasion," Beatrice said shortly.

"The story of a monster would need the dark of the theater to lend credence. It wouldn't work in the open air. A theater gives a certain privacy, to see life on display and have our chance to consider."

"No." Beatrice sat up and slammed the book on the desk. "You're wrong."

She walked away, gathering books to return to the shelf as she went.

He followed her. "Miss Walsh, I do wish you'd reconsider your stance on the theater. So much could be accomplished if you were to become its spokesperson."

She scoffed as she climbed the ladder to the highest shelf to return books to their places. "No one in this town cares about my opinion."

"That's not true," Mr. Wylie mused. "I rather think everyone is in awe of you. They know you are smarter than they are. If you were to actually speak, you'd have the ear of everyone in this town."

She climbed back down where he waited for her with both hands on the sides of the ladder.

Leaning close to her face, he spoke in a tone full of charm. "And don't tell me you are just the librarian spinster, either. A spinster has her hair pulled as tight as her morality. She has wrinkles and pinched lips and spectacles, with a nose so high in the air she wouldn't see an available man if she stumbled over him in the street. You have mystery, romance and adventure in those black eyes of yours, but not a single drop of spinsterhood."

"Please let me go," Beatrice said, more annoyed than afraid as she pushed past his arms.

"Alas, I have not caught your romantic eye." He took a book from the shelf and idly leafed through. "Still, it is an alliance I seek, not a match."

She glanced at him with suspicion.

"You are the town musician. You play the piano like an angel. If you were to tell the townspeople they need a theater, they would listen."

"I have no intention of telling them anything. Least of all that they need a theater." She sniffed and walked back to the desk.

He nodded. "I suspected as much. But do not expect me to give up or let go of my vision for a theater in Dempsey. I have investors to repay. I've taken risks in order to achieve success. I believe in this cause! I won't apologize for it. And I won't let anyone, including you, stand in the way."

She flipped the catalogue on the desk so she wouldn't have to look at him.

"I won't give up on you, either. You don't think I haven't noticed this stack of books you're reading about architecture and building? You are a woman of similar interests to me, and I need your help. It's simply providential." He flipped through the book on the top of the pile until she took it and closed it, holding it to her chest.

He was undaunted. "You have no good reason to deny the town this privilege. You should appreciate what I am doing. I know you don't have any interest in profit, but you value vision and entrepreneurship. It is my goal to have you on board and it will happen. Mark my words."

She fiercely met his gaze. "It will not happen. Ever. I will never say this town should have a deathtrap for their entertainment, and I will do everything in my power to stop you. Mark *my* words."

He ignored her challenge, his tone softening into one of consideration. "You do not believe I would build a safe theater?"

She narrowed her eyes. "I *know* you would not."

He shook his head. "My dear, I will see every standard of safety met. No one will die in this theater."

She shook her head slightly, unwilling to believe him. She had no response, so she walked briskly to the water closet at the back of the building and firmly shut the door. She'd wait him out. After a few moments, she heard the click of his heels on the tile floor and the resolute bang of the door as he left.

Something was definitely different about Evan.

Beatrice played the notes harder, trying to steel herself against the truth. Evan had overcome his infatuation with her. Shouldn't she be glad?

She covertly glanced at him. He was talking with Widow MacGregor, Edna Mae, who couldn't be a day over twenty-five. Whose rosy cheeks, strawberry locks and sea-blue eyes were presently staring adoringly up at Evan's handsome face.

Beatrice missed a note.

She should be charitable. Edna's husband died in a train explosion the year before, leaving her with a toddler and a baby.

A ready-made family.

Beatrice struck a chord too loudly. Evan's eyes flickered her way, but he didn't focus on her. His gaze remained locked on Edna's as he reached out a finger for the baby to grasp.

Beatrice couldn't swallow back the lump in her throat. She finished the song and set the book aside.

Is he toying with me?

She would despise him until the quickly coming day she died if he was. She hated games and she would not be controlled in such a way. If he was playing a game with her, he better hope Edna was ready to take up with him because she certainly wouldn't stoop to his level.

Not that she had any intention, anyway, she reminded herself.

She fought back emotion. It would do her no good. Feelings couldn't change a single thing, and they were not to be valued above reason. Evan finding Edna was for the best, even if it secretly aggravated her.

She walked toward the door, attempting to keep her back straight and her chin up. Before she could escape the building, Amelia caught her arm and squeezed.

"Beatrice, how pretty you are looking this morning!"

Beatrice frowned and glanced at her navy walking skirt and white blouse. She wondered if Amelia was referring to someone else. But then, her outfit did match Amelia's almost perfectly.

Amelia's thinly veiled emotions surfaced, and Beatrice wished to get away. She had no interest in feeling the suffering the other woman was surely experiencing at the loss of Kathleen's baby. In some ways, Beatrice felt that she and Amelia had similar temperaments. But Amelia had a much harder time keeping emotion controlled and hidden, and for this, Beatrice was on her guard.

Amelia must have noticed her hesitation, because she let her arm go and folded her hands in front of her, smiling. "I just wanted to thank you for how you tried to save Ruth. You gave Kathleen time to say goodbye. She will always be grateful for that."

Beatrice wasn't so sure. Kathleen had been missing from church for the fourth week in a row. Joshua and his boys sat alone, and his expression was forced. He had dark shadows under his eyes. What did it matter if their baby had lived a few extra minutes? It hadn't fixed anything.

"Dear Evan is taking the boys for a couple days. Joshua and Kathleen need time. They have to make a way through this storm."

"And you?" Beatrice asked the question to be polite and to keep the conversation on neutral ground. But Amelia misunderstood.

"I'm sad, of course, but God is so very good. Thank you for asking. It helps to be here and take care of little Ellen. Kathleen has had a hard time looking at her, but I love seeing an exact copy of Ruth's face. It reminds me she is safe and happy with Jesus."

"I'm sure," Beatrice said. She cleared her throat, watching the twins leave Joshua's side and run for Evan's arms. He laughed and gathered them up so they were both perched on a shoulder.

"Who's going to Uncle Evan's house tonight?" He jiggled them until they laughed. Edna smiled, bouncing her own baby as she watched him play with the boys.

Beatrice couldn't blame Edna for her rosy cheeks and breathless smile. She felt like she'd had the wind knocked out of her when she saw Evan smile, too. His whole face lit up. If he could love his best friend's children so much, what kind of father would he make?

"Are you okay, Beatrice?" Amelia put a hand on her shoulder. "You look pale. Should you sit down?"

Beatrice shook her head. "I just… I should be going."

Amelia followed Beatrice's gaze to Evan and Edna. Understanding dawned in her wise expression. "What would you have him do, Beatrice?"

Beatrice frowned at Amelia's quiet comment. "I'm sure I have no idea what you're talking about," she lied.

She didn't wait for a response. She walked past Evan and Edna without a further glance.

Eighteen

Evan had new respect for Kathleen. How did that woman entertain the twins all day? He'd had them for four hours and he was completely exhausted.

They'd played baseball in Evan's backyard. That lasted less than ten minutes. Then Ben and John decided they were hungry. Evan made them sandwiches, from which they each took exactly one bite. Following that, they tore around his house on a mission of destruction. John was scratched by the cat, and Ben got a goose egg on his head by running headlong into a doorframe.

The child cried for ten minutes. When he finally stopped, Evan's ears were ringing. Somehow, he managed to get both boys to nap for an hour. It was the most blessed hour he could remember in quite a while. He fell asleep on the sofa and woke an hour later to the boys sitting quietly in the corner of the room.

Pulling every string out of his guitar.

It was only four in the afternoon, but Evan determined it was past time for dinner. "Come on, boys. We're going to the hotel to eat."

"You make dinner, Unca Evan," John said, squashing Evan's nose with his sticky finger.

"Uncle Evan isn't a great cook." Evan tried to straighten up their clothes.

"Where your mama?" John asked, shrugging his shoulders as

if the answer to the problem seemed obvious to him. Ben glanced around as if she might be hiding in the corner.

My mama's dead, Evan thought immediately, though he didn't say it. "Do you mean my wife? I don't have a wife."

"You need a wife," John said, and Ben nodded his solemn agreement.

"I sure do," Evan agreed emphatically.

They walked for exactly half a block before both boys decided it was taking too long and neither could take another step or they might die. Evan carried both of them the other three blocks to the hotel.

His arms were burning by the time he deposited them on seats in the hotel dining room. He looked up as the waitress approached.

"Mrs. MacGregor," he said in surprise when he looked up to see her shy smile.

"Hello, Mr. Masters," she said, her cheeks turning pink. He felt a little breathless at how pretty she looked.

"I didn't expect to see you here," he fumbled for words. "Where are your children?"

"They are with a woman who stays in the hotel room next to ours. We've been living here since I had to sell the house. She kindly watches the children three days a week. I need the extra money. I miss them so much, but I don't know what else I can do." Edna's smile faded, but she found it again quickly. "I'm sorry, please don't mind me. Shall I get you gentlemen the special?"

"Yes, thanks."

"Milk!" Ben shouted.

"Me too!" John tried to yell louder than his brother.

Evan felt eyes turn their way. "Three milks, please."

"Coming right up," Edna said before she hurried away. Evan couldn't keep his eyes off her as she went. She was a beauty, and there was no denying it. And it was also obvious she was in need of a husband.

But something about it felt wrong, like he was being unfaithful.

Ben and John spent several quiet moments nibbling on their fried chicken. Then they mashed their potatoes to the plate. Then they threw their peas on the floor. John's milk spilled across the table and Ben's spilled down the front of his shirt.

Edna immediately came with towels. "This happens all the time," she said in a cheerful voice as Evan apologized. She made a game of cleaning up. The boys smiled and sang along to her made-up song.

"You're good with kids," Evan said.

"I guess mothers know what to do." She shrugged, blushing again and shyly avoiding his gaze.

Evan considered her. Did he dare ask her to dinner some night? Could he really go so far? Would Beatrice care if he did?

Whether she cared or didn't notice, it was time. He must be resolute. Everything must end, for he'd been pursuing Beatrice long enough to know it wasn't going to work between them. This was his second chance. Who knew if he'd get another? He couldn't waste it.

"Mr. Masters."

He looked up in shock to see Beatrice standing next to the table, her hands folded in front of her and her gaze more direct than it had ever been before.

"Miss Walsh," he said. He cleared his throat and motioned to the boys. "Ben, John, say good evening to Miss Walsh."

"Eav-ing, Miss Wash," they both said around bites of food that never seemed to be swallowed. They squirmed in their chairs and tried to take off the napkins Evan had tucked into the front of their shirts.

"You have your hands full," Beatrice observed with a reserved smile. "I... I was wondering if I might talk to you."

Evan ignored the expectation that immediately set his emotions off their hinge. He shrugged and gestured to the empty seat next to him.

Ben chose that moment to leap from his chair and start running laps around the table. It was only seconds before John had joined him.

Evan grabbed them and pulled them both into his lap. He handed them crusts of bread from his plate. They quieted, and he kissed their heads in thanks before he looked up at Beatrice and waited for her to speak.

She sat rigidly and twisted her fingers in her lap. Her expression was haunted. Her lips parted. She stared at him holding the boys as if she was noticing something new. Something that moved her.

He swallowed back the grip of hope that wanted to snake around his heart. He'd given her up. He'd told the Lord he wouldn't pursue her anymore. He'd move on and find someone to share his life. He couldn't go back on that promise now.

"What did you need?" He tried to sound passive.

She shook her head slightly as if she was clearing away whatever had captivated her. "I wondered if you could think of any way to halt this plan of Mr. Wylie's to build a theater in Dempsey."

Evan considered her. "I'm leery of it, too. I suspect the kind of man he is. But what I can't figure out is why you're so dead-set against it. You've spent the past twelve years trying to avoid this town and everyone in it. Why are you worried about Dempsey now?"

Beatrice's eyes flashed. "Don't presume to know me."

"How could I presume that?" He asked in frustration. "You've kept yourself completely hidden."

She stood quickly, and he sighed, sorry he'd started an argument. She smoothed her skirts and let the cool expression of indifference he knew so well take over her features. "I don't owe you anything."

"I never said you did." Evan took a deep breath and released his irritation as he exhaled. He wouldn't get frustrated. It didn't matter what Beatrice thought. He'd moved on. He'd set his sights on Edna.

"I am to *presume* you won't help me stop this theater from

being built?" She glared at him.

He shrugged. "I never said that. I'd just like a little more information before I agree to anything."

Beatrice folded her arms across her chest. Edna came from behind her with Evan's bill in hand.

"Was everything to your liking?" Edna asked, glancing at Beatrice but not speaking to her.

Evan forced a smile. "Of course. Mrs. MacGregor, may I introduce Miss Walsh?"

Evan glanced at Beatrice's stormy expression, exasperated. He'd only introduced them, as he should if he was being a gentleman.

"I don't believe we have met. It's a pleasure," Edna said with a welcoming smile. Beatrice's frown remained in place.

"Likewise," Beatrice mumbled.

"Can I get you something?" Edna asked uncertainly.

"No."

Evan glanced from one woman to the other, feeling completely awkward. "Thanks, Mrs. MacGregor."

Edna managed a weak smile in his direction. "See you around, Mr. Masters."

"Yes, I'll see you at church for prayer meeting, won't I?"

"I'll be there."

Edna turned to leave. Evan surprised himself by reaching out and grabbing the corner of her apron. She turned around in surprise.

"I wondered if you might like to sit together. At prayer meeting, that is."

Edna glanced at Beatrice as if she needed her permission. Beatrice's glare became more menacing.

"I'd like that." Edna gave him another hesitant smile before she hurried away. Evan didn't blame her.

"What do you think you're doing?" Beatrice's voice had gone low and harsh.

"What are you talking about?" Evan was stumped. He truly

had no idea what she was talking about, and he had to admit he was a little afraid of the menacing look on her face.

Beatrice appeared convinced he was as dense as a rock. Meanwhile, the twins began running the perimeter of the room. Evan pulled several dollars from his pocket and left them on the table, being sure to leave a little extra for Edna. He grabbed one twin by the arm and the other by his suspenders.

"Let's step outside," he said, not waiting to see if she would comply. He needed to get the boys out of the hotel before they destroyed something and left him with the bill.

When they were outdoors, the twins noticed Ezra Hamilton's ornery mule standing on the corner and immediately started to tease the poor creature.

Evan admonished them to be gentle before he turned to Beatrice. "Now what were you saying?" He was almost positive he didn't want to hear her answer.

She fumed. He could see her color deepen and her full lips become a tight, thin line. "You are using that widow to make me jealous."

"You're jealous?" Evan would have been less surprised if she'd conked him on the head with a frying pan.

Nineteen

You hear me, Evan Masters. I am not the kind of girl you want to play games with. You will only convince me I was right all along.

Beatrice was too angry to speak the words as she glared into his flabbergasted expression. She turned on her heel and stuck her nose in the air, determined to leave while he was fumbling for words.

He caught her arm and firmly whirled her around to face him again. "I wasn't trying to make you jealous. I had no idea you would even show up. You've got this all wrong."

Heat rose quickly to her face. "I have it wrong? I suppose I've had it wrong for ten years? Did I misunderstand your intentions and now you mean to make me the fool?"

Evan wasn't good at angry confrontations, she could tell. He hesitated too long. She figured she'd won the argument, so she tried to leave again.

"Hold on, Beatrice," he said quietly. "You aren't playing fair. Give me a chance."

She folded her arms across her chest, but she stayed. For some reason she couldn't explain to herself, she stayed rooted to her spot.

"There was a time I would have wanted to make you jealous. It would have given me hope for us. Made me think I hadn't wasted my life caring for you." He exhaled. "But I had to let you go, Beatrice. It was what the Lord wanted of me. I can't go back on that, not without a change of heart on your end."

It was her turn to be speechless. An unfamiliar emotion seemed to squeeze her lungs. Was she feeling disappointment at his declaration that he no longer held any interest? That he'd let her go?

Her tears betrayed her and stung her eyes. "You're saying you asked Edna to sit by you… because you like her."

He nodded. "I did. And I do like her. Very much."

She heard the tenderness in his tone, but also a firm resolve. She felt desperate to leave. She took a step back, but he reached forward and held her elbow.

"Hold on," he said, his voice softer. "Just because I have an interest in Edna doesn't mean I'm not your friend. I'll pray about the theater situation. Give me a couple days and we'll talk."

Beatrice gave a short nod and pulled her arm away from his grasp. "Good day, Mr. Masters."

She hurried away. But before she turned the corner, she glanced back. She had expected to see him standing there, watching her with that forlorn expression she'd seen so many times before. Instead, he collected the twins and headed in the opposite direction.

Since he couldn't see her, she watched them until they walked out of sight. With his immense stature, both boys had their arms extended all the way up in order to reach his hands. He looked at them as he talked to them, laughing at their responses.

She suddenly felt alone. It was a creeping feeling of darkness, which reminded her of lying on that table in the restaurant, barely alive in a world without her family and her love. Doctors discussed her condition as if she wasn't there. They didn't care she'd lost everything. They only had a responsibility to keep her heart beating and her lungs breathing, whether she had any interest in continuing to live or not.

Now she was back on that table, watching the world pass by

her. She was all but dead, and still she lived on.

♫

Evan kept the boys busy the next morning. He didn't want them to go home with extra energy. After lunch, he walked them all the way to the Whitley farm, ensuring they would be ready for a good long nap when they arrived at home.

The farm was quiet when he knocked on the back door. Amelia answered.

He smiled. "Hello, Mrs. Morehouse. I've brought Ben and John home."

She nodded and kneeled in front of the boys. "And did we behave like gentlemen while we were guests at Uncle Evan's?"

Ben and John both glanced at him, unsure. He smiled and tousled their hair. "They were just fine."

"I am so pleased. Now, up to bed with you both after you say hello to your father in the parlor."

Evan followed them into the parlor. Joshua was reclined on the couch, staring up at a picture on the mantel. Baby Ellen slept on his shoulder, her tiny thumb in her mouth.

The twins greeted their father before Amelia took them upstairs. Evan sat down on a chair across from Joshua.

"How's it going?"

Joshua met his eyes and didn't speak for a long moment. "I won't lie. This has been the hardest thing I've ever been through. Harder than my ma leaving me. Harder than losing Grandpa and Gran. Harder than learning to love a saloon girl and make her my wife."

Evan nodded. "I don't claim to know what's like to lose a child, but I can imagine it's the worst kind of suffering in the world."

"The worst part is watching Kathleen," Joshua said wearily. "She can barely stand to nurse Ellen. She cries when she looks into her face. I don't know what to do – I don't know how to help her. I'm worried I'm losing my wife to her grief."

Evan shook his head. "I'm so sorry, Josh. How can I help? I

could take the boys again –"

Joshua shook his head and sat up, staring at the mantel once again. Evan stood and went to the fireplace, picking up the picture on the mantel. "This is you and Mary and your grandparents."

"Taken not long after we came to live with them. I keep staring at their faces. Trying to imagine what they'd tell me to do."

Evan put the picture back. "No telling if they'd even know. Did your Gran ever lose a child?"

"Not that I know. But they knew God. They never questioned his ways. I need that kind of faith, and I'm realizing I don't have it the way they did."

Evan considered Joshua's words. "I wouldn't say you don't have faith. They were further along in their journey. I think God wants you to do the next right thing. Love your wife like Christ loves the church and sacrifices for her. Look after your family and fill in the gaps Kathleen can't manage right now. He'll give you the strength as you admit your weakness and lean on him. I know you, Joshua. You can do this, and you will get through it."

Joshua sighed. "That's awful astute of you, Evan Masters. Did you go to preacher school or something while I was out tending the fields?"

Evan smiled. "I did. Graduated top of my class. Taking over for Pastor Merchant this Sunday."

"Looking forward to it. You gonna preach how spinsters should marry the sad-looking giant that follows them around for a decade?"

Evan's smile fell. "I've let it go, Josh."

Joshua nodded. "I know. I'm sorry. And I know you aren't a stranger to loss. You know what you're talking about."

Evan thought of the dark place where God had first found him. "It's not anywhere near the same."

"It's not so different, either."

Evan sensed Edna peeking at him. He sat up on the church pew and tried to focus on Pastor's words. He ignored the glare he was getting from the little woman seated at the piano. Where was the Spirit's voice? He needed to listen hard so he'd know what God would have him do next.

When prayer service was over, Edna gathered her children. "How is your week going, Mr. Masters?"

"Call me Evan," he said, reaching a hand to the back of the cooing baby she balanced on her hip.

"And you may call me Edna," she said sweetly. "Did you survive your time with the boys?"

He chuckled. "We all made it through alive."

"Good." She fussed with the collar on her daughter's dress as the toddler stood in front of her.

"You been all right?" Evan tried to focus only on Edna's face, though he could see Beatrice watching him from behind her.

"I've been trying. But it's hard, being on my own," Edna said, then smiled apologetically. "I'm sorry. I don't mean to go on about it."

"I understand. I know it's hard living alone." He gestured to the children. "I'm sure it's even harder raising kids on your own."

He noticed her pink cheeks and felt a surge of affection for her. She looked down at the floor. "I would rather not, in fact. Live alone, that is."

Beatrice had gathered her things and passed them briskly in the aisle. She bypassed the rest of the crowd and headed for the door, disappearing into the night.

He sighed, steeling himself. It still hurt him to see her walk away. Reject him. He could pretend he didn't care until the cows came home, but he wondered if he'd ever really be free of the pull he felt to Beatrice. He shook his head. It was time to make different choices.

He focused on Edna's face. "Will you spend Saturday with me?"

She tried to hide her smile. "Why, Evan Masters, I do believe I will."

Twenty

Beatrice woke to the sound of hammer and nails.

At first, she thought it was her weary heart, beating out its last rhythm, sending her off to eternity. But her eyes opened and sunlight flooded her vision. She sat up and blinked.

Life still went on. She would have to face another day of her prison, resigned to her fate. But now she would have to do it as she watched the love of her life woo and win someone else. And Edna was a woman far more suitable.

She frowned. When had Evan become the love of her life? She had expected Edward would always carry that position.

As she went to the washbasin and peered into the small mirror, she recoiled at the dark circles framing her eyes and the angry expression marring her features. She glared at her reflection in annoyance.

Didn't Evan deserve a beautiful, vibrant wife with health and strength? Didn't he deserve to be a father? It would be ridiculous to spite Evan his chance at happiness.

"Go ahead and live, Evan," she insisted in an irritated whisper. "Don't throw away everything on account of me."

Of course, it would be easier if she would just die. Maybe if she had any courage at all she'd take that knife in the kitchen and plunge it straight into the heart that refused to let her live, but that denied her death at the same time.

As she contemplated it, she heard the faint sound of applause.

She dragged herself from her bed and went to the window. She heard the sound of laughter. A man speaking. She feared what it meant.

She dressed and pulled her hair back before she descended the stairs and followed the sound. If only it weren't true. If only she would find something else – something good and positive. But when she arrived at town square and turned her eyes north, she saw Jacob Wylie at the helm of a crowd of onlookers.

"Dear citizens, because of your generous support and your relentless enthusiasm, today we break ground on a revolutionary theater. This will put your town on the map. You will see wonders you could not have imagined. You will put away the daily grind and take on life as you have never known it before! Step forward and invest in the future of this great town. Hats off to you who will not be deterred by tradition or backward fear.

"We break ground today, and as long as the weather holds, we will soon build your theater."

Beatrice sighed as a bitter taste rose at the back of her throat. The workmen had arrived on the scene. Dirt had been cleared from the empty field next to the saloon, and men were stacking beams in the lot behind. Whether Beatrice approved or not, Dempsey had decided to keep up with the big cities in their pursuit of the arts. They would press on into the new century.

Beatrice felt a wave of foreboding.

Once, when she was just a little girl, her family had visited her aunt in Mount Vernon, Illinois. A tornado had ripped the town apart. It had come out of nowhere, whirring and spitting debris as it took a haphazard course, disregarding life with a violent display of power.

She'd had the same ominous feeling the day she saw the tornado ravage everything in its path – a feeling that this could only end badly. There was nothing she could do to stop the force of the storm that would take them down.

As she turned to go home, she heard someone shout her name.

She turned back to see Jacob Wylie running toward her.

"Miss Walsh," he said, stopping to catch his breath. "I wasn't sure you were going to stop."

"I'm just leaving," she said stiffly.

"Wait. I just wanted to see if you'd given any more thought to what I'd asked you."

"Will I be your spokesperson for the theater? Surely you know the answer to that question."

He sighed and looked back at the busy site, his hands on his hips. "I wish you'd co-operate."

"I won't. You can count on it. In fact, I'm trying to think of a way to stop you. I've asked the help of others who aren't so sure of this plan of yours. We'll find a way to stop you."

He looked back at her, and she saw the flash of hostility behind his pretentious smile. "I wouldn't suggest going up against me, Miss Walsh."

She heard a clear warning in his statement, but instead of shrinking back in fear, she took a step toward him.

"I've already hung a statement at the library warning people that theaters are notorious firetraps. I've cited several tragic fires that have killed hundreds. If I have anything to say about it – and I will, Mr. Wylie – everyone will withdraw their support from this endeavor immediately."

"No one will listen to you," he seethed as she started to step away from him.

She turned back and eyed him evenly. "You inspired me, when you told me they would listen to me. Now I'm counting on it."

"Then you can count on me to fight back."

She ignored him and turned for home.

Once there, she sat down to read as she always did on Tuesday mornings, but she could not concentrate. It was so quiet in her apartment she could hear the tap of bare branches against her window in the early December wind.

Usually, Beatrice loved the quiet. She appreciated thinking

more than any other pastime. But on this day, with her anger residing just below the surface of her psyche, she quickly became agitated.

Finally, she threw aside the encyclopedia she had been reading. It fell to the floor with a thump that echoed through the empty room. She went to the window and looked out over the back lawn and the creek behind the church. Her apartment felt stale and closed up. Perhaps a brisk walk by the water would be a welcome distraction.

Come unto me, all ye that labor and are heavy laden, and I will give you rest.

Words she had heard in her youth came to her suddenly. She had not heard the still, quiet voice in some time. Had she taught herself to avoid the words of Scripture – the very breath of God?

She ached to answer.

Darkness had been growing within her. It had been a gradual process that began the day God stripped everything away from her. She could barely hear his voice anymore. Why was he speaking now?

I could respond. I could ask him why he did this to me. Maybe he would give me a reason.

But what if he didn't? God was the one who had allowed her to lose so much. Why should she trust him? Why should she open herself up to more pain? She must face facts: the faith of her youth had been destroyed that night. It had been burned and trampled just as she had been.

And yet, what a sweet Savior she had known in her youth! How she missed his tender voice.

"No," she whispered, turning away from the window. She would not walk and talk with him. She had other plans. The Dempsey theater must not be built. Her life was over, her hope had disappeared, but she could make sure no one else had to endure what she had.

She could stop others from discovering the vengeful nature of their Creator. It would be her last offering.

♫

Evan had trouble sleeping when it got cold. He sat up in bed with a sigh.

Come. Walk. Talk to me.

He pulled on his clothes and coat and left the house. He walked into the street, his hands in his pockets. The light of the full moon lit his path.

He wanted to pray, but the words wouldn't form in his mind. He stared up at the moon, suddenly struck by the wonder of the world God had made.

"What am I doing wrong, Lord?" He spoke aloud, his breath forming a frosty mist in the air. "Why am I still thinking about her?"

He walked a ways before a thought occurred to him, from his childhood, from the voice of a mother who no longer breathed or spoke and hadn't for twenty years.

Evan, my son, when you give yourself to the Lord, you must be wholehearted. God only wants all of you, not just the parts you're willing to give up. And when you give your life and your plans to him, speak the words. Say it aloud, not for his sake, for he knows your every thought, but for your sake. Say it so you'll remember you made the promise and abide by it. Just like the Bible says, confess with your mouth and believe in your heart.

He stopped and cleared his voice. "I'm sorry, Lord. I've been holding back." He hesitated, wondering if he could speak the words.

"I give her to you. All my hopes and dreams I've had for our future together. All the love I feel for her. I give Beatrice to your loving hands and I vow to you tonight not to make any more effort to change her mind. I pray you'll show her your way through her heartaches and trials."

Relief flooded his being. He exhaled long and deep. "Thank you, Lord. Thank you for leading me out of great trouble and putting me here where I belong. Thanks for keeping me from bitterness. I need you, Lord. Every moment."

I am with you always.

Twenty-One

Evan stuck his hands into his pockets as he walked the rest of the way down Dempsey's main road, reveling in the release he felt.

It was short-lived. He stopped to eye the structure that was forming on the site of the future Dempsey theater. The skeleton of the building stood in the darkness, evidence that the salesman's dream was taking shape. Evan frowned. He'd had a picture in his mind of something much smaller. This building would have a much grander scale than any other building in Dempsey.

He had a bad feeling about it. Surely it wouldn't cause as many problems as Rita's saloon, but what if the theater was a more subtle form of evil? Would Dempsey's residents gradually become lazy and distracted from their jobs and families? Would Dempsey become like Chicago or New York, where anything went and corruption was as common as potatoes?

A ticking caught his attention. He strained his eyes to see in the dim light. Was there movement at the far end of the worksite? He pulled his coat tighter around him and headed for other side of the lumber pile.

Sparks shot up into the dark, cold air, followed by a small flame. A figure bent over a pile of newspaper shreds, watching the flame quickly turn the scorched papers to ash. The person intentionally blew on the infant blaze, sending it toward the pile of lumber.

"Beatrice?" he said in shock.

She whirled around, gasping in surprise. He moved forward and quickly stamped out the fire before it had a chance to spread.

"Have you taken leave of every last bit of sense in your head?" Evan wanted to shake her. "What in the world do you think you're doing? Trying to burn down the town?"

Her eyes narrowed.

"Give me a reason not to go straight to the police, Beatrice. *Please* give me a good reason why you're out here setting fires in the middle of the night, because the explanations I'm coming up with only put you in a pretty bad light."

She stepped forward, her fists clenched tightly at her sides. "I had no choice. There is no other way to keep this theater from being built."

He shook his head, grappling with the knowledge that she intentionally set the fire. "I told you I'd help you. But we have to go about it the right way. Getting yourself locked up for arson isn't going to stop Jacob Wylie."

He noticed a flinch in her expression. "Are you going to turn me in?"

It took him a long moment to answer. "Should I?"

She sighed impatiently. She looked away from him, as if she was fading back into some memory. When she spoke, her voice was haunted. "If you had been where I have, you'd be helping me set this fire."

"Okay, so tell me. Make me understand."

She hesitated, but suddenly she met his gaze with a fierce expression. "No one should have to go through the hell I did."

Evan was intensely curious, but he didn't press her for details. "I get that you don't want Wylie to build this theater. But what if your fire had gone out of control? There's a brisk wind tonight, you could have burned down the entire street. What if you'd killed someone, Beatrice? Did you consider that when you came out here to do this?"

She didn't back down from her icy glare, but at least she didn't try to justify her actions.

"I'm taking you home." He reached for her arm.

She shook away from him and moved back. "I can find my own way."

"No, you can't, Beatrice." He sighed. "Not when you're lurking around town setting fires. I'm going to see you home, and I'm going to keep an eye on you from now on."

"You will leave me alone, Evan Masters."

He said nothing more, but when she tried to walk away from him, he grabbed her arm and refused to release his hold. He marched her in the direction of the church. She rigidly walked beside him. He could sense her iron will in every tense muscle of her arm, but he noted with satisfaction that she glanced warily at the police station as they passed it.

He took her up the stairs to her door. "Don't get any funny ideas about waiting until I'm home to go back and finish what you started. Keep in mind: if there's so much as a whiff of smoke or a scorch mark, I'll know where to send the sheriff."

He didn't give her a chance to respond. He left, descending the steps and walking a good ways down the sidewalk before he heard the click of her door as she closed it.

What had she been thinking? Was the woman he'd thought he loved an arsonist and murderer? Could he have been so foolish? Evan felt sick at the thought. It was right to give her up. He could see it now. God had directed him away from Beatrice toward Edna, hadn't he?

He swallowed back a huge lump in his throat as he faced disappointment on a scale he'd not known in a long time. It felt like the end of an era. The breaking of relationship. The realization of his worst nightmare.

Beatrice Walsh was a criminal, and he was the only thing standing between her and a jail cell.

Beatrice didn't sleep well after Evan left her at her apartment.

She tossed and turned, the images of terrified children and a trampled baby returning to plague her mind. When she finally dozed around three in the morning, the children met her in her dreams.

"Why didn't you just grab my hand?" the boy asked, stricken. "I wanted to live. All you had to do was grab my hand."

"I tried!" she argued, swiping away her tears.

"Why couldn't you stop that man from knocking us over?" One of the little girls stepped forward, pulling the other girl by the hand.

The baby squirmed on the floor, between theater seats, crying pitifully until he fell silent. His eyes were open, yet unseeing. Smoke wafted around his little body and he turned to ashes before her eyes.

"I'm sorry!" she cried again. None of them seemed mollified.

"You could have saved us!"

She blinked, and she was standing in the center of the theater worksite. Her entire hand and arm were engulfed in flames that she reached out and held to the wooden structure. She screamed, terrified of the fire melting away her skin, but glad as the flames caught on the wood.

A deafening explosion shook the very foundation of the structure. Beatrice covered her ears and screamed again.

A moment later, she looked up, finding herself in her bed inside her dark apartment. She sat up. The ticking clock beside her bed revealed it had been only fifteen minutes since she had fallen asleep.

She was about to lie back down when she heard what sounded like a steam whistle. It cut through the silence of the night, causing her heart to start racing. She could think of one thing that made a sound like that.

The steam pumper truck. The one the volunteer fire department used in case of a blaze gone out of control.

She went to the door, opening it. The acrid smell of smoke accompanied faint sounds of voices. A stab of fear pierced her heart.

She dressed and hurried toward the center of town. Men in their long johns and trousers lined the street, passing pails from the fire hydrant as the volunteer firemen in long black coats attempted to get the engine pumping. Hosing lay in a tangled mess on the graveled road.

She didn't want to, but her eyes searched for the source of the fire. Her breath caught in her throat as she saw the smoke billowing from the theater structure.

She tried to breathe. The smoke and flames reaching angry fingers into the night brought a terror that made her heart pound and her entire body go limp. The faces of the doomed little ones taunted her. Blamed her. She felt a rush of guilt so staggering she couldn't catch her breath.

In shock, she watched the hose from the pumper come to life and send a shot of water high into what would have been the rafters of the new community theater. As they looked on, the structure gave way and fell.

"The hotel!" She heard the shout and knew whose voice it was. She searched the crowd until she saw Evan, clad in his volunteer fireman's uniform. He pointed up at the third story of the hotel, where smoke drifted from the window closest to the theater site.

"Someone get a ladder," another firefighter called. They hoisted a long ladder to the side of the building. Evan pushed the other man out of the way and grabbed the rungs.

"Let me go, son. You have your whole life ahead of you," the older volunteer shouted as Evan began to climb.

"I think I know the woman and children in that room," Evan said, breathless.

Beatrice's throat went dry. She sank to her knees and clutched her chest as she willed Evan to save Edna and her children before it was too late.

Twenty-Two

Evan wasn't sure how he knew Edna and her babies were in that room. Had the Spirit told him? He was sure of one thing – he would save that family or die trying.

He made it to the top of the rickety ladder that should have been replaced years ago. He poked his head into the room full of smoke, barely able to make out a form crumpled on the floor. Edna must have passed out from the smoke. He saw the toddler trying to lift the baby on the other side of the small space. He climbed inside and grabbed both children, balancing them on his shoulders as he climbed back down the ladder.

The other firefighter, Tom, met him halfway and took the kids. He quickly returned to the window and jumped back inside, coughing from smoke that was now so thick he couldn't see a thing. He crawled to the place he remembered seeing Edna and pulled up her limp body, heaving her over his shoulder and making a quick exit.

All the way down the ladder with Edna's dead weight on his shoulder, Evan thought of one image. Beatrice, leaning over that pile of newspaper shreds, blowing it toward the wood.

She'd done this. She'd caused this fire and Edna might be dead because of her.

When he reached the bottom, he ran across the street and gently set Edna on a bench, motioning to Luke. The doctor hurried to her side.

Evan couldn't do anything to help, so he scanned the street for Beatrice. He was sure he'd seen her a few moments earlier. She'd probably been there all along.

Sure enough, he saw her kneeling in the street. Her arms were across her chest and a desperate, panicked expression marred the features of her pale face.

"What did you expect?" he muttered. "This is what happens when you play with fire."

"Evan," Luke said from behind him. "Will you carry her to the clinic?"

Evan saw that Luke had Edna's children in his arms. He took care as he lifted Edna and followed Luke down the boardwalk.

"Is she going to be okay?" Evan stared at Edna's face, dark with soot and so still.

Luke glanced back. "Only time will tell how much damage the smoke has done."

"But she'll live?"

Luke opened the clinic door and held it for Evan. "I'm always hopeful. I couldn't bear not to be."

Evan didn't like his evasive answer. He stayed with Luke and tried to wash some of the soot off the children's faces while they eyed their mother, lying still on the table. Luke cleared the ash from Edna's nose and mouth and listened to her breathing with a solemn expression.

Finally, Edna sat up and coughed hard. She kept coughing until her ashen skin began to turn pink again.

"Thank the Lord," Evan breathed as he crossed the room, holding her baby and leading her daughter by the hand.

"We were worried we might lose you," Luke admitted as he checked her pulse.

"No one… to take care of them," she said in a hoarse, gasping voice, nodding to her children.

Evan nodded. His throat felt thick.

"You'll need to find someone temporarily," Luke advised.

"You are going to need a few days to recover."

"I'll help," Evan said. "I can get Mrs. Merchant to watch them while I'm at work."

Edna leaned back into her pillow as if he'd just removed stress that was keeping her upright. "Thank you."

His heart lurched at the sight of her grateful tears.

"How did the fire start?" Luke asked as he prepared medicine at the counter across the room.

"I intend to find out." Evan's demeanor darkened. "I'll be right back." He showed the little girl the bench by the door and handed her a child's book from the bin of toys Luke kept in the front room for patients. He handed the baby to the nurse, an older woman who helped Luke during emergencies.

He almost barreled into Beatrice as he left the office. She stood just outside the door, her hands clasped together at her chest. She met his gaze with a haunted expression.

"I didn't do this, Evan. You have to believe me. I didn't go back there."

He wanted to believe her. He did. But he'd found her standing over a fire at the same site less than an hour before it had gone up in flames. She'd admitted she was there to burn it down. It was difficult to get around the facts.

"Why should I believe you?" He couldn't look at her anymore. He didn't want to stare into those familiar black eyes, so determined and intelligent. His heart would deceive him if he did. He'd believe anything she said. "You had the motivation."

"I didn't want to hurt anyone! The whole point of me being out there was to *keep* people from being hurt. *That* was my motivation."

"I'm not saying you intended to hurt them –" His voice caught and he stopped talking as Edna's face filled his mind. "Don't say another word, Beatrice. Please. Don't make me responsible to turn you in."

His voice had gone low. He could hear his desperation, so he was sure she could as well. He tried to walk away, but she caught his arm in a fierce grip.

"I didn't go back, Evan. I swear I didn't." Her voice trembled. "Do you think… do you think perhaps the fire wasn't completely extinguished?"

He squeezed his eyes shut, but he could still see her vulnerable, wide eyes. His ridiculous bleeding heart told him to protect her, no matter what she'd done.

After a long moment, he clamped a hand around her arm and pulled her into the small alley between the clinic and the mercantile. Her back hit the brick wall and she gave an involuntary gasp. He ignored the sound and leaned as close as he could without actually touching her face with his. "Do you realize the position you've put me in?"

His voice was a whisper. It would not go well for her if anyone were to overhear their conversation. He'd heard men at the scene promising to find who was responsible and make them pay. Not one of them would care enough about Beatrice to accept her claim of innocence if anyone found out what she had been doing before the fire.

She glared back at him, not cowering or resorting to tears despite the danger. "Are you sure the fire was out?"

He stared into her eyes. "I survived on my own in the wilderness from the age of twelve. I know when a fire is out. The only question I'm asking is why I should believe you didn't go back there and pick up where you left off."

Being so close to her, he could feel her entire body relax. She sighed in what looked like incredible release.

"You're relieved," he said, the realization causing him to doubt his suspicions. "You were worried."

The color began to return to her face and her breathing slowed down. She seemed to notice how close he was for the first time, but she didn't try to get away.

"I was so scared. The fire… I don't do well with fire." She fumbled for an explanation.

His eyes caught on her mouth. Her lips opened. He tried to

look away, but he ached to kiss her. Physically ached. No matter what she'd done.

"Evan," she whispered, and he felt undone at the sound of her delicate voice.

He dragged his gaze away from her mouth and forced himself to take a step back. "Are you okay? Your heart, I mean?"

"I'm fine," she said, clearing her throat and looking down, which told him she was lying.

"You're not," he acknowledged. "I want to believe what you're telling me. Enough that I'm going to keep what I know to myself for now. But that's a risk to me, too, because I'll be implicated right along with you if anyone finds out."

Beatrice nodded. "I didn't do it. So nothing will point to me."

"It already does, Beatrice. Enough that I'm ashamed of myself for not taking this to the sheriff this minute."

She didn't answer. Either she could lie better than anyone he'd ever known, or she was telling the truth. For now, he'd believe her. He couldn't yet face the alternative.

With the conversation over, she leaned back against the wall. Her eyes closed and he heard her labored breathing.

He nudged her and gestured toward the clinic. "Doc should look at you, too."

She didn't answer. She watched him for a moment, then turned and walked to the end of the alley, disappearing from his sight.

Twenty-Three

Evan was sure everyone on the street could read his thoughts. Men still worked to contain the last of the blaze, but it didn't appear the rest of the hotel was in danger. The residents and staff of the hotel stood outside on the street, most in their pajamas, covered only with thin blankets to keep out the cold. Some were angry, some were still in a panic, and young children cried for the sake of boredom or hunger.

At least they were all alive. That much he could be thankful for.

He needed to collect Edna's things and get her children settled, but he felt a pressing need to speak to Joshua first. The farm was too far out, but it occurred to him maybe he could call him on the telephone and at least let him know what had happened.

He walked with purpose toward the telegraph office. His mind was still reeling from everything that had happened. Maybe talking to Joshua would help him sort it out and make sense of it. Maybe Joshua would tell him what to do.

As he turned the corner, he stopped short. Jacob Wylie was standing outside the office with a group of men around him. They were all talking at once and he was trying to calm them.

"Now, now, folks, do you think I would have left the theater uninsured? This may delay the opening of the theater by a month or two, but it will not affect your investment or our plans."

"You took my life savings, Wylie, and I better see a return on that money."

"I should have known better than to give money to a traveling salesman."

Wylie held up his hands. "Trust me, gents. Everything is in hand. My good man Daniel here will see that the theater is built in a timely fashion."

Wylie clapped his hand on the shoulder of a younger man standing next to him. When Evan moved to pass the large group, he brushed the arm of the man standing next to Wylie. The man turned around and looked Evan in the eyes.

Evan stopped short, struck by a sense of familiarity. "Do I know you?"

He was almost sure the eyes of the other man flickered in recognition, but he shook his head and stuck out his hand.

"Don't believe so. Daniel Barrington. I'm Mr. Wylie's foreman."

Evan shook his hand. "Evan Masters. Excuse me; I'm in a bit of a rush."

Barrington stepped out of his way and watched him pass by with a curious expression. The encounter made Evan feel even more unsettled. Where had he seen that man before?

He went inside the office and reached for the phone on the wall. But even as his hand slid around the cradle, he couldn't pick it up. What could he say to Joshua over a public line?

He let go of the receiver and sighed in frustration, running his hand through his hair and pacing to the door. There was nothing to be done except to go back to the clinic and take those children so Edna could rest and get better. He'd have to deal with everything else later.

♫

Beatrice didn't come out of her apartment for two straight

days. She didn't eat or drink much. She sat on the floor in front of the window and thought anxious, regretful thoughts that made her stomach churn and her heart flutter.

How had she come to this? She had been ready to commit arson and possibly murder. What if Evan hadn't stopped her?

And what if he was wrong about the fire being out? Could she be responsible for the damage and the injuries?

She considered her meager bank account. Her resources would dry up soon. She had no way to begin to pay back the hotel or make amends for Edna and her children.

"Why didn't you let me die?" She demanded, her fierce prayer breaking the silence in the dark room. She wouldn't take all the blame. Not when God had been the one to leave her to cower alone in an upstairs apartment and go mad. Wouldn't it have made more sense for her heart to have stopped beating December 30 of 1903?

The room mocked her with silence. She would have no answers to the questions she was asking. She shut her eyes and willed away the misery, but felt no relief. Making use of the knife in the kitchen had never been more tempting, but she couldn't face God. Not when she was so angry with him. Not when he refused to talk to her.

At some point, she fell asleep and slept for so long she wasn't sure what day it was when she woke up. She heard a deep rumbling in the room below her. A man, not Pastor Merchant, was having a conversation with Mrs. Merchant.

She had little strength to move, but she managed to go to the door and creep part way down the stairs. She sat just above the window that Mrs. Merchant had cracked, because it was baking day, and listened.

"Doc was wondering how the burns were doing on the baby."

Beatrice recognized Evan's voice, taut with concern.

"I've been applying the salve," Mrs. Merchant answered. Beatrice leaned over and saw her point to a line of blisters on the baby's arm. Beatrice's eyes fixed on the marks and she couldn't look away.

"I think they look better," Evan said. "Don't you?"

"Of course. He'll be fine, dear. How is their mother?"

"She's improved. Doc thinks she might be able to go back to work by the end of the week. The undamaged part of the hotel is full, though, so she'll have to find a place to stay."

"It's good of you to help her. We'll think of something."

"It's the least I can do."

The least you can do, knowing what you know, Beatrice added silently. It was what he meant, after all.

Evan hesitated before he spoke again. "Has she come out?"

Mrs. Merchant sighed. "No. I haven't even heard her move. She must be out of food by now. Several times, I went up and peeked in the window. I was afraid she might be –"

Her voice stopped, and they were both silent. Beatrice fought guilt.

"I'm afraid of it, too," Evan admitted, so softly Beatrice barely heard him speak.

"She's just sitting on the floor in the middle of the room. Maybe it would help if you talked with her."

Evan sighed. "I can't right now. I need to work through a few things first."

Beatrice went back upstairs. She'd heard enough.

The next morning, a warm day for February, a knock at the door woke Beatrice. She sat straight up in bed, gasping for air. It had to be Jacob Wylie, followed by the sheriff. They must know what she'd done.

"Beatrice?"

She heard the voice of Amelia Morehouse on the other side of the door and sighed in relief. "I'm not feeling up to visiting," she said loud enough for Mrs. Morehouse to hear her.

The handle turned and the door creaked open. Amelia peeked through the crack. "I'm sorry. I hate to bother you, but I'm in desperate need of your help at the library. Mrs. Reynolds is still away and the twins have colds. Kathleen needs me."

"I'm sorry to hear that," Beatrice mumbled. She got up and

went to put a pot on to boil as Amelia stepped into the room and closed the door. "No need to let all the winter air into your apartment, I suppose. Can I join you for breakfast?"

"Sure," Beatrice said with a shrug. She found some bread and buttered it.

"Wouldn't you know it, but I was at the hotel this morning and they offered me some leftover eggs and sausage from breakfast to take with me. I wouldn't want it to go to waste, would you?"

Amelia sat down and gestured to the other chair at the table. Beatrice smelled the food and her stomach gurgled. She had no hope of resisting Amelia's plan to get her to eat.

The water boiled and Amelia made two cups of tea from a tin she had in her basket. "Isn't this nice?"

She blessed the food without asking Beatrice for permission. Then she put the generous portions of food on plates and handed Beatrice one of them. "They do something to these eggs. I wish I knew what it was," Amelia said. "I think it is some sort of fancy cheese."

"Cream." Beatrice forked a small bite.

"Cream? Really?"

"My mother used to make them this way. She used cream."

"Isn't that something?" Amelia stopped eating and watched Beatrice with her perceptive gaze. "Tell me more about your mother."

Beatrice shook her head. "I don't like to think about her."

"Why would you not like to think of your mother?" Amelia frowned.

Beatrice stared hard at the food on her plate, which suddenly seemed to make her stomach turn. "I lost her. She died when I was nineteen."

Amelia nodded, waiting for her to go on. When Beatrice went silent, she spoke. "Why would you want to stop thinking of her just because you lost her? We have to keep memories alive, lest we forget."

Beatrice shrugged. "What would you know about it?" Even as she said the words, she remembered the other woman had lost much.

"Plenty." Amelia took another bite of breakfast. "I watched my mother wither away and die of tuberculosis when I was twenty-two. I still think of her every day."

Beatrice didn't answer.

"Your mother was a kind woman, wasn't she? Did she take good care of you?"

Beatrice nodded.

"Then you must keep her memory strong. You'll need to tell your children about her one day."

"My children?" Beatrice laughed, a caustic sound that echoed through the empty room. "I will never marry. I will never have children. It's a ridiculous notion."

Amelia watched her curiously. "It wouldn't be the first ridiculous idea I've ever come up with. But that doesn't mean it won't happen."

"A person can't live life with their head in the clouds. Dreams don't usually come true. Not for me, anyway." Beatrice set her fork down, no longer hungry.

Amelia nodded. "You're right. This world is most definitely broken. I learned that first when I lost my mother and then when my husband was murdered ten years ago. But I refuse to lose hope. I refuse to stop dreaming. God is bigger than any evil in this world. He will have his way."

"Not with me," Beatrice said, ashamed that she was speaking the dark words aloud. There was a long pause, as if Amelia could not believe she'd said it.

"My dear, God is bigger than you and nothing you say or do is going to change that fact." Amelia's tone came as a soft warning. That she spoke the words gently caused Beatrice more guilt than if she'd shouted them at her. She stared at the floor. She wanted to discount Amelia's statement. But the words stuck in her mind and wouldn't shake loose.

Amelia set down her fork and picked up her teacup. Her voice was strained when she spoke again. "Tell me you'll help me out at the library. I think it would be good for you. Get you out of the house."

"Maybe I don't want to get out of the house."

"That much is clear. But that is exactly why you must. Believe me, the idea of being all alone and not having to worry about the feelings and thoughts of other people is a constant temptation to me. But God wouldn't have me be a hermit, and he doesn't want us to be perpetually alone. Our minds can be affected when we are by ourselves too much."

Beatrice remembered how she had gotten it into her head to "save" Dempsey by setting fire to the theater. Maybe she'd already gone mad.

"You've done a great job reorganizing behind the desk at the library," Amelia said in an obvious attempt to lighten the conversation. "Between you and me, Mrs. Reynolds had a completely indecipherable system."

"I hope she isn't too angry when she returns," Beatrice said, though she didn't really care how Mrs. Reynolds felt about it. They both became quiet, and Beatrice felt threatened by the silence. She cleared her throat. This might be a good time to complete some research associated with a plan she was considering. She eyed Amelia with curiosity. "I've been reading your new novel."

Amelia nodded, her cheeks turning red. "*A Purpose to Find?* What did you think of Natasha having to travel out into the woods to hide and living there all alone?"

Beatrice would have to be careful speaking to the intuitive woman. She had a definite ulterior motive in speaking to her about that particular novel. "I found it fascinating to consider. How did you know the details of what Natasha would need in the wild and what dangers she might face?"

Amelia leaned back in her chair and folded her arms across her chest. She considered Beatrice closely. "The wheels began turning when I read Thoreau's *Life in the Woods*. I used many of his experiences as inspiration for Natasha's adventures."

"I'll have to read it."

Amelia looked out the small window over the kitchen sink. "*I went to the woods because I wished to live deliberately, to front only the essential facts of life, and see if I could not learn what it had to teach, and not, when I came to die, discover that I had not lived.*"

"Thoreau said that?"

Amelia nodded. "He did. I admit I haven't taken him at his word, besides in my imagination. I would like to go into the woods and live simply, but I am not on friendly terms with insects."

Beatrice allowed a tiny smile. A grain of hope buried itself into her soul. Could she salvage the remainder of her days and find meaning in them?

More importantly, might she do a better job of avoiding civilization?

It was a welcome prospect.

Twenty-Four

Evan loved kids. He always had. He'd always wanted a whole passel of them. And Edna's kids were no exception.

What he didn't love was midnight crying, bottle warming on the stove and leaky diapers. God had specially created mothers to see to their babies' needs without losing their minds over it.

So, it was with a bit of relief that he returned the kids to their mother three days after the fire.

She had returned to work the morning Luke released her from the clinic, so she was just finishing her duties as he brought them to the hotel. He cringed when he saw the blisters on her hands and face, far from healed. But when he brought her children to her, her tired, overwhelmed expression lit with true joy.

"My babies! You've no idea how much I missed you!"

Evan watched them bury themselves in her arms. "I'm glad you're doing a little better," he said. "You don't look right yet, though. Are you sure you should be jumping back into things so quickly?"

Edna gave him a sad smile. "I don't have a choice. You're right. I'm not better yet. If it were just the pain from the burns or the smoke in my lungs, it would be one thing, but I keep having horrible nightmares about the kids being lost in the fire. I haven't been sleeping well."

"I can understand that." Suddenly, a baby waking him up in

156

the middle of the night seemed a small thing compared to what this young mother was experiencing.

Edna looked around the busy hotel porch and cleared her throat. Evan could tell by the sound that her lungs were still working to clear out the smoke. He could also see she was embarrassed by the conversation, or at least by the timing of it, standing on the hotel porch in her service uniform.

"I'm sorry," Evan said quickly. "Would you like to take a walk and talk some more?"

She didn't answer right away. "Are you asking because you want to take a walk or are you just being polite?"

"I'd be honored if you joined me." He chuckled. "I'm concerned about you, Edna. You've been through a hard time and I don't want you to feel like you're all alone."

She smiled, though her expression remained uncertain. "I'd like that."

They followed the walk around the side of the hotel and to the back where a quiet path wound along the creek. He offered his arm, so she balanced the baby on one hip and took it with her other. Her little girl, Rose, skipped ahead of them.

She asked the question he'd hoped she wouldn't. "Did they find out who started the fire?"

It wasn't Beatrice.

He swallowed back the words. He wasn't convinced they were true. "Uh... the newspaper had an article today saying the city council confirmed the investigator is fairly sure the fire was intentional. He's still working on a suspect."

"How does he know?" Edna asked curiously.

"He believes an incendiary was used. Kerosene, to be specific."

"Who on earth would want to burn the new theater?" Edna shook her head in disbelief. "I haven't even heard of anyone who doesn't want it, have you?"

Evan licked his lips and didn't answer, pretending to have his attention stolen by greeting someone coming the other way on the path.

When they reached the pond, he motioned for Edna to sit on the bench and lifted her little girl to the seat next to her. He pulled a wild daisy near the water and handed it to her to play with.

"Say thank you, Rosie," Edna said as she adjusted the baby so he could snuggle against her chest.

"Thank you." Rose smiled shyly at Evan.

"You're welcome, sweetheart." Evan reached a hand to her mop of honey-colored curls. He stared out over the water, knowing it was time to have a discussion with Edna he didn't want to have.

"I've enjoyed getting to know you, Edna." His voice caused her gaze to fall on him and she waited for him to continue.

"And...?" she finally prompted.

He glanced at her. "And... I think you're a wonderful, strong woman. You've been through so much but you don't let it ruin you or make you bitter. You've got grit, and I'm awfully impressed with you."

She smiled. "Thanks, Evan. I think the world of you, as well."

He shrugged. "So, I know you're in a rough spot and you're probably looking for... long-term solutions to your problems."

"I am." She spoke honestly, though her cheeks went pink when she caught his meaning.

"I've been thinking about it." His heart started trying to pump right out of his chest.

"So have I," she said softly. "My aunt has offered for us to come and live with her. She sent me tickets. The train leaves next Tuesday."

Evan frowned. "Where does she live?"

"Boston."

"So, it's now or never," he said, trying to process this new turn of events and wondering how he should respond. He cared about her and he wouldn't mind making them his family, but now that she had an alternative, the choice wasn't as clear-cut. Did he care about her enough to permanently sever all other ties?

"Evan, you've been so kind to me. I hope you don't believe I'm trying to trap you. The timing is awful, I realize that. We can go to Boston, even if I had hoped Dempsey would be my home."

He chuckled. "Ironic that I've been hoping to leave Dempsey."

She stared at him in confusion. "I didn't know you weren't happy here in town. You're leaving?"

He shrugged. "I have no plans. I've never even told anyone I wanted to leave. I've always wanted to go out west and ranch or farm. Live off the land and get out of a suit and office. And hat. I hate this stupid hat."

She gave a short laugh, but her expression was wary. "I've never been much for farming. Not to say I couldn't learn."

They were quiet for a time. Suddenly, Evan gently took her bandaged hand. He banished the stubborn image of Beatrice and thought of nothing else but Edna and her children and what was best for them.

"I'll make this offer to you. You don't have to give me an answer today. You can get on that train and never say another word to me if it's easier. But if you're willing to marry a man you barely know, I'm willing to be your husband and a father to your kids. If you wanted to stay in Dempsey, I'd cheerfully work at the train and telegraph office for the rest of my life. That's my promise to you, Edna."

"Are you asking me...?" she stammered, tears filling her pretty blue eyes. He was touched that she honestly seemed not to have expected the proposal. It said much about her character.

"I'm asking you to marry me."

"Oh, Evan." Her hand fluttered to her chest.

"I've never been a husband or father before. But I promise you I'd learn to do it right, the good Lord helping me."

She let go of his hand and reached a palm to his cheek. "You are a dear man. And you *would* be a good husband and father. I know it, without a doubt."

He knew it, too. And once he'd said the words, everything

seemed easier. Love was a choice, after all. Hadn't Joshua and Kathleen proven that? He could choose to love Edna for the rest of their lives, and he had no doubt they'd be happy.

If Edna chose to stay with him, he'd keep his word. And he'd never give the hope he'd had for Beatrice another thought as long as he lived.

Her hand fell to her son's back and she looked away from Evan with a self-conscious smile. Should he try to kiss her now? Would she know he was serious if he didn't?

She saved him from wondering. "I don't expect anything more from you now, Evan. I'll have an answer for you by Tuesday."

He tried to stifle his sigh of relief. "It's not that I wouldn't like to kiss you, Edna. Trust me, I would. It's just a lot to take in so quickly."

"I know." She nodded. "I feel the same way. But I also know why this is so hard for you. I understand this is a rather large sacrifice on your part."

He knew she was speaking of Beatrice. He shook his head. "Marrying you is no sacrifice, Edna. You'd be a sweet reward for any man in his right mind."

Her smile grew wider. "Thank you."

He stood and leaned over to kiss her cheek. "See you around."

He waved to Rosie and left them. He'd either just made the best or worst decision of his life. Whatever Edna ended up deciding, he'd stick to it. *It's in your hands, Lord,* he prayed. *Help her make the right choice.*

Twenty-Five

Beatrice didn't want to go out, but she needed the money. She arrived at the library early and tried to brace herself for the day.

It seemed all of Dempsey had developed a sudden need to conduct research or find a novel to fill up the long days of winter. She only spoke if spoken to, but that didn't stop patrons from speaking to each other. She managed to hear a year's worth of town gossip in an afternoon, no matter how many times she shushed them.

"Word is—the fire was set on purpose. Jacob Wylie has promised to press charges if a suspect is found."

Beatrice continued to replace the biographies on the shelves as two women spoke in hushed tones in the reading room.

"Heaven help the person who did it."

Two younger girls on the other side of the shelf had news of a different nature. It was news that nearly caused her to fall off the ladder.

"Did you hear about the Widow MacGregor?"

"Edna? The woman injured in the hotel fire?"

"The very one. Luanne at the hotel said Edna told her in confidence that Evan Masters asked her to marry him this very week. She'll decide by Thursday whether she'll go live with her aunt or marry Evan."

"How is there any choice to be made? He's a catch by any

standard, to be sure! I'd marry him today if only he'd ask me."

"Me, too!" The other woman giggled as Beatrice clung to the rungs and tried to breathe.

They continued to snicker as they returned to the reading room and sat down at one of the round tables to continue their gossip.

Beatrice climbed down and sat on a stool. Evan – who had loved her completely and unashamedly for as long as he had known her – was really moving on. He would give his devotion to a more worthy woman.

She wondered if the incident at the theater site had finally caused him to let go of her. No matter when it had happened, she was alone. No one would care now if she lived or died. And should the evidence trail lead to her doorstep, no one would be around to advocate for her. She would pay for a crime she did not commit, yet attempted nonetheless.

It made her decision to go ahead with her secret plan an easy one. She would leave Dempsey. There was nothing to hold her back now. Nothing to fear. As Thoreau promised, she would find solace and clarity if she left civilization for the woods.

She would go as soon as she had the funds to purchase the things she would need.

♫

Thou wilt keep him in perfect peace, whose mind is stayed on thee: because he trusteth in thee.

As Evan drifted to sleep, his prayer was for Beatrice. She hadn't known a moment's peace in all the years he'd known her.

"Help her learn to trust you, Lord. Don't leave her all alone. Do whatever it will take to make her know your peace," he whispered.

Morning seemed to come quickly. Evan rose with more energy than he'd had in some time and headed to work a full half-hour earlier than usual.

The day passed quickly, and before he knew it, the clock told him it was time to go home. He complied.

He heard the sound of hammers and calls of construction

workers when he reached the main street of Dempsey. It hadn't taken Wylie any time to begin rebuilding. The man had a drive to get that theater done in record time.

Jacob was there, barking orders to workers who couldn't move fast enough. At the same time, he saw an unsuspecting Beatrice turn the corner, her head down and her arms clutching books. She must be headed to the library.

Jacob saw her the same moment Evan did. A slow smile that didn't seem a bit friendly spread across his face. He moved to overtake her and grabbed her arm.

Evan walked faster. Jacob turned as Beatrice struggled against his grip. Wylie gave a shrill whistle, causing passerby to stop and give him their attention.

"I have a sworn statement by a hotel worker that this woman intentionally set the fire that destroyed the theater and hotel."

Gasps and murmuring followed Jacob's declaration. Beatrice turned pale, but her narrowed eyes searched the crowd until she found Evan. Her glare accused him.

You told him.

He shook his head. Obviously, someone besides him had seen her that night. He watched helplessly as Jacob dragged her toward the police station. Her books slipped from her arms and clattered to the boardwalk.

Evan picked up the books as the crowd followed Wylie and Beatrice. How could he fix this? No judge in their right mind would ignore the damning evidence Jacob would present, especially if he had a witness. No one would take her word for it, as he had, that she had not gone back.

He saw only one option. He would have to find out who really did set the fire.

The bystanders and gawkers quickly overwhelmed the small police station and jail. The sheriff told the crowd to go home as he directed the rest of them across the street to the courthouse.

Evan stood near the back of the courtroom, wishing Joshua

was still a part of the police force. The current sheriff of Dempsey was a fair man, but he did not possess the integrity Joshua had displayed as deputy in charge ten years ago. Sheriff Mavis was more concerned with Jacob's ire than the welfare of Beatrice.

Beatrice shook off Wylie's grasp and glared at the sheriff. "I insist you forbid this man to touch me again!"

Mavis didn't answer her. He directed his questions to Wylie. "What's the trouble?"

"Albert Mavis. So good to see you again. Terrible circumstances, though." Wylie leaned over the desk the sheriff was standing behind in order to shake his hand. Evan wondered if Jacob was pretending to know the sheriff.

"Of course, Mr. Wylie. Tell me your grievance against this girl."

"Sheriff, I have an eyewitness who can testify that this woman was seen setting a fire on my construction site the very night the fire occurred."

"Where is your witness?" Evan asked from the doorway.

"She is working at the hotel at the moment. She was seeing to a guest's need and happened to see Miss Walsh through the window, blowing on strips of newspaper to make a fire."

Evan's heart sank. Someone *had* seen her.

"Miss Walsh, what do you have to say for yourself?" Mavis asked sternly.

She lifted her chin in the air, her fists balled tightly at her sides. "I didn't do it."

Evan shook his head. If she told the whole truth, maybe it would go better for her. She'd still be in plenty of trouble, but it would be the truth, and he believed as sure as they were standing there the truth would set her free.

But he couldn't speak for her. And no one else in the room planned to, either. Not the sheriff. Not the deputy. Not the few citizens who'd found their way to the back of the courtroom and were curiously peaking in the doorway. No one would speak to her character. Why should they? She'd shut herself away. No one knew her. Not even him. And everyone wanted someone to blame for the fire.

"I say we lock her up," the deputy said. "It will give folks a chance to settle down, now that we have a suspect in custody."

Mavis shifted and cleared his throat. "Since there is a witness prepared to testify to your guilt, I'll have to arrest you, Miss Walsh. But you'll need to bring your witness in for a statement, Mr. Wylie. Now."

Evan saw the first sign of fear in Beatrice's expression. But she didn't cower or grovel. Her dark eyes continued to flash and her gaze stayed focused on the sheriff. He only saw the fear in the slight trembling of her lip.

Evan couldn't stand to see her so humiliated. He walked forward. "Do you really think that's necessary?"

"You've been whipped over her for a dozen years," Jacob replied. "Nobody in this room besides you believes this woman is incapable of destroying my theater."

A low grumble of agreement passed through the gathering of people who had followed them into the courthouse. The sheriff sent Evan an apologetic look that also held an element of warning as he took Beatrice's arm. "Miss Walsh, you're under arrest for suspicion of arson."

Evan watched in disbelief as the sheriff slowly pulled iron cuffs from the back of his belt. He held Beatrice's hands behind her back and locked them around her delicate wrists. When he came to the door, he waved the onlookers away. "Move along, now, folks. There's nothing else for you to see here."

They slowly dispersed. The sheriff pointed at Evan and Jacob. "Go home. I'll put her in a cell overnight and we'll discuss this further tomorrow morning."

"Don't do this," Evan said, trying not to sound as desperate as he felt. "What if she's innocent? She'll be terrorized by spending the night in jail."

The sheriff glanced at Evan evenly, his mouth twisting behind his bushy mustache. "She won't be harmed. You go on home."

Evan's gaze fell to Beatrice. She hadn't said a word. With a frustrated sigh, Evan took the sheriff's arm and pulled him aside where Jacob would be less likely to hear his words. "She has a heart condition. Please keep a close eye on her and call Doc Thomas if she has any trouble. I'll check on her tonight."

"We'll take care of her. The doc is just around the corner if we need him."

Beatrice had been staring at Jacob, fuming. She dug in her heels as the sheriff tried to move her. "*He* did it."

The sheriff chuckled. "Why would Mr. Wylie burn down his own work site?"

Beatrice seethed. "To frame me. He knows I've been working to convince people to withdraw their support."

The sheriff shook his head. His incredulity echoed through the chamber as he spoke. "That doesn't sound like much of a defense, little lady."

"What if she's right?" Evan asked.

Wylie smirked. "This is utter nonsense."

"I'll be back," Evan reminded the sheriff.

"Doesn't mean I'll let you in, son," the sheriff said.

Evan shook his head and pushed past Jacob, coming to stand close to Beatrice. He took her shoulders in his hands.

"Deep breaths. You're going to come through this. I'm not going to let you go through it alone." He kept his voice low so only she would hear him.

She didn't answer. She tried to appear disdainful and irritated. But he knew that was her way of dealing with stress. He believed his words would reassure her, deep down.

The sheriff led her away.

Evan stopped Wylie on the sidewalk outside. "I'm going to make sure the truth comes out," Evan said. He breathed deeply to avoid punching the smug salesman right in his big mouth.

"Are you sure you want the truth, Masters? You know as well as I do your girlfriend is far from innocent. You weren't the only one watching that night."

Evan took a step closer. "I know what you're doing. I'm not going to let you blame her for this."

"And I'm not going to let some overgrown Romeo get in my way," Jacob snapped back. "That's the only warning you'll get. Stay away from me, and stay out of this."

Evan leaned into his face. "Not a chance."

Twenty-Six

Beatrice didn't want to be intimidated by the jail cell. She wanted to remain poised and indifferent and scoff at the deputy every time he came by. But being terrified made her goals difficult.

The harsh white interior of the cell spoke to her on behalf of the citizens of Dempsey.

You are guilty and the guilty must be punished.

"I didn't do it!" she whispered fiercely into the silence.

But I almost did. I would have, if not for Evan.

Her guilty soul convicted her, even if she could not admit it. Someone could have died because of what she had been ready to do.

It made her sick to consider, so she focused her attention on her outrage at Jacob Wylie. Why had he framed her? Was it a matter of spite, or did he intend to silence her opposition so he could cut corners and build the theater at a lower cost? If that were the case, people would die in his theater. People like her parents and brother. Her fiancé.

She felt cold. She shivered and brought her arms around herself. She cowered in the corner as she heard the station door open. Someone with a heavy step came through the door, stomping off snow that must have fallen since she had been brought inside. She didn't have to wait long to know who was there. Suddenly, Evan was standing in front of her, holding the bars of her cell. Neither of them spoke for a long moment.

"I'm sure you think I'm pathetic." She couldn't look him in the eye.

"I think you need a friend," he answered without hesitating.

"I don't need you, Evan. How many times do I have to tell you that?"

"I'm not leaving you alone."

She stood up and rushed at him, grabbing the bars in her hands and shaking them. "Why not?"

He looked at her with a sorrowful expression. "Because there's no one else here."

Tears stung her eyes. She knew she had created her own problems. She was responsible for it, so she should take the blame. It made her angry that he wouldn't face the facts and leave. "You shouldn't put your life on hold. I created this mess. You have other concerns."

"What do you mean?" he asked warily.

"You're marrying Edna."

"How did you know that?"

"It's all over town, Evan. I overheard it at the library."

He sighed. "I told her I would marry her if she was agreeable. She'll tell me yes or no tomorrow."

Beatrice nodded, working to control the avalanche of emotions within. "She'd be crazy not to marry you. And that's why you have to leave. It isn't right for you to be here with me. Just let me go, like you said you would."

Evan shook his head. "That would be easier if I understood why. Explain it to me."

"Time's up, Masters." The deputy's voice invaded their conversation.

"Just give me a minute," Evan called. He turned back to Beatrice. "Tell me."

"I already did," she said.

She could see he was frustrated and on edge. His near-whisper was fierce. "You said you believe you are dying. That you have believed this for many years – as long as I've known you. What I don't understand is why that would cause you to stop living your life. If it happened to me, I'd want to live it as fully as I possibly could."

"I'm not you, and you didn't go through what I did," she hissed.

"Then tell me what you went through!" His voice rose and they heard someone approach.

"Why don't you head out, Evan?" The deputy's question sounded more like a warning.

"Yeah, I'm just about finished, Jimmy." Beatrice saw the sheen of tears in Evan's eyes as he turned back to her.

"Beatrice, just tell me what happened to you."

"I can't," she said around a sob that seemed lodged in her throat. "Please don't make me."

"I need to understand why you think I should just give you up to the likes of Jacob Wylie."

Because I don't want you to be destroyed along with me.

"Because my life is none of your concern," she said instead.

"Beatrice," Evan pleaded, leaning his head against the bars. "Don't shut me out. Please."

"Go."

She turned and went back to her stiff cot, turned toward the wall and ignored him. The deputy came over to stand beside Evan.

"Time to go."

She could feel Evan's eyes on her. "It's not right to leave you defenseless against a criminal. What you did that night, you did out of an honorable notion to protect people. And I believe you. I *believe* you, Beatrice. You didn't start that fire. He probably did, and if that's the truth, that's what I'm fighting for. I have to believe in truth. I won't stand by and let him destroy you with lies."

When she didn't answer, he finally let the deputy show him the door. "I'll be back in the morning with Joshua Whitley. He'll know what to do."

Beatrice gave herself up to the tears, though she did not allow herself to make any noise. Her face burned as the tears fell. How she longed for Evan to return! To take her hands, to stroke her hair. She wanted to feel his touch and know she wasn't completely alone.

But feelings were an indulgence she could not afford. She didn't deserve comfort, so she wouldn't beg for it.

She held her aching head in her hands. It would be a long night.

♫

"I feel bad calling you to town when your family's been through so much lately, but I didn't know what else to do."

Joshua had met Evan in front of the courthouse early the next morning. He shook his head. "It was right for you to call me. Amelia closed the library until further notice. She's with Kathleen. And if I'm being honest with you, I sure don't mind an excuse to get out of the house."

Evan was certain there was more to Joshua's statement. "I'm sorry, Josh. Things aren't any better?"

Joshua forced a smile. "We're not here to talk about me. Tell me what's going on. Something about Beatrice?"

"She was arrested last night."

Joshua folded his arms across his chest. "That right? For what?"

"Arson. But she didn't do it. Jacob Wylie is framing her because she opposes the theater he's trying to build."

"Sure do miss quite a bit when you live out of town," Joshua murmured. He frowned and shook his head. "Ain't you supposed to marry Edna MacGregor?"

"She hasn't officially given me an answer."

"But if she says yes, you're going to marry her?" Joshua raised his eyebrows. "I'm just trying to understand."

Evan sighed and looked away. "Yes. If she says yes, I intend to marry her."

"Then are you sure you want to get involved in all this?"

"If I don't, who is going to stand up for her? No one else will believe her."

"Why is it so hard to believe she's innocent? She's never given anyone any trouble before." Joshua shifted his stance and eyed Evan. "You haven't told me the whole story."

Evan hesitated. "Beatrice did have a notion to start a fire. Because she wanted to stop the theater from being built. I think it has something to do with how she was injured, but she won't tell me. She wanted to protect the people of Dempsey."

"So, she did start the fire?" Joshua stared at him in confusion.

"No! I stopped her."

"You just happened along when she was starting a fire and stopped her?"

Evan sighed in frustration. "I know how it sounds, but it's true. I talked her out of it and stamped out the fire completely. Then I took her home and warned her to stay in her apartment. I think Jacob saw what happened and took the opportunity to set his own fire so she would take the blame and be out of his way. You know she's been spreading the word that she thinks the theater's a bad idea."

Joshua took a long time to answer. "Evan, I know you care about her. But I don't see how you're going to get her out of this one. If someone saw her start the fire, I don't see how she wouldn't be convicted."

"It isn't justice if she gets blamed for something she didn't do."

Joshua nodded. "I agree. And I believe you. Wylie had motivation. Could even be he has some insurance policy against destruction caused by foul play. The man seems powerful determined to make a buck."

Evan considered the idea as they walked across the street to the courthouse.

Inside the courtroom, Beatrice already sat in the defendant's seat across from the only defense lawyer currently practicing in Dempsey. His name was Robert Overton, and he had a reputation.

"That man is a bigot, and he hates outspoken women," Evan said under his breath. "He's not going to be overly interested in representing her. Especially since she can't pay him."

The sheriff stood in front of the judge, leaning against the divider that separated the judge's bench and defendant's seat from the rest of the courtroom. He was speaking to the circuit judge, Elliot Graves. "I've got enough to hold her until trial."

The judge sent a stern look Beatrice's way as Joshua stepped forward and stood next to the sheriff, his hands in his pockets.

"Morning, Judge."

"Morning, Whitley. Haven't seen you in town."

Joshua nodded casually. "Been dealing with family issues. I came in to speak on this woman's behalf. Miss Walsh has a spotless record. She's the pianist at the United Brethren Church and has been for over ten years. The evidence is hearsay, and you only have one eyewitness who was possibly influenced by Wylie. I'm no lawyer, but it sure seems like a shaky case. At least give the woman bail. She's probably distressed enough by spending the night in jail."

Evan was relieved at Joshua's calm confidence.

Judge Graves nodded. "I've always respected your opinion, Whitley." His bushy eyebrows hung severely over his eyes and his long beard twitched along with his generous jowls. "Bail is set at a thousand dollars. The trial begins a week from Monday. I should be back in Dempsey by then."

Beatrice swiped a stray strand of hair from her face. Evan saw the tremor she tried to hide. "I don't have that kind of money."

The judge shrugged. "You may be able to hire a bail bondsman."

"How would I do that?"

Evan could take no more of her terrified expression. "I'll post bail."

Every eye in the room turned his way.

"You sure that's a good idea?" Joshua leaned toward Evan and spoke quietly. "What about Edna?"

Evan ignored him and kept his eyes on the judge. Judge Graves shrugged. "You have the money?"

"I have a house worth three times that amount," Evan said.

"Then it shouldn't be a problem. You can post bail in the office of records across the hall. Dismissed."

Beatrice lifted her chin and her eyes flashed as she looked at him. "I didn't ask you to do that."

"Would you rather stay in jail for another week?"

She had no answer, though she seemed no happier with the decision. She followed him across the hall where he signed the necessary papers. As she followed him outside the courthouse, her shoulders began to slump as if the weight of the world rested on them.

An early spring storm gathered in the sky. Loose hair blew around Beatrice's face. He'd never seen a more perfect representation of her personality, beautiful, delicate and vulnerable, yet as spun up and fierce as she'd ever been. The attraction he felt nearly knocked the breath out of his lungs.

She suddenly came forward and beat her fists against his chest. "Why can't you just leave me alone?"

He caught her arms. "Why can't you just let me help you?"

The reserve she guarded so carefully had cracked. Emotion seeped from her spent spirit.

Her voice cracked with weariness. "Please just leave me alone."

He couldn't leave her there on the street to fight her way home in the storm. His hand moved against his will and went under one of her arms and around her back. The other swept under her skirts and brought her petite form up into his grasp.

All the fight left her and she leaned into his chest.

He stepped out of the street and followed the path by the creek. The skies opened up and rain fell hard, washing away any evidence of her tears. When they came to the apartment and he climbed the stairs, he opened the door and brought her inside, setting her gently on her bed. He found a towel by the washbasin and wrapped it around her soaked shoulders.

Her expression was broken. She lifted a tentative gaze to meet his, and her hand stole up his chest. He couldn't think. He couldn't remember why he should leave, why he shouldn't comfort her.

"Beatrice," he whispered, kneeling in front of her. His face hovered near hers. She didn't move away. He was sure he must be imagining this entire encounter – it felt like one of his daydreams – but it sure seemed like he could see *longing* in her expression.

He could kiss her. He sensed the invitation. He could give comfort and receive it in return until they both found some measure of peace. They were two souls that had been alone far too long.

His lips hovered close to hers. He felt the sweetness of her warm breath on his face. She waited, sorrowful, tear-stained eyes watching him, all the fight gone out of her.

But the nagging sensation remained, warning him. Something was wrong. But what?

Edna, for starters.

Evan jumped up, backing away. "I'm sorry," he said in a breathless voice.

She shook her head and looked down at her empty hands with a profound sadness that shattered his heart. "Go."

He left her. He had no choice. He had pledged himself to someone else. What he was about to do would have been wrong.

He ran home through the rain. As he passed the hotel, he imagined he saw Edna through the front window, staring at him.

Guilt crept over him like the dark skies rolling overhead.

Twenty-Seven

It was time for Beatrice's wasted life to end. Couldn't God see it? Hadn't there been enough misery?

She stood at the window for hours, watching the snow melt away and the spring rains flood the creek. She intended to go ahead with her plan to leave town and go live on her own in the woods. It would be better to wait until it was warmer and the weather was more predictable, and she still didn't have enough money for supplies, but her journey into the wilderness was the only option left.

She would wait another week. She would sneak out by night and travel so deeply into the woods no one would ever find her. One more paycheck from the library should give her enough funds to purchase her most basic supplies. She would have to endure the first day of her trial, but she could if she knew she would be escaping.

She felt a nervous excitement, but also a measure of guilt. If she left, she would cost Evan his home. But had she asked him to post her bail? He should have known better. It would serve him right for trying to save someone who was already drowning. Surely, he knew she would pull him under.

A knock on the door quieted her dark thoughts, though she did not answer it. She heard the sound of a key unlocking the bolt before the handle turned.

"Hello, dear," Mrs. Merchant stuck her head inside. "I've come to see if you need anything. And to tell you how we've missed you playing the piano at church."

Beatrice nodded. "I'm sorry, Mrs. Merchant, but I don't believe anyone else has missed me. I'm rather a pariah at the moment."

Mrs. Merchant came inside and crossed the room to join Beatrice at the window. "You have more friends than you want to admit, dear girl."

Beatrice glanced at the older woman.

"You have a rare talent in your mastery of that instrument," she went on in a cheerful tone. "Every one of us wants you back where you belong."

Beatrice didn't answer.

"I want you to know – some of us listened when you warned the town about the theater. I don't take that lightly, and I know I'm not the only one." Mrs. Merchant smiled and nodded before she left the apartment.

Beatrice was left to deal with the ache the woman's words had brought to her heart.

If she wasn't desperate for the remaining funds, she wouldn't keep going to the library. It terrified her to be in full view of anyone in town. No one on the street was shy about gawking and whispering as if she couldn't see them or hear them. It was worse in the library. She never knew who might come through the doors, or who might find her alone on a quiet afternoon. The two she feared the most were Jacob Wylie and Evan Masters, though she was embarrassed to admit to herself she rather hoped for the latter.

Her worst fear happened the second day back. Jacob Wylie pushed open the heavy doors. He stood just inside, watching her where she sat at the front desk. She tensed her jaw and stared back at him with all the ferocity she could muster.

"Get out," she seethed.

"This is a public building. I have every right to be here. You are the one who belongs in jail." He walked toward her.

"You are the one who set the fire," Beatrice replied in a sharp tone.

"I'd like to see you prove that. Why would I set fire to my own theater?"

"To blame me for it and probably to collect insurance funds as well. I know you weren't happy that I was attempting to spread my own opinion about the theater."

He scoffed. "Utter nonsense. Neither I nor my foreman are happy about having to set back our opening several weeks because of the destruction you caused. Don't think you'll get out of this either. I have a spare eyewitness if I need to employ her services." He leaned close and whispered the words next to her ear.

She understood his meaning well enough. "You are a liar," she said as a chilling sensation traveled down her back. "You set that fire and paid your witness off to lie for you."

He smirked. "Paid for by the money I saved from breaking into your hummingbird jar and your bank account, no doubt."

She seethed. "You stole my money. I'll see every penny returned."

"You know, it's really too bad." He smiled. "You don't meet too many broads as smart as you, and now you'll be spending the rest of your life in jail."

"I'm smart enough to know you won't get away with this. Witnesses that can be paid to lie can be convinced to turn on you just as easily."

Jacob Wylie suddenly reached across the desk and grabbed her by the front of her shirtwaist. He jerked her toward him. She fought him, but he kept tight hold of her. "Listen to me, doll, and hear this well. You won't gain the upper hand on me. I've been in this business far too long to let some floozy put me in the pen. I'm all in now, so watch out."

His expression was pure menace. She felt panic tighten around her throat like a noose. He forced her even closer. "You're quite the looker. Definitely a shame."

"Leave me alone!" Her voice sounded strangled as it echoed

through the large room. "Help!"

He smiled. "There's no one here. Do you think I would be so careless?"

He twisted his hand so the neckline of her blouse began to choke her. She tried to push his hands away, but he was stronger than she was. Her heart began to beat erratically. To her horror, his face came closer and his mouth possessed hers, greedy and harsh. The taste of cigar followed her into blackness.

♫

Evan was going crazy sitting at his desk sending telegraphs about feed orders and great aunts visiting. Why he'd ever agreed to take this job instead of managing the railroad workers, he didn't understand. What had he accomplished with the extra money? Nothing. He had nothing to show for his life. Nothing that mattered, anyway. Nothing that made a difference for him or anyone else. This wasn't what he'd had in mind when he started out on his own, determined to make something of himself.

He stared out the window. "God, it seems like you should be helping me forget about Beatrice and focus on Edna about now," he murmured in a low voice.

"Talking to yourself, Evan?" Isaiah asked from across the room.

"Just taking up a matter with the Lord." Evan sighed and reached for the stack of telegrams that needed to be delivered.

"Best place to take it," Isaiah answered.

Movement outside caught his attention. He looked up and saw Jacob Wylie step out of the library. The man stopped, looking either way as he straightened his vest and tie.

Evan stood up. If that man had done anything to her…

"Gotta check something out. Will you listen for the wire or the telephone?" Evan called to Isaiah as he grabbed his hat and coat.

"Sure thing," Isaiah said without looking up.

Evan caught up with Jacob before he'd made it a block past the library. He stood in front of him, causing Wylie to shrink back with a startled expression.

"Why were you in the library?" he demanded.

Jacob sneered and held the lapels of his coat. "To get a book, of course."

Evan knew by the look on his face Jacob had done something to Beatrice. He fumed, breathing in and out of his nose like a bull about to charge. "If I find out that you hurt her – in *any* way – I'll be the eyewitness to your assault trial."

He saw Jacob flinch. He was sure of it. But Wylie smirked and straightened his tie as he regarded Evan. "You saw nothing."

"Like you, I don't mind making up the details."

Jacob glared, but he didn't speak again. He pushed Evan aside and set off in the direction of the theater worksite.

Evan ran into the library, throwing open the doors. The building seemed empty.

"Beatrice?" He ran along the edges of the shelves, scanning every aisle for signs of her. "Are you here?"

When he came back to the desk, she was suddenly standing there, watching him.

"Where were you?" he asked. "Did he knock you down?" Rage lit him on fire and he had an itch to throw a chair through the window.

"I was looking for something in the cabinet under the desk," she said, but he noticed she wasn't looking him in the eye.

"Don't lie to me," he meant it as a command, but it sounded like a plea.

Her face was white, as he'd seen it before when she had her heart episodes. Her blouse was wrinkled at the neck. His breath came faster as he leaned forward and examined her, seeing red lines under her neckline.

She pushed his hand away as he tried to move her collar out of the way. "Just let it be, Evan."

"Why won't you tell me the truth?" He tried to make his tone gentle, but controlling his rage seemed a monumental task.

"What good would it do?" She pulled the gathers of her

undone collar together and buttoned it. Her jaw tightened, as if she was trying to keep her emotions contained.

"Did he choke you?" Evan's own voice sounded obstructed. When she didn't speak, he had his answer. "Beatrice, don't let him win. You have to fight."

She shrugged with a miserable expression. "Why does it matter?"

He gripped the edge of the desk, feeling like he had enough pent-up frustration to unhinge the entire thing and crumble it to pieces. "Your life *matters*, Beatrice."

She met his eyes with a small, weary smile born of irony. "Look around, Evan. You're the only one in the world that thinks so."

"What about God? He made you. He put you here for a reason."

She held up her hand, silencing him. "Don't talk to me about God. He's the one who did this to me."

Evan was speechless. He'd no idea the hymn-playing, church-going, prim and proper Beatrice Walsh had a vendetta with God. How could he help her if she had rejected faith?

With sadness, he realized why he had let her go. Why he had proposed to Edna. He was helpless to do anything for Beatrice.

He sighed, trying to release the anger. If she wouldn't tell him the truth, if she wouldn't reach out, he was powerless.

"If you want to tell me the truth, you know where to find me," he said quietly.

She gathered her arms around her middle and lifted her chin in the air. "I have nothing to say."

♫

Evan went to the Whitley's farm after work. He found Joshua in the barn, moving bags of feed. He could tell Joshua wasn't in a good place to see to Evan's problems, but Evan didn't know where else to turn.

"Jacob Wylie tried to strangle Beatrice in the library today. She was out cold on the floor when I walked in."

Joshua didn't speak. Evan could bear the ire no longer and took out his fury on a support beam. He immediately regretted it as he shook his burning fist and yelped in pain.

Joshua sniffed. "Don't break my barn."

"How am I supposed to help her if she won't talk?"

Joshua lifted his Stetson to scratch his head. He leaned back against the horse stall and crossed his ankles and his arms. "Evan, I could just be remembering it funny, but I sure do seem to recall you saying you were going to give that woman up. And it also occurs to me you proposed to another woman two days ago."

Evan paced across the barn floor, his fists on his hips. "You seem to think I'm doing this on purpose. I don't *want* to care. I want to wash my hands of her and walk away and never look back."

"Prove it."

"I can't! It's like telling fish not to swim with the current. It's like... like telling you to walk away and give up on Kathleen."

A dark expression spread across Joshua's face. "That ain't fair, Evan Masters."

Evan stopped pacing and held his head between his hands. "I know. I know, Josh, I'm sorry. I'm just so frustrated."

"I can see that. You're like an animal on the prowl for a mate. Sometimes the fool creature can't accept the girl isn't interested."

Evan rolled his eyes. "That ain't fair, either, Josh."

"You deserve it. No more bringing Kathleen into this. It's a sore spot right now, and I don't mind saying so."

Evan worked to soften his tone. "I realize that. I'm sorry for laying my self-induced problems on you when you're facing such a hardship."

Joshua tried to speak and stopped. After a moment, he sauntered to the door and stared up at the stormy sky. "I don't know how much more I can take. She's sent away all the saloon girls and didn't even tell me first. It's like she's not here. She's going through the motions. But I need her, Evan. I need my wife. Not just because I got a passel of young'uns that depend on her. I

182

can't get along without her, either."

"I know," Evan said.

Joshua was quiet again for a time. "You're all fired up because Beatrice is doing everything – including breaking the law – to get rid of you. But maybe you should be thanking the good Lord he's kept you apart. A woman like that, Evan… she could have been the death of you."

Evan took a deep breath and released it slowly. "How can I help you and Kathleen?"

"I wish you'd pray for me, brother. I don't feel like being the husband I'm supposed to be. If I'm being honest, I feel like heading into town and finding a blasted saloon for all the comforts a man craves when life goes sour."

"You know that's not an answer," Evan admonished quietly.

Joshua nodded, but the way he kept staring up at the sky didn't convince Evan he'd heard.

"I've also been wondering if I should head to Columbus and sign myself up to fight in this war everybody says we're going to have to get involved in. Least then I'd be doing something."

"Don't leave, Josh," Evan said. "Your family is the priority."

Joshua didn't answer.

"Lord," Evan began in an awkward voice. "You know Josh's heart better than I do, and that's saying something. And you know what's keeping Kathleen from moving past this trial. I pray you'd help her out of this rut. And most of all, I pray you'd give Joshua every ounce of patience he's going to need to keep doing the right thing. I know you're going to answer, and I thank you, Lord Jesus."

Joshua didn't say anything, but he nodded gruffly.

"I'm going to head up to the house and see if the women need anything. Take some time." Evan reached out a hand for Joshua to shake. Joshua stared at it for a moment before he shook. His grip was unrelenting. Desperate.

Evan squeezed his shoulder. "It's going to get better."

"I'm hoping. It sure can't get much worse."

♫

Evan found Kathleen in the kitchen. She was peeling potatoes, but judging by her disheveled appearance, Joshua was right to be worried.

"Hey, Kathleen. I came to see if you or your aunt needed anything."

Kathleen glanced up in surprise, as if she had not seen him come through the door. "Evan?"

"Hey."

She dropped the peeler on the counter. "Were you talking to Joshua? Did he send you in here?"

Evan shook his head. "We were talking, but he didn't tell me to come up here."

She crossed the kitchen and sank into a chair. "I wouldn't blame him if he had."

"He mentioned you were having a rough time of it."

Kathleen laughed, the sound completely void of humor. "I'm in a terrible spot."

"I'm sorry."

Kathleen sighed so deeply Evan thought she might sink into the floor. She leaned over and covered her face with her hands. "Is Joshua going to leave me?"

Evan frowned. "No. Josh wouldn't do that and you know it. He's going to stay by your side. No matter what."

She regarded him with incredulity. "You don't sound convinced any more than I am."

"Kathleen, Joshua is your husband. He's not going anywhere."

"But he's had enough of me and my sadness."

Evan tried to word his response carefully as he joined her at the table. "He wants you to find happiness again. I don't think that's a secret."

Kathleen nodded. "I want to find it, too. But it's out of my grasp. All I can think about when I hold my baby Ellen in my arms is what Ruthie would look like if she were still here. It makes me want to avoid my daughter. What kind of mother am I, who can't love her own baby? I'm so tired. I'm always crying. I've neglected the boys – they're running wild and driving their pa crazy. Aunt Amelia does everything she can, but she can't heal the wounds."

"It's a valley you're passing through," Evan said, remembering a similar time in his life. "Things will get better. I promise."

"But I'm so afraid," she whispered. "I'm afraid his love has limits."

"Joshua's love doesn't have any limits," Evan said confidently. "And even if it did, God's love doesn't."

Evan murmured the words as Beatrice returned to his thoughts. Had he taught her to count on him and in the end, walked away to another when she needed him most?

But he'd made a promise to Edna. How could he go back on that, especially since she was in need as well?

"Josh won't leave you. I know it because he made a promise. We gotta keep our promises or life don't mean much. If we didn't have to forgive so often, we wouldn't need so many promises. But God knew we'd need to be held accountable. Joshua understands that. You understand it. God will get you through together."

Kathleen nodded through her tears. "Thank you."

"That's what friends are for," Evan replied.

"Aunt Amelia says I have to choose to allow joy to walk hand-in-hand with my grief. I don't know how. It feels wrong to be happy. Like I'm saying I didn't love my baby."

Evan was surprised by her candor. He saw the wisdom in Amelia's words.

"I know my aunt has known loss. And I know you have, too." Kathleen folded her hands in her lap and stared at them.

Evan felt a rush of memories. A town overtaken and terrorized. Armed men surrounding them. Women abused. Children forced to watch their parents tortured and executed. All in the name of gold.

It was painful to consider the faces of his parents and his

sisters. What they had endured! It would never leave him. Never stop haunting him.

Yet, he knew what Amelia had been saying to Kathleen. God had worked on him long and hard through the loving influences of the Merchants and Joshua and his family. He had learned to know joy again. The joy supported his grief just like the stakes Kathleen used in her garden to hold up the tomato plants. Without that measure of joy, and peace that passed understanding, he would have crumbled. He'd have shriveled up and died before he grew to adulthood.

"Your aunt is right. The only way through it is by the grace of God. That peace the Bible talks about is real. He'll give it to you, Kathleen. Just ask him. Expect it. He'll answer your prayers."

When he was alone in the darkness, walking home, Evan prayed.

Lord, I made a promise to Edna. I'll honor it if you don't direct her away from me. But you'll have to give me the strength to turn my back on Beatrice. And you'll have to take care of her some other way.

You have to take care of her.

Twenty-Eight

You can choose to let your hurts help grow you or tear you out by the roots.

Where had Beatrice read the words? Maybe in Amelia Morehouse's novel? She thought about them all morning as she sat in the defendant's chair of the courthouse and watched Jacob Wylie give his ridiculous testimony.

He painted her with vile brush strokes and colors, making sure everyone else in the room, including the judge and jury, hated her as much as he did.

Her fate was sealed, she knew it. Her own lawyer glared at her the same way everyone else did. Beatrice Walsh had taken their hard-earned money and burned it to ashes. She'd been reckless and nearly stolen the life of a poor widow and her children. If the fire department hadn't responded so heroically in the dead of night, she could have killed hundreds.

She was guilty.

She focused her attention on the Merchants. On Joshua Whitley, who made scoffing noises at Wylie several times, so loudly the judge asked him to stop.

And then there was Evan. Dear, faithful Evan. He stared at her with so much intensity she wondered if he was trying to devise a way to take her place. He cringed at every scathing accusation.

Finally, Jacob Wylie sat down next to his fancy lawyer from

Columbus, Mr. Alexander. They shared a satisfied smirk only Beatrice seemed to notice.

"Does the defense wish to call anyone?" Judge Graves asked solemnly. Beatrice waited for Overton to reply, but he frowned as if he had no witnesses planned.

"Defense calls Evan Masters," Overton finally said. His tone assured Beatrice the balding lawyer did not approve of Evan testifying.

Evan quickly went to the witness stand, briefly meeting Beatrice's gaze. The bailiff held out the Bible, on which Evan placed his right hand. He swore to tell the truth and sat down.

Overton didn't stand, but read questions from his notebook as if it was the least important thing he'd do all day. "What is your connection to Beatrice Walsh?"

"We're friends. I've known her for twelve years, ever since she came to Dempsey and started playing piano in my church. I've never heard anyone play as well as her."

Overton glared over his glasses as if he did not appreciate the extraneous details. "Do you have any reason to suspect Miss Walsh's character?"

Beatrice glanced at Evan. He had plenty of reason to suspect she was a criminal. Of all the people in the room, he was the only one who had the right to judge her.

Evan met her eyes. "I do not."

Beatrice shook her head slightly. She didn't understand him. Why would he lie for her? Why would he protect her when he knew she wasn't worth his efforts?

Apparently, Overton could think of nothing else to ask. He waved to the other side.

The city lawyer stood and adjusted his expensive tie. His mustache twitched with humor as if he enjoyed Beatrice's humiliation.

"Mr. Masters, were you with Beatrice Walsh on the night in question?"

Evan hesitated. Beatrice didn't wonder why. He might

sacrifice his own good name along with hers if he wasn't careful.

"I was out walking that night. Couldn't sleep. I came upon Beatrice. We spoke in front of the worksite, where she shared her concerns about the theater not being safe for the residents of Dempsey. We discussed appropriate and inappropriate measures to take in order to keep the townspeople safe."

Beatrice almost smiled at the clever answer.

"Did you leave Miss Walsh there at the site? Did she possess any means of setting a fire?" Alexander asked.

"I saw her home," Evan continued. "All the way to her door. I left her there. Before I had arrived back at my own house, I was summoned by the volunteer fire brigade."

The lawyer glanced at Jacob as if Evan's answer had unnerved him. The crowd murmured. Beatrice saw the determination in Alexander's eyes as his attention returned to Evan.

"Mr. Masters, is it not true that you have been in love with Miss Walsh for twelve years? That even though she has rejected your advances on many occasions, you have continued to pursue her to the point of insanity?"

Evan hesitated. Beatrice saw the crack in his composure. He shook his head and fumbled for an answer. "I think insanity is a harsh word. I used to carry a torch for her, but that's over. I've moved on. I asked someone else to marry me."

Mr. Alexander smirked as if he was torturing a captured insect. He stuck his thumbs through his suspenders. "You ask this court to accept your testimony based on your assurances that you've recently *moved on*? Judge, this man's testimony should be disregarded because of his skewed perspective. He has romantic feelings for the defendant."

The judge glanced at Evan, but shook his head. "Overruled. Evan Masters is in good standing in this town. I've no reason to suspect his testimony isn't valid."

Evan breathed a small sigh of relief as he exchanged a glance with Beatrice.

After Evan stepped down from the witness stand, Alexander

called his witness. "Prosecution calls Miss Elvira Langston to the stand."

Beatrice recognized the short, dark-haired girl. She'd worked at the hotel for a few months after drifting into town from who knows where. It wasn't hard to read the woman's motives. She'd probably say anything for a payoff.

"Miss Langston, you saw someone set fire to the construction site the evening in question."

"Yes. A woman. I was cleaning up a mess after someone got sick in the night. When I was taking supplies back to the kitchen, I saw a woman blowing on a small fire that had been set in a pile of newspaper and kindling."

"Can you identify the woman for the court?"

"Sure. Miss Walsh, just there." Elvira pointed at Beatrice.

"Liar," Beatrice couldn't help whispering. The judge eyed her sternly.

The judge looked at Overton, who merely waved his hand. "Defense rests."

Beatrice held no doubts about what the jury's verdict would be when the trial was over. She knew what she had to do.

♫

Tuesday dawned wet and cold. Evan's feet seemed to drag on the way to the hotel to meet Edna. His thoughts had been far from his marriage proposal. Beatrice needed protecting. He had to do something to clear her name. His mind was spinning as he hurried toward the hotel.

"I take it the trial didn't go well?" Edna was standing outside the hotel, her hands folded in front of her. She wasn't wearing her uniform, but she didn't have travel bags with her. He could feel his heart pounding as he climbed the stairs to stand in front of her.

"No, it didn't. Wylie is lying about what happened, and I don't know how to keep her from going to prison."

Edna shifted. "Evan, are you certain she didn't do it?"

"She didn't." Evan tried not to take offense.

Edna hesitated. "I got up that night to tend the baby. I was

190

standing by the window. I heard you and Beatrice talking."

Evan could imagine what she'd been thinking this whole time. He nodded as he fingered his hat in his hands. "Beatrice was concerned about the theater. She was trying to think how she could stop it, but I talked her out of doing anything drastic she would regret. Jacob must have seen the whole thing and set the fire himself, or he had someone do it for him."

Edna played with the buttons on her jacket. "I can see how it would be a possibility, though I'm not sure it's the truth. I'm willing to give you the benefit of the doubt, anyway. But what I can't seem to get past is the more obvious problem here."

"What's that?"

"I need a husband and a father for my children. But I'm not willing to share that man with someone else. I think marriage should be exclusive, don't you?"

Evan nodded. He was embarrassed he'd proposed in the first place. "I'm sorry, Edna. I wish I could be what you need. I hope you find someone."

She reached a hand to his and squeezed. "Evan, you're a good man. The way you love is admirable. I wish you all the best, and I truly hope you find a way to save her. But I can't be second place. I don't think any woman deserves that."

He couldn't look her in the eye. "You're right."

She let him go and turned back to the hotel.

"Can I at least take you to the station?"

She looked back at him and smiled. He knew the sight of her pretty face would stay with him for a long time to come. She was a beauty, inside and out.

"That would be nice, Evan. Thank you."

Twenty-Nine

Beatrice emptied into her lap the entire amount of bills she'd hidden in a sack between her mattress and bedstead. It included the remainder of her bank account, which she had closed.

She had enough money to leave.

She headed for the newer grocery store recently opened on the edge of town. Hopefully they wouldn't care who she was or what she bought.

She went over her list as she walked, checking and rechecking to ensure she had thought of everything. When she came into the mercantile, she went straight to the counter with her chin set confidently in the air.

She laid down her list in front of a nervous little man who eyed her as if he had better things to do than wait on her. He perused the list, glancing at her. She almost said she was going west with her husband, but decided she need not explain. She glared back at him.

He read the list aloud. "Hatchet, hunting knife, canteen, five boxes of strike-anywhere matches, flint and steel, one length of sturdy rope, one pair of the smallest trousers, with smallest men's work shirt and suspenders, three pairs of wool socks, one pair small sturdy work boots, bandana, two warm blankets, eight yards of canvas, beef jerky and dried fruit." He took off his spectacles. "Going into the wilderness, are you?"

She didn't answer. She placed all her money on the counter as her eyes caught on a selection of sheet music on a shelf next to the counter. She reached for the closest one and opened it.

Turn back the universe and give me yesterday;
Unclasp the hands of time that hold life's golden ray.
Take back the bitter hour when our love passed away,
Turn back the universe and give me yesterday.

Pressure built behind her eyes as she laid the music on the stack of items he was collecting on the counter. "I'll take this, too."

"Never seen a piano in the wilderness," the intrusive little man mocked.

♫

Beatrice was thankful she could carry the load home with everything wrapped in the canvas and tied with the rope. She only had a few cents to her name, but she wouldn't need money where she was going.

She walked past the church, lost in her thoughts. It was growing dark, but light shone from the church as she came closer, illuminating the cool March evening. She wanted nothing but to go inside and touch the piano one last time.

Pastor Merchant was closing the door to his office as she stepped inside and put down her burden of supplies. "Good evening, Miss Walsh. Have you come to play?"

She forced a smile and nodded.

"That's wonderful," he said as he came down the aisle toward her. His eye fell on the canvas at her feet. "May I ask... are you okay? I know things didn't go well today. My wife and I are concerned for you."

She shifted her stance and looked away. "Thank you for your concern, but I'm fine."

He hesitated, but finally turned away and went to the door, his hat and Bible in hand. She waited until the door clicked before she sat down at the piano and opened the music.

The piece was simple. Far below her abilities. But the simplicity compelled her. Something about the song touched a part of her she had hidden for too long.

If only I could turn back time. Tears blurred her vision. *If only I could go back and keep my family from going to the theater that afternoon. How different everything would be.*

She barely noticed as tears rushed along her cheeks and fell from her chin. Her nose and throat swelled, but it didn't stop her from playing every note of the wistful melody. As the last note faded away and the large room went silent, her resolve failed and she buried her damp face in her hands. Her shoulders heaved in labored, silent sobs that caused her heart to race. She felt breathless. She should get control or her grief might end her life. But the release was more necessary than breath. The pain had to be expressed.

"Beatrice."

She gasped, standing up quickly and scanning the large room. In the balcony, Evan stood up. He leaned on the rail and watched as she wiped away the evidence of her tears.

"What are you doing here?" She asked, her voice still trembling from emotion. Her whisper easily carried through the empty room, loud with silence. He only watched her, not speaking, not moving. She exhaled and steeled herself against her pain. "Please leave."

"Sorry. I was fixing a gas light up here. I tried to motion so you wouldn't be scared, but you were possessed by the music." He gave her another thoughtful look before he headed to the stairs. A moment later, he appeared in the auditorium. He stayed at the back of the room, but he didn't leave. "That was a beautiful song."

She shrugged.

"It seemed like the words affected you," he acknowledged, but she refused to confirm or deny. He turned to go, but only took a few steps before he shook his head and turned around. "I feel strange. Like I shouldn't leave you alone."

194

She ignored the ache of her heart. How did he read her mind? Was he so wise about everyone or just her?

"I'm fine." She chose her words carefully. "I'm resigned to my fate."

She was lying, of course.

"I'm here," he reminded her.

"You have other things to be concerned about."

"No," he said. "Not anymore."

He turned and walked away, his hands in his pockets. She wished the last she would see of Evan was his smile, but she was to be left only with his sad, uncertain expression that broke her heart. When his silhouette reached the doorway, she covered her chest with her hands.

"I'm sorry," she whispered in a broken tone.

Beatrice woke up before dawn, second-guessing her plan. She could go back to sleep and pretend she'd never come up with the idea to go off into the woods by herself and wait to die.

But she'd tried it the easy way. She'd tried to live among them, yet apart. She'd waited for death for twelve years, and it had never come. How long would she have to wait? How would she protect Evan's heart if she stayed?

She closed her eyes and remembered every declaration he'd ever made. How many times she had seen the yearning in his eyes as he stared at her. Did he ever suspect she had felt it, too?

If she stayed, she would relent. She would give in to him, and let him ruin his life trying to protect her. She couldn't let that happen. She wouldn't.

Love for Evan was what brought her out of bed. His happiness motivated her to don the trousers and boots, pack her supplies in the canvas and tie it with string. She poured water in the canteen and ate the remnants of her food supply as a final breakfast. Before she left, she wrote a note.

Dear Merchants,

Thank you for allowing me to live in this apartment for so many years, though I offered no real contributions to this town or the church. Forgive me for leaving without a proper goodbye. I am moving on.

Beatrice

She debated adding a note for Evan. But wouldn't it just make it harder for him? If she stayed aloof to the end and owed him no explanation, wouldn't it be easier for him to move on? Maybe if he hated her, he would be able to let her go.

She imagined the words she would have written to him. Words she could only say to her own faltering heart.

Evan,

I can't say I have loved you as long as I have known you. My heart was hurting too much to love you when we first met. But I did notice you. You were so young then. Your hair curled around your ears just like a boy's, and your big brown eyes were full of hopes and dreams.

I can say I love you now.

I wish things could be different. I wish I could be well and whole and give you everything you deserve. Because I can't, I release you to live your life. There's no sense in you spending your prime caring for an invalid wife, wondering when you will become a widower. I want so much more for you. I always have. Edna will be a good wife. Go get her. Love her. Forget about me.

Be free, my strong, gentle Evan. Live.

Beatrice

Thirty

Beatrice sat on a large rock with a knife in her hand. She was completely still. Waiting.

She'd been at her camp deep in a forest ravine for a week, and her inability to capture something to eat had left her quite hungry. She was determined not to go back to camp this time without a prize.

It was a full hour before anything came close to the river to drink. But finally, a rabbit passed within reach and drank, watching her with wariness as it did.

Before the animal could react, she threw the sharp blade with the precision she'd learned practicing on the tree stump in front of her tent. To her relief, she hit her mark and the rabbit fell, motionless.

"I did it!" She stood up, breathless. She reached out for the animal and held it by the knife, away from her.

As she was releasing the knife from the rabbit, pulling on the still warm fur, her shaking hand slipped, causing her to drop the rabbit. Her knife clattered to the rock and teetered on the edge. Another inch and it would have fallen into the mad spring current and been lost forever. She left the rabbit by the tree on the bank and went back, careful as she reached for the knife. She was dependent on that knife. Her death would come much faster and more unpleasantly without it.

She grabbed it, sighing with relief as her fingers closed around the handle. But as she inched further out on the rock, her boot hit a patch of wet, slimy rock and her feet slipped out from under her. Pain shot through her ankle. As she screamed, she slid off the side of the smooth rock and into the river.

The furious flow of water forced her under. She managed to come up for a breath, but she was quickly moving downstream and too far from the shore to swim back against the current.

"Help!" she screamed, but knew her cry would go unheard. She had ensured she was completely alone. There would be no rescue. If she was going to get back on that shore, she would have to make it happen herself.

She grabbed for a fallen tree log and caught the tip of it. She held on with every bit of strength she possessed, putting her knife handle between her teeth so she could hold on with both hands. Her ankle protested the current with blinding pain, and she fought the feeling that she might pass out.

Maybe I should just let go, she reasoned. *Forgo this delaying of the inevitable.*

"Beatrice?"

The familiar voice was distant. Perhaps behind the tree line. But she knew whose voice it was.

"Evan!" she screamed.

It was a matter of seconds before he pushed through the overgrown bushes at the side of the creek. He saw her and set out on the log with steady footing and no hesitation.

Her fingers started to slip. For one terrifying moment, she thought he might be too late.

But just as she lost her grip and her fingers slipped off the branch, his hand reached down and clamped around her wrist with a grip of iron. He effortlessly lifted her out of the water and set her on the log. She cried out and lifted her ankle, and would have gone back into the water if he hadn't still had a grip on her.

Evan understood without her having to explain. Without hesitating, he swept her up into his arms, keeping perfect balance on the log as he walked back to the bank. He hopped off the log onto the path. He smiled as he went and grabbed her rabbit.

"Good catch," he said, holding it up for inspection. "I didn't know you hunted."

"I didn't, until a week ago," she said, reveling in the way his chuckle resounded in his chest where her ear rested.

"Where's your camp set up?" he asked. She directed him and he walked back, not even out of breath when he set her down by the fire in front of her tent.

"Where does it hurt?"

"My left ankle."

He kneeled in front of her and reached for her leg, giving her clothes a pointed glance. "Nice outfit."

She looked down. She'd stuffed her oversized shirt into trousers she had rolled twice and held up with suspenders. "This was the smallest size they had."

"Maybe you should have asked for children's sizes."

She frowned at him as he smirked. He pulled up the hem of her trousers to her knee. She cringed and gasped aloud when he removed the boot. His eyes darted along the shape of her leg, but whatever he felt, he reined in as he examined her injured ankle.

"It's pretty swollen and red, but it doesn't feel broken," he mused. His fingers gently slid along the sides of her ankle and down her foot. "I think you have yourself a sprain. I'll wrap it up tight so you can't move it and it should heal in a few days."

"A few days? I can't be hurt that long out here. Survival depends on mobility."

He smiled. "I don't know that you have a choice."

He pulled a length of flexible bandage from his pack and wound it around her ankle. Though he took care not to hurt her, his touch was firm and she had to steel her jaw against the pain. After he tied it, he sat back against the log she used for a seat and reached for the rabbit. He held out his hand for her knife until she handed it to him, then skinned and gutted the animal with skillful precision.

"I guess you've done that before," she said.

"I have."

He looked over at her for a long moment. "You cost me my house."

She remembered then that she had broken the terms of her bail. "I didn't mean to make trouble for you. But it's your fault for putting up security for me in the first place. You had to know it was a possibility."

He nodded, but the reproachful expression didn't leave his features. "You should have talked to me first. I'm on your side. I've always been on your side."

"Last I knew, you were getting married," she reminded him, indignant. "Are you married now? Did you leave your wife and children to find me? Or are you here to drag me back so your house will be returned?"

He stared at her evenly. "Edna went to live with her aunt."

Beatrice was surprised. "Well, you could still get her back."

He didn't reply, so she stared at the fire for a time as he speared the rabbit and placed it over the fire. Finally, he spoke. "Why'd you leave?"

She shivered. The afternoon sunshine had been warm enough, but evening shadows were causing her wet clothes to bring on a chill.

"You're cold. Of course you're cold, you're sopping wet."

"I'm fine," she disagreed. She covered her chest with her arms and tried not to allow her teeth to chatter.

"Beatrice, propriety isn't worth catching a chill. Especially not for you."

She knew he was referring to her illness, which irritated her. "I said I'm fine."

"You got long johns on under there?" He reached for the hem of her shirt. She protested and tried to get away, but she couldn't go far with a sprained ankle. He caught hold of the hem and pulled it up.

"You do have long johns. Good thing." He smiled as she

pushed her shirt back down and glared at him. As she started to lecture him, he unhooked the suspenders and quickly pulled the trousers off. As she gasped and sputtered in offense, he pulled on her sleeves and took the shirt as well. He calmly stood and hung them over a bush to dry by the fire. He turned around and eyed the long johns.

"No!" she warned. They both knew she was at his mercy.

"Hmm," he said as he eyed her.

"I'll sit close to the fire. They'll be dry in no time." She promised, sure that he was on the verge of whisking off the last of her clothes along with her dignity.

"They'd better or they're coming off." He sat down next to her.

"That was completely uncalled for, by the way," she huffed, unable to look him in the eye. Her cheeks were on fire.

He only shrugged as he handed her a blanket from his pack. "You're welcome."

She dragged her leg out straight and grimaced at the pain. "I don't understand why you keep showing up," she said stiffly. "I've never met someone so stubborn."

"I could say the same," he replied.

He grabbed her cast iron pan and set it in the fire to heat. "Why did you do this, Beatrice? Do you just care that little for me, that you wouldn't even leave a note explaining yourself?"

Duly chastised by his quiet, wounded tone, she only shrugged. If only she could explain. She wanted to tell him everything and see that light of understanding dawn in his charming brown eyes.

He sighed when she didn't answer. "Rabbit tastes better in stew. This won't be the best fireside meal I've ever prepared, just so you know."

"You've prepared many? Sitting at your desk in your suit and tie sending telegraphs?"

He glanced at her, reproachful. "I've only done that a few years. There's plenty of history before that."

"Not a lot of call for survival skills in Dempsey," she

reminded him.

"Nope," he answered. "But plenty of call out in Wyoming Territory where I was born."

She was curious. "You were born out west?"

He seemed surprised by her interest, but he didn't question it. "My pa had the pioneer spirit, even though the west wasn't as untamed as it had been when he was a youngster listening to his grandpa tell tales. As it was, he had to look for some time before he found a place without people. He didn't trust anyone. In the end, he was right not to.

"We ended up in Wyoming during the cattle boom. Pa had a cattle farm but he didn't like dealing with other ranchers and sales. We moved out into the wilderness. Lived in a canvas tent not much bigger than yours for months until Pa built us a house. We grew or hunted our food, did our own doctoring, and went months without seeing another soul." Evan chuckled. "Sounds rough, but those were good days."

"What changed?" She sat up and adjusted the blanket. "Why did you end up back east?"

Vulnerability spread across his features.

"They died. When I was twelve."

She remembered him saying it before. She knew by the myriad of details he left out that there was more to the story. A twinge seemed to twist her heart. "I guess we have more in common than I thought."

"Maybe," he said, noncommittal. "We moved from the wilderness to a small town called Chaney. Times were hard and there wasn't enough food to eat, so Pa said he'd look for work until things turned around. Said I'd probably have to get a job, too. But things went bad in Chaney. Really bad."

Evan frowned a troubled, pained frown. Again, he seemed to leave out a chunk of the story. "I came east after that. Lived on my own a few years before I walked into Dempsey and found people I could trust. I never wanted to be alone again."

She stared at the fire until Evan spoke again. "Why'd you

come out here?"

She shrugged and didn't look up. "Something Thoreau said."

"The author?"

She nodded. "He said he went to the woods because he wanted to live deliberately with only the essentials. He thought it might teach him something about life, so he wouldn't come to his death and discover he'd never lived."

He only watched her with his brow furrowed. Curiosity got the better of her. "What are you thinking?"

He tilted his head to the side as if to consider her from a different angle. "That's pretty deep. If it's the truth, it's a good plan. At least it would be if you weren't breaking the law."

"Is that why you chased me out here?"

"I came after you because you made me lose my house," he reminded her. "That and you didn't say goodbye."

She scoffed, though her cheeks warmed.

"Maybe you should have asked me to come with you."

"You wear a suit and bowler hat and sit in an office all day. I didn't think you'd be interested in surviving. Besides, it's improper for us to be alone together."

He smirked. "The stars and the bears don't have any sense of propriety."

She couldn't help a shy smile, until she felt an uncomfortable squeezing in her heart. She took a deep breath and lifted a hand to her chest.

"Are you alright?" he said in a melancholy tone.

"No," she said. "I'm not. Remember?"

"I remember," he replied. "That doesn't mean I'm going to buy what some doctor told you a decade ago."

She sighed and folded her hands in her lap. "Dr. Thomas confirmed it. And it doesn't matter whether you accept it or not, Evan. It's still the truth."

"It hasn't been proven." He sat up, adjusting his position.

"I don't know what else I have to do to prove it. Besides die, I mean."

His eyes flashed. "Don't be flippant about this."

"I'm flippant because I've accepted it."

He stood up and took a step closer to the fire, his hands on his hips. "Why? Why do you have to accept it? You sitting out in the woods hiding from life... I just don't understand why."

She sighed. "I don't see why *you* have to keep bringing it up. How many times have I told you to stay away from me? What do I have to do to convince you I'm not interested?"

He turned around and glared at her. For a moment, they were still and silent, staring at one another. The next thing she knew he had come to her, kneeling in front of her. His arms went around her, though he rested them on the log behind her and didn't touch her. She was trapped by this giant of a man.

He leaned into her face with irritation still clear in his features. "All you have to do is prove there's nothing here, nothing between us. Make me believe I don't mean a thing to you and I'll never bother you again."

As he stared at her, she saw his irritation dissipate. He still frowned, but his eyes fell to her lips. His breathing hitched in his throat. She felt it as well, and heart raced.

"Don't, Evan," she warned him.

He backed up about an inch. "Are you scared I'll hurt you?"

She shook her head. "I know you won't hurt me."

"Then what is it?"

She felt his breath on her mouth and saw the muted shadow of his lips over hers. She craved making the effort to close the gap. The thought of it made her heart ache.

"Please," she said, desperate. Did he know she was completely at his mercy?

His eyes tore away from her mouth and met her pleading gaze.

Suddenly, he pulled away and retreated to the opposite side of the fire. He started to speak, but before he could get a word out, she felt blackness swallow her.

"Beatrice?" Evan shook her. Her face and lips were white and her breathing was shallow. He felt for a pulse. It was weak, but steady. "Beatrice, wake up."

After what seemed like a lifetime, she finally opened her eyes. She groaned and sat up.

"What happened?" he demanded, gasping in relief.

"I fainted," she admitted. "It happens."

"You fainted because we were talking? I don't understand."

She pushed him back. "We were not just *talking*. You were in my face and breathing all over me. I asked you to stop and you didn't listen."

"You're saying I made you faint?" He sat back and frowned.

"Not exactly." She pulled the blanket around herself. "But the ideas you were giving both of us were not helpful."

He stared at her in disbelief. "You were thinking it, too?"

She narrowed her eyes and refused to answer.

"You were thinking it, too." He could hardly comprehend it.

She hesitated. "Even if I admit I am… affected by you being near me… it doesn't change anything."

"Do you mean you're attracted to me?" He felt a silly grin spread over his face, which she obviously did not appreciate, since she only scowled in response.

"Wait, but why doesn't that change anything?" he demanded. "I think attraction should count for something."

She stared at him as if he were a foolish child. "Not when I'm dying."

He shrugged, a little weary of the same argument. "So a stranger said a decade ago."

"I fainted because you were talking too close to me. What would happen…" She clamped her mouth shut, her cheeks going red.

He enjoyed the sight. "What would happen…?"

It took her a long time to get the words out, and he had to strain his ears to hear her answer. "If we were to go any further."

She had him there. The hope he'd been feeling did a nose-dive, and they lapsed into silence.

"Get some sleep," he finally said. He leaned back against the log and closed his eyes.

♫

She sat by the crackling fire a long time, watching him sleep. She memorized every indentation of his skin, imagining she was running her fingers along every inch of his face and stopping at the perfect dimple in the middle of his chin. Edward had been clean-shaven with short, greased hair, so she could only imagine what Evan's stubble and shoulder length hair would feel like. But she had to admit to herself, she enjoyed the wanderings of her imagination.

When the fire faded to embers, she stood up, took her clothes and her blanket and climbed into her small canvas tent. But even as she lay in the quiet under the stars, she couldn't sleep.

She wanted to belong to Evan, but life had been so cruel, and she had been so foolish. How could she make up for the problems she'd caused? He'd even lost his house because of her. According to the citizens of Dempsey, she was an escaped fugitive. With a start, she realized her disappearance could add charges to her case. There would be no chance of her escaping a prison term.

Why would you let me live to do this, God? Are you just taunting me?

God seemed as silent as ever. She'd nearly forgotten what his voice sounded like. Did God only speak to people who hadn't made major mistakes? Who were without scars? Was she too broken? Had he rejected her as she had rejected him?

Did she really blame him if he had?

Thirty-One

When Beatrice peeked out of her tent the next morning, the day was clear and comfortable. The cool spring breeze tousled the branches covered in buds ready to break open into new life.

The beauty and the peace only felt like a mockery.

She sat up, recognizing the smell of wood smoke mingled with something tantalizing. She peeked out of her tent and saw Evan squatting by the fire, tending something in a cast iron pan she had not brought with her.

"Fish were biting this morning," he said with a friendly smile that only touched his mouth but lit up his eyes with warmth.

She frowned. "I didn't ask you to make breakfast."

"I was hungry," he said with a shrug. He flipped a fish out of the pan onto a wooden trencher of some sort. He added a handful of greens and handed it to her. "How's the ankle?"

She tested it. It was painful when she put her full weight on it, but it didn't feel as swollen. "I think it's a little better."

"Good."

"Did you make these?" She examined the board that served well as a plate.

"Sure." He continued to make his own plate.

She ate a bite of the fish. "This is much better than your rabbit steak, I have to say."

"I warned you rabbit was best in stew."

She smiled. "I never thought of you as a chef before. Why do you eat at the hotel every night if you can cook?"

"You have no idea my talents," he teased. A sheepish look crossed his face. "I only know how to cook over a campfire. I'm lost in a kitchen."

She chuckled.

"So, what's next?" He sat on the log and ate, watching her.

"What do you mean?"

"Well, I assume you have a plan. A schedule?"

"A schedule for what?"

"You came out here to survive, didn't you?"

"I was thinking more the opposite, actually."

He gave her a dark expression, but did not comment on her words. "What I mean is that when you go out into the wilderness to survive, you have to make a plan. You make your camp more habitable. Safer. You find a good source of water away from predators where you build a shelter. You find animals to provide you with food, like eggs and goat's milk."

"I've never heard of wild chickens or goats," she said, laughing.

He grinned and watched her silently for a long moment. "I like your laugh. I don't think I've ever heard it before."

She hid her smile. "I don't believe there are chickens and goats out here."

"There probably aren't chickens," he agreed. "But there are plenty of wild turkeys, and turkey eggs make the tastiest omelet you'll ever have. And there aren't wild goats, but chances are, sooner or later, you'll come across a feral goat or sheep. They're easy to capture and keep."

She stared at him. "And to think that everyone in Dempsey thinks you're a telegraph operator."

He shrugged and poked the fire.

"You do look different out here," she admitted, noting again his wild, free hair and his shadow of a beard. He wore a plaid flannel shirt and jeans, more rugged than she'd ever seen him before.

"This feels more right, if I'm being honest," he said. "I grew up in nature."

Beatrice watched Evan poke at the fire to the point of distraction and remembered the things he'd told her about his childhood. Had she ever considered him before? Where he'd come from and what he'd been through?

She set the trencher aside and stood up. "Fine. If you're such an expert, show me your world. Show me how to survive, Evan Masters. I challenge you to keep me alive."

He raised his eyebrows and smiled at her as her stomach did a funny little flip. He stood and held out his hand. "Challenge accepted."

♫

It took over a week for her ankle to heal enough to travel. When the pain and swelling were gone, they carried out everything they had and set off to find a good place to survive.

Evan had brought a bigger pack than her canvas bundle, but he seemed undaunted as he slung the heavy bag over his shoulders.

"What do you have in there?" She couldn't help her curiosity.

"Tools. Basic supplies. Little things you can't find in nature that come in handy."

She followed him as he walked steadily all morning, leading her deeper into the heart of the forest. Whenever her heart began to pound, they would rest and drink from their canteens. But she noticed the longer they traveled at the slow, steady pace, the better she began to feel and the longer she could go between breaks.

After lunch, Evan led her into a beautiful little clearing, complete with a stream full of big rocks.

"Perfect," he said with great satisfaction.

"Perfect for what?" She dropped her pack and sat down on one of the rocks to catch her breath.

"Perfect for your own little cabin in the wilderness, of course." He smiled.

She chuckled, thinking he was joking. "You're going to build me a cabin, are you?"

"Nope." His smile grew wider. "*We're* going to build it."

"I don't know how to build a cabin. Don't you need to buy siding and windows and plumbing fixtures?" She wondered how delighted he would be if she admitted she'd always been interested in architecture. The very thought of building a house with him made her more excited and motivated than she'd been about anything in a long time. She didn't mention the fact that he should be taking her back to Dempsey to face trial, if he was any sort of model citizen.

"Pshaw." He waved off her words. "Everything we need is right here in the forest."

"Have you built a cabin using only forest supplies before?" she asked doubtfully.

"I have," he answered. Then he looked sheepish. "But the first one was a sorry mess. I was only thirteen, so I was just proud that I'd built it all on my own. Never mind it leaked and shook back and forth in the wind. It was mine."

Evan set up her canvas tent for her and sent her to bed. "We have a lot of work to do tomorrow."

The next morning Evan was awake with the sun, calling for her to get up. They spent the morning finding and hauling ten-foot trees back to the campsite. While they searched for tree candidates, Evan taught her how to identify poisonous plants and plants with medicinal value.

"Now this is a find," he said as they headed down the path to their clearing with a bundle of logs. "I've been looking for it, but I hadn't seen it yet." He kneeled over and pushed aside the brush.

"Is that Lily of the Valley?" She recognized the characteristic large leaves, though there were no flowers yet. "My mother planted Lily of the Valley in front of our house. She told us never to touch it or put it in our mouths, though, because it was poisonous."

He nodded, pulling several out by the root. He stuck them in his pocket without further explanation.

Later that night, Evan put Beatrice to work scraping the bark off their pile of trees. He went to the fire and took out the leaves he'd saved. He pulled the plant back and took a portion of the root and leaves, then put them in a pot which he placed in the fire. He filled it with water from his canteen.

He didn't say what he was doing, and she didn't ask. After the water had boiled for a few minutes, he took it off the fire and let it cool. He helped her scrape the trees for a time before he went back to his mixture, dipping a spoon into the pan.

"Come here," he said, holding up the spoon.

She frowned, but she approached him. "What is it?"

"Medicine. For your heart."

She wondered if it was a trick, and he was attempting to sedate her and drag her back to Dempsey. Or he was exacting his revenge on her for losing his house by poisoning her.

He smiled knowingly. "Trust me. My mother was trained in the art of healing. I've seen this work for people with weak hearts."

She scoffed. "If it's so amazing, why have I never heard of it?"

"Because your doctors most likely weren't taught about healing herbs. Not all of them, anyway. And as you said, Lily of the Valley is known to be a poison."

"Are you trying to kill me?" She stepped closer and sniffed the liquid in the pot. "It's a good thing I'm not opposed to dying."

He frowned at her glib words. "Just take it. It's not poisonous the way I made it."

She sighed. "Fine. I'll humor you." She leaned over and took the spoon in her mouth, swallowing every bit of the bitter liquid.

"Good girl," he said, watching her face as if he expected to see it work immediately. "You'll take some every day. In a few days, you'll start feeling better and stronger."

She doubted it, but she didn't voice her arguments. When they had a good stack of trees smoothed and shaped, Evan dug holes and used rocks from the stream for the foundation of the cabin.

"That's enough for today." Evan was drenched in sweat. They sat by the firelight as the sunlight disappeared behind the trees. He unwrapped her ankle and examined it as she watched his features with great interest.

"You really do know what you are doing out here," she acknowledged, grimacing as he gently rotated her ankle.

He considered her words. "I've never felt as alive as I did during the years I lived on my own."

"Then why come to town and end up in an office answering the telephone, of all things?"

He sighed deeply as he peered into the mesmerizing glow of the red-hot logs. "I was lonely."

Her first reaction was scorn, but she tried to consider his perspective. "I don't think I've ever been lonely. I prefer my own company."

He chuckled. "I've noticed. But I wanted a family, and I wasn't going to find someone to share my life with if I was living out in the woods by myself."

She was contrite. "You should have found someone. You shouldn't have waited so many years for me. I'm too broken. You should have found someone energetic and ready to take on the world with you. You could have chased all your dreams."

"My life would be a lot different if I had," he said, nodding. "But Beatrice, how could I think of anyone else after I'd met you?"

She huffed. "I don't believe that. I'm not a nice person. I'm reclusive. I'm the type who thinks it's okay to set fires in order to stop things from being built. I'm a criminal on run from the law. When they find me, I'll be sent to jail for the rest of my life."

He scoffed at her declaration. "No, you won't. Even if it were likely, I wouldn't let it happen."

"It doesn't matter, anyway. I'll die soon. Maybe before they find me."

"I wouldn't be so sure about that." He finished rewrapping her ankle, then leaned forward toward the fire and draped his arms around his knees. The movement drew her attention to his form, and she suddenly ached to be close to him. To lean against his chest once more and hear the rumble of his voice.

"You've been hauling and scraping logs and clearing brush all day. I haven't seen you stop for breath too many times. I'm guessing you feel stronger than you have in some time."

She couldn't deny it, now that she thought about it. She felt better than she had in twelve years.

"That medicine is going to make you even better," he promised.

"Maybe," she said quietly.

"You don't seem very excited about getting better."

She shook her head. "I've spent so much of my life waiting for death. I can't even begin to imagine how to live."

Her words caught his attention. He met her gaze for a long moment as a small smile crept over his face. "I have a good starting place."

She heard the hitch in his voice and her heart skipped a beat. He reached a long arm across the space between them and fingered a lock of her dark hair. He took his time, letting the strands fall through his fingers until they reached the end of it and it fell back against her shoulder.

"You keep saying you don't know why I think so much of you, but if you could see what I see, you'd get it."

His palm came to rest on her cheek.

"You are the most beautiful woman I've ever seen. But I didn't even know half of the loveliest parts of you when I first laid eyes on you." His voice was soft, almost melodic. She knew peace in the stillness of the night surrounding his quiet, tender tones.

He smiled. "I didn't know then that you were so smart. Or how deeply you think about ideas. How sensitive your spirit is. Your body may be delicate, but your soul is furious. It rises up inside you and bursts out of every part of you like sunbeams. You can't hide something like that."

She gasped a rather unsteady breath at the heady feeling he was inspiring. His finger ran a feather-light line along her jaw until it rested underneath her chin.

He gazed at her. "You're a work of God, and there's no denying it. I saw it the first glimpse I caught of you, and I've never been able to look away since. I don't see how that's going to change."

Beatrice had never wanted anything in her life as much as she wanted to throw out her principles and fears into the sea of forgetfulness. She wanted to belong to Evan for whatever time remained. But it wasn't safe. It wasn't practical. It wasn't her plan. It would be messy. She was too tired to face the repercussions of living up to Evan Master's spectacular expectations of her.

"I'm going to sleep," she mumbled as she fell away from his hand and crawled toward the opening of her canvas shelter.

He caught her by her good ankle. "Beatrice, besides the obvious things, why are you so afraid of me? What's really at the heart of this?"

His words stopped her, and she turned back. "When did I say I was afraid of you?"

"You're not?" he asked, thoughtful.

She considered the question. It sparked a memory of her mother, and her eyes closed in pain as the beloved face came to mind. How her mother's features had darkened and faded away from her mind over time. She would give anything to see her again.

"Are you afraid?"

She hesitated. "Yes. But it's not fear that drives me."

"Are you sure?"

She thought of the conversation she'd had with her mother when she was only eight. "I used to be afraid. I'd cry every night to sleep with my parents because I was afraid of sounds in the house. I thought a robber or a goblin or a ghost might get me. Probably something I read."

Evan smiled. "What happened?"

She sighed. "My mother told me that the secret to fear is not letting it get the best of you. If I heard something that frightened me, I should seek it out. Go to wherever I heard it come from and see what it was. That when I found out the noise had some sort of explanation that didn't harm me, I wouldn't be afraid anymore."

"Did it work?"

She shrugged. "Not at first. But I never forgot what she said. And when I finally had the courage to follow her instructions, I discovered she had been right."

"So why are hiding from your fears now?" Evan shook his head with a confused expression. "Why not run toward them and find out they're not as scary as you thought they would be?"

Because it would be selfish. Because you would be hurt.

"It's not that simple. You must forget me," she pleaded. "I'm not the prize you think I am. I'm full of darkness and regret."

He reached and grabbed her hand with both of his. He pulled it to his lips. He kissed it as tenderly as if it was the downy soft head of a newborn baby.

"Good night, Beatrice. I'll meet you in my dreams."

Thirty-Two

Evan noticed Beatrice stopped talking after their talk by the fire. He tried to fill up the silence with chatter, thinking it would make her more at ease. When Beatrice shunned his conversation, he started talking to the squirrels, who tolerated him well enough as they scampered around burying their treasured winter stores.

He used his ax and auger to define the edges of the logs and notch them before he and Beatrice hauled each one to the cabin site and fitted them together on top of the rock foundation they had laid. After a few days, they reached the final row of logs. Evan straddled the top of the wall, fitting two opposite notches into place. He was about to hop down to retrieve the last log.

He was stunned to see Beatrice propping it up to him. He took it and fitted it before he hopped down. "You just lifted a hundred-pound log in the air," he pointed out.

She blinked in surprise. "I guess I do feel stronger. I feel fine, really. My heart hasn't faltered all morning."

He grinned. "Thank the Lord."

She cleared her throat and covered her chest with her arms. "So, what do we do now?"

"I'm going to make the roof, and then you get to chink it."

"How do I do that?"

Evan showed her how to make a mixture of mud, dried grasses and water and fill in the gaps between the logs. Then he set to

216

work framing the roof.

"What are you going to do for things like tar paper, shingles and nails?" She stopped her chinking and wiped her forehead with her arm, giving the skeleton of the roof a curious perusal.

"You'd be surprised how well pine boughs work to keep you dry in the rain."

They spent the rest of the day finding pine branches and dragging them back to the cabin.

♫

Beatrice had not a single moment to appreciate the silence of the forest. Thoreau would have taken a pine bough to Evan's head by now. The man would *not* be quiet.

Presently he thought it necessary to explain to her the advantages of a pine bough roof. Apparently, his family had weathered some rather severe storms and remained cozy and dry, all because of their remarkable pine bough roof. Beatrice didn't dare argue with him lest he was encouraged to talk more. She ignored him. He didn't seem to mind, as he continued to talk while he built the mud cement chimney with rocks from the creek.

As tedious as his constant conversation might be, her attraction to Evan had undeniably grown. Seeing him in his element, she realized how resourceful he was. The clever ways he overcame his lack of tools and supplies delighted her. He was persistent in his attention to detail, from the V-shaped notches he cut in the logs to the carefully formed window and door openings. When he was done with the structure, he took his ax and went off to find more wood for furniture and a porch. She sat by the fire and enjoyed the pleasure of owning her very own little house in the woods.

She also enjoyed the break from his ever-running mouth.

A few days later, though, she didn't mind it as much as she pretended. As long as he didn't expect her to respond, she came to appreciate the talking after so many years of silence. She could hear and consider the thoughts of another person without the pressure of conversation. Within her mind, she explored the differences in their personalities and opinions with curiosity.

Yet there was a black spot on her soul, for she knew she was stealing these days not meant to be hers. At some point, the beautiful dream would end and she would have to face the reality she had created by her circumstances. She didn't dare dwell on it, but the dread found her in her dreams.

As Evan crafted a rugged table and she cleared and swept the dirt floor of the cabin, she watched him. She watched the sinews of his muscles strain his shirt as he worked. She wanted to reach out and touch those arms with her fingers, or put her hands in his hair, damp from a dip in the creek. She longed to sit in the circle of his arms and let him love her as completely as she suspected he still did.

Thoreau had been right in his conclusions. Living in the woods provided a different set of instructions for living. Everything became simple. People didn't build theaters in order to take people's money in exchange for safety. No one suspected her of trying to murder them by fire. Finances weren't stolen and they weren't important at all, and family didn't die at the hands of the greedy or the self-seeking.

Oh, to stay here forever.

"Beatrice, we need to talk."

She cringed. So much for the beautiful fairytale.

"I know you'd probably disagree, but I could live like this for the rest of my life." He came to sit next to her on the log by the fire.

She nodded, but her heart sped up, realizing he wasn't finished.

"We have to go back. I think you know that."

"Why?" She hated the cynical and harsh tone of her voice. She didn't want to start a fight, but she saw her reaction frustrated him. He stood and went to the doorway of their cabin, reaching a hand to smooth away the sawdust from the beam above his head.

"We can't stay here like this. It isn't the way. If we want this life, we have to go back and deal with the problems and make things right."

She knew he was correct, but her entire spirit rebelled. "You can leave if you want. I'm staying."

"You can't live this way," he said, turning around to look at her, his arms crossed over his chest.

"What way? Surviving? I've come to love this life, Evan, and I haven't loved life in many years. I'm going to plant a garden. Get better at hunting. I'll keep taking the Lily of the Valley tonic. Everything I need is here."

"I agree. Being out here and building this cabin with you has reminded me how much I love this life. I'm not saying we shouldn't live out here together. I'm just saying we have to go about it the right way."

She frowned.

"You gotta consider *why* you're out here, Beatrice. Why do you resist being part of things and depending on others?"

She was quiet for a long time. She hesitated to tell him the truth, but part of her wanted him to know. Evan had proven his ability to knock through the walls of her self-protective spirit. He had sheltered her. He'd begun a process of healing within her, and not just in a physical way. He deserved the truth.

"I have lost so much," she whispered. She feared that if she said anything more, she would lose control of her emotions.

He watched her, his eyes shining. "I understand that. Believe me. But neither of us can let ourselves be held hostage by the past."

"And what makes you the authority?" Beatrice huffed. But she knew he had reason to make the statement, even if she didn't know the details.

Evan looked into the fire. Beatrice glimpsed something raw and vulnerable in his expression, and her heart fluttered with sudden empathy.

After a long moment of silence, Evan sighed deeply. "I know what it feels like to say goodbye forever. I've held my loved ones in my arms and realized there wasn't a blessed thing this side of glory to save them. I've looked at their faces, knowing it was the last time, even though that morning I'd done the chores and gone to school with everything right in the world." His gaze was fixed on some distant point in the woods; his voice was small and soft in the expanse of the trees. "I argued with my father that morning. He wanted to go back into the wilderness, and I wanted to stay in town. Just a bit longer."

They didn't speak for many long moments. "I know what it's like to lose everything, Beatrice," he admitted.

Beatrice swallowed hard. The faces of her parents, her brother and Edward appeared foremost in her mind. The pain swelled in her jaw until she gave a sharp intake of breath.

He continued. "My ma and pa and my sisters, they were all talking and present and living one moment, and gone the next. Just... gone. I had everything, and then I had nothing. And I couldn't understand why God didn't take me, too."

God, why didn't you take me, too?

Tears escaped, so she swiped at them. "You were twelve?"

He nodded. "I'd just turned twelve the week before. My ma made me a cake. My older sister knitted me a cap." He smiled through tears. "I still wear it."

"What took them?"

Evan closed his eyes. At first, he seemed unwilling to speak of it. She wanted to reach for him. Hold his hand. It took all her strength to refrain.

"I don't like to think on it," he confessed.

She nodded, understanding his hesitation. "I know. That's how I feel. I lost everything in ten minutes' time."

Evan looked at her then. His warm hand enveloped the entire left side of her face. "What happened, Beatrice? Tell someone, for Pete's sake."

Her heart fluttered. Could she speak of it? He waited, patient. Always so patient.

Eventually, in faltering tones, she tried to speak her truth. Her tongue was numb and her throat resisted allowing air to pass through. Evan didn't speak, but brought her the tonic. After several minutes, she took a deep breath. Her lungs filled with air and her heartbeat slowed.

"My mother, my father, my ten-year-old brother, Jamie, and my fiancé, Edward, all died on the same day. It was a day that was supposed to be happy. Fun."

Evan nodded, sharing her sorrow by his understanding of loss. He pushed the tendrils of her hair back from her forehead, which had become damp during her episode. She must have looked like an overexerted child. He didn't press for details. He was an artist at knowing when to ask questions and when to be silent.

"I'm sorry," he said with certainty she needed to hear. He wasn't too weak to take on her pain. His shoulders were strong for the burden.

"It makes sense that I have always been drawn to you," he said with a certain sense of awe in his voice. "We are kindred spirits."

She dared to look into his eyes and was undone. It was as if a giant knot in her soul loosened at the force of his supportive companionship.

She nodded. "We are."

He smiled with tenderness. "It's been a good two months, Beatrice. We need to go home. Make things right."

She felt fear. "Would they hang me?"

He breathed a soft laugh. "I don't think there are too many public executions these days. Anyway, the fire didn't kill anyone, even if there was any proof you'd set it."

"If they convict me, I'll be sent to jail. Maybe for the rest of my life."

He frowned. "The fire was set at night, which makes it more serious. But since you didn't do it, not a shred of evidence exists to prove your guilt. Trust me; truth has a way of working itself up to the surface. It will prevail. I promise."

She wasn't convinced. "I'm afraid."

He grasped her hand tighter. "I know. But I'm going to be right by your side every step of the way. And you're forgetting something. Someone – probably Jacob Wylie himself – *did* set that fire. And that means there's evidence of it. We just have to find it."

After a moment, he spoke again. "Besides, what did your mother tell you to do if you were afraid of something?"

She smiled in spite of herself.

Thirty-Three

Evan knew he was giving the Dempsey citizens more credit than they deserved when he convinced Beatrice to return. They were stubborn people, some with backward ideas. And none of them trusted Beatrice. He didn't tell her the judge had been far from understanding in the matter of his house.

He didn't care so much about losing his house in town. The little hand-made cabin in the wilderness meant more to him than the yellow bungalow on Vine Street. He'd packed the few belongings that meant anything to him and taken them and his cat to the Whitley's before he left to find Beatrice in the woods. He had quit his job as well, and it had been freeing.

Now that he was thinking about it, walking along the path with Beatrice, he had cut most of his ties to Dempsey.

It made him think of the existence he'd shared with his family as a child, before they had moved to town because his ma wanted a church and school. His parents had several heated discussions about it, but Evan had secretly sided with his ma. He wanted to go to school. He wanted to have chums. If only he'd known how bad an idea it would prove to be.

They walked in silence as they made their way back through the woods toward Dempsey. Beatrice was pensive. He cast several sideways glances at her. She looked cute in her trousers and suspenders. She reminded him of his ma out in the wilderness of

Wyoming. She'd worn trousers as well. They didn't associate with anyone in society, and pa didn't care what she wore.

"What?" Beatrice demanded, her eyebrows drawing together.

"Nothing." He helped her over a tree that had fallen over the path. "You remind me of my ma."

"How did she die?"

He glanced at her. "Quite horribly."

She was quiet for a time, and he wondered if she was considering the deaths of her own family members. When she spoke, her tone was harsh. "Death is always horrible. It's merciless. If you manage to escape it, you change into someone you would never have imagined."

"Maybe," he acknowledged. "But it doesn't have to be that way. There's forgiveness."

She gave a mirthless laugh. "I suppose you've forgiven me?"

"Nothing you did is worth holding a grudge over."

"Even when I made you lose your house?"

He laughed. "Especially then. I hated that house."

She looked at him as if he was crazy. "You might not feel that way when we get back to Dempsey and you have nowhere to live."

He raised an eyebrow. "I'll just live in your apartment. I lived there before you did, you know."

She narrowed her eyes and reached over to pinch him hard on the arm.

"Ouch!" He rubbed the spot.

"You will *not*. Living together in the woods is one thing, but living together in town would be completely inappropriate," she said indignantly.

He shrugged. "We won't be together, because you'll be living in jail."

At first, she was surprised, but eventually he saw a flash of humor. She pinched him again.

"Ow! You're going to get it!" he protested.

For a moment, they hesitated, staring each other down. Then, to Evan's surprise, Beatrice ran off into the brush with a shriek of laughter.

It took him a moment to comprehend what she was doing. But when he figured it out, he dropped his things with a grin and went after her.

She shimmied down a ravine and into a clearing before his long legs caught up with hers. He grabbed her around the middle and lifted her into the air as she kicked and screamed, giggling.

"Did you really think you could get away from me?" he admonished as she struggled.

She managed to reach behind her and tickle his sides until he had to let her go since he was hardly able to breathe from laughing. She ran, but she tripped over a log and fell into a bed of leaves. He caught her foot as she tried to squirm away. Pulling her back, he captured her in the circle of his arms. She wriggled against him until her giggles faded away, and then she was silent. She smiled at him, and he couldn't breathe. She was so beautiful, all flushed and happy and breathing hard.

"Your heart is racing," he said.

"So is yours."

"Oh, Beatrice," he breathed. "I want to …"

She nodded, still smiling. "Then do it," she said.

He stared at her, unhinged by her invitation.

He almost took her up on her offer. Almost. Her lips parted and she watched him with a sort of challenge in her expression.

"Blast it!" He sat up and pulled her with him. He couldn't do it. Not like this. They were blowing off steam and avoiding hard conversations. A moment like this one – one he'd dreamed about for years – shouldn't be stolen too early.

"There's going to come a time," he promised her, "when I'm going to collect on your invitation."

He stood up, pulling her with him. Without a word, they turned and headed back to the path.

Thirty-Four

When they arrived outside Dempsey and saw the town bustling, Beatrice's courage failed her. She stopped walking. Was there time to run away without Evan catching her? She ruled it out when she remembered how fast he'd overtaken her in the woods.

She felt his hand on her elbow and heard his voice soft in her ear. "You won't be alone."

"I'd rather be alone," she argued. "In the woods."

As she followed him into town, she realized her priorities had changed. If they hadn't, she wouldn't have come back. Why was she now willing to face the demons? And could she put Evan's heart at such risk for the sake of her sick one?

"What are you thinking about?" he asked, his fingers brushing against hers.

"You."

She didn't offer another explanation. She moved forward resolutely. There was no use prolonging the inevitable.

"Wait," Evan caught her arm. "Go home first, Beatrice. Take a bath and change. When you turn yourself in, the sheriff will need to lock you up because you jumped your bail."

She had known it, but she had needed the reminder. And she appreciated the extra time to prepare, though part of her just wanted to get on with it. He led her along the creek where they wouldn't be seen, right to her apartment door. Before he left, she reached on tiptoes to kiss him on the cheek.

"Thank you for everything, Evan."

"Don't talk like it's all over," he said. "We'll get this worked out and then we'll talk about what's next."

She gulped. She could hardly contemplate the next few days, let alone years after that. And she couldn't expect Evan to be further involved with her if she were sent to the women's reformatory all the way over in Marysville. But since she didn't wish to argue with him, she nodded. "Okay."

An hour later, when she had pulled all the leaves from her hair and washed away the dirt, she felt more socially acceptable. She dressed in her skirt and blouse and gathered her belongings – a few books and items of clothing, her mother's brooch and her father's pocket watch – and left them in her mother's carpetbag by the door. If anyone else needed the apartment, it would be easy to move her things out. She took one last look around the stark room and closed the door firmly behind her.

She carried her stack of library books to the bottom of the stairs, intent to return them before she went to the police station, but Evan came around the corner as she was heading out.

"I'll take care of those." He took the books and went to set them inside the Merchant's front door. When he returned, he gestured to the horse and buggy waiting on the street in front of the parsonage. "We're going out to the Whitley farm before we go anywhere else."

"Why?" Now that she was prepared to meet her fate, she didn't like the thought of putting it off any longer.

He held out his arm. "Because if I know you, you haven't had a bite to eat since those berries we found on the way home."

He was correct. She didn't give him the satisfaction by admitting it.

He helped her into the small buggy and went to the other side. His presence filled any remaining space in the seat. He rested a foot on the dashboard and his free arm behind her back. With the flip of the reins, they were off for the farm.

As they entered the woods, alive with green leaves and the smell of blossoms permeating the air, she was reminded of their little log cabin and felt a wistful pull at her heart.

He pulled out a mason jar of liquid. "I made you some more tonic."

She smiled and took the jar. "Thank you, Evan."

"Someone's got to take care of you."

His hand came forward behind her and squeezed her shoulder. She closed her eyes, her senses warning her that being this close to a man would make her think of her Edward. Instead of attempting to get away, she gritted her teeth and waited for the sad, desperate feeling to pass. To her surprise, it did. This was not Edward holding her. This was Evan, and he was strong and real and alive.

She turned suddenly, before she could change her mind or overthink what she was doing, and buried her head against his chest. She listened to his heartbeat, strong and steady. His hand slipped to her waist and pulled her closer to him, kissing the top of her head.

"It's going to be okay, you know."

"This won't be easy. I'm not going to lie to either of you." Joshua drummed his fingers on the kitchen table as Beatrice and Evan sat opposite him. It wasn't hard for Beatrice to see he was concerned about her odds. Her heart sank, not for her sake, but for Evan's.

"The people in this town are still put out about the fire. More so since you disappeared. They figure you ran because you're guilty," Joshua said in his blunt, gruff manner.

"She didn't do it," Evan reminded him. "She ran because she knew she wasn't going to be given a fair chance."

Joshua regarded Evan, but his perceptive eyes trailed back to Beatrice as he continued to drum his fingers. Ba-dum. Ba-dum.

Kathleen brought the meatloaf and potatoes to the table. "Aunt Amelia took the boys and Ellen to the summer kitchen to eat their dinner," Kathleen said as she sat next to her husband and gave them a brave smile.

Beatrice saw weariness in Kathleen's eyes and didn't miss the tense exchanges between the married couple. A rush of sympathy surprised her. They had lost so much.

"Beatrice, I'm going to do what I can to help you; mark my words." Joshua folded his hands and blessed the food.

When supper was done and Beatrice had finished helping Kathleen with the dishes, she excused herself to visit the outhouse before Evan would take her to the police station.

But when she came out of the latrine, she was startled by a group of angry looking men standing at the back door of the house. The group was led by Jacob Wylie.

"There she is! Catch her!"

She didn't move, so the sheriff hurried forward and awkwardly placed handcuffs around her wrists. They were too large and she could have easily slipped her hands out of them, but she didn't. She lifted her chin and glared at him.

"What are you doing?" Evan demanded from the porch.

The sheriff grabbed her arm and pulled her in the direction of the police automobile. She stumbled in the gravel, falling to her knees since she couldn't break her fall with her hands. She cried out in pain.

Evan was quickly by her side, holding her arms and helping her up. He brushed off her skirt for her, since her hands were bound, and then he stood in front of her, facing the men. "You should be ashamed of yourselves."

"We're just apprehending a suspect, Evan," the sheriff said in warning. "Out of the way or I'll have to arrest you right along with her." He leaned around Evan and took Beatrice's arm again, though this time he let her walk at her own pace.

"I'll have you know that Beatrice was on her way into town to turn herself in. I'm the one that insisted she have a decent meal first."

"How in the world you going to prove that, Masters?" Wylie shrugged, amused.

"It's true." Joshua stood on the brick path with his arms

crossed over his chest. "I had her in my custody. You know that's good enough, Sheriff Mavis."

Mavis put Beatrice in the car and eyed Joshua for a long moment.

Wylie stepped closer to Sheriff Mavis. "He's obviously covering for her. All of these people are in on it. They should all be arrested." Beatrice heard the forceful intent in his voice.

"I want to give you all the benefit of the doubt," Mavis said. "But the truth is, there isn't a way to prove what you're saying. I've plenty of cause to arrest her. Bail jumping, failure to appear in court. Those are serious crimes, and you, of all people, know it, Whitley."

"Doesn't change the fact she's innocent to begin with," Evan shot back.

Jacob scoffed. "They're harboring a fugitive."

"Watch your mouth, Wylie. These are good, honest men. I won't have you maligning their good names. Get out of my way and let me be about my business."

Jacob stepped out of the way, but he fastened narrowed eyes on Joshua and Evan. As Mavis sat down in the front seat and turned on the car, Beatrice watched Wylie lean close to Evan and whisper something in his ear. Evan rushed at Jacob, but Joshua grabbed his arm and pulled him back.

She watched him sadly as he turned and met her gaze. She wanted to tell him so much. That she was doomed. That their beautiful dream together was over. That she was sorry.

She knew now it was no life, what she'd chosen. She'd been wrong to isolate herself. She had left herself completely at the mercy of Jacob Wylie, and there was no one but herself to blame for it.

She deserved what she got. And she would accept whatever might come.

Thirty-Five

Reason told Beatrice she was safe in her cell. Her nerves, however, could not be convinced. She jumped at every sudden male voice. Her heart pounded whenever the deputy sauntered past her cell and leered at her.

The humiliation grated on her. She reminded herself more than once that she had done wrong. She'd set a fire intending to burn the construction site. She'd run from the law at great expense to Evan. She deserved her incarceration. But it still irked her to be treated as a dangerous criminal.

Evan had complained long and quite loudly. He had stood at the sheriff's desk for a good hour arguing about her being left there overnight without her medicine.

"I've never heard of this *medicine* you keep talking about. Far as I know, Lily of the Valley is poison. How do I know you're not trying to help her kill herself to avoid her trial?"

"You really think I'd do that?"

"I know you talked me into letting her out on bail and she took off. Cost you your house."

"I also brought her back, didn't I?" Evan said, impatient.

"No one knows what happened for sure. Jacob Wylie is convinced you were caught trying to help her escape."

Evan had roared in frustration, which probably didn't help her case. "Jacob Wylie is a manipulative trickster!"

"So says you."

Beatrice listened from her cell as Evan paced the floor. "If she doesn't have that tonic, the stress may be too much for her. She has a weak heart."

The sheriff sighed. "I'm sorry. But I asked Luke and he said he didn't know anything about lily water being good for the heart. I have to take his word for it. He's the doc, not you."

"I'll talk to him."

The sheriff was quiet for a moment. "Can I just suggest you go home and rest?"

"I don't have a home," Evan reminded him.

"Well, go somewhere and put your feet up for a few hours. We'll work it out in the morning. The circuit judge is here and she is his only case. I won't leave her in there longer than necessary."

Beatrice had listened for Evan's response. He said nothing.

"Masters, you have to start being realistic." The deputy spoke from a different corner of the room. "If the judge or jury finds her guilty – and you know it's likely – she'll be sent to the reformatory. You'll probably never see her again."

"Why are you telling me this?" Evan demanded, his frustration almost palpable in the air.

"You should prepare yourself."

Beatrice had nodded sadly. The deputy was right. Evan would be better off letting her go.

Just let me go.

Now, in the still of night, when the only sound was the snoring of the town drunk, Beatrice went to the iron bars. They had rusted and been painted over. The paint was chipping off in places. She grasped them tightly until the rough edges dug into her skin and made her eyes sting with tears.

It occurred to her as the moonlight poured down and struck them. She was like those bars. She wanted to be presentable. She wanted everyone to think she was in complete control of her own destiny. But inside, deep in the recesses of her broken heart, her spirit had rusted away. Her hope had chipped and broken off, falling piece by piece onto the floor of her existence.

The condition of her soul was appalling. But she had no idea what to do about it. How did one go about mending damage from horrors such as those she had witnessed?

She surprised herself by whispering, a raspy sound in the dark, quiet room. "Lord."

She inhaled quickly. She had no right to speak that name. Part of her had no desire, either. But she pressed on, before she could talk herself out of the prayer.

"Lord, Father used to tell us to *go forward in faith*. He always said trusting in Jesus was the answer to any problem. But I don't know how to do that. I feel worn away. Useless. If you want me to live, and if there is some way through this, I need you to do the work for me. I need you to be strong in me."

A rush of emotion accompanied images of the tragedy. Her heart raced and her hands trembled on the bars. She sank to her knees and pressed her forehead against the cold iron. She faced her coldest, darkest night and wondered what would become of her in the morning.

God has forgotten me. He has given me up to my grief.

She awoke in the same position on the cold floor. As soon as her eyes opened, she gasped and clutched her aching chest.

"Come on, Miss Walsh, up and at 'em." The deputy opened the cell with a series of clanks and hauled her up as if she was a rag doll.

She tried to keep up with him as he led her across the street to the courthouse. Her heart started to race and she stumbled. He greeted acquaintances and tipped his hat to ladies, apparently unaware of her struggle. When he finally dragged her inside and deposited her in a chair by the door, she was seeing black around the corners of her vision. She gasped for every tiny breath of air.

"Better get Luke. She looks a little peaked." Sheriff Mavis told the deputy as he looked over from the judge's bench where he was talking to Judge Graves.

Beatrice determined she would not stand to have this trial put off and have to spend another night in that cell. She took deep, slow breaths, willing her heart to slow down. She tried to imagine the stress on her heart blown away with each exhale. How she wished for a spoonful of Evan's tonic.

By the time the doctor arrived, her condition had improved. She was not well, but she could at least walk up to the defendant's chair in front of the full courtroom without someone having to carry her.

"Better stay close," the judge told Luke.

"I will," Luke said, holding Beatrice's wrist a bit longer than was needed to take her pulse. He glanced at her with sorrow. Was he disappointed in her? Did he think she was guilty, too?

"Thank you," she said quietly, surprising herself as much as the doctor. She wanted him to believe the best about her. He'd always been kind and honest and she was grateful for it.

Jacob was the first witness for the prosecution. Before he sat down, he gave the crowd a charming grin. "Let me just say that despite the opposition, the theater has made strides and is set to open a week from Friday. Dempsey will join the ranks of the elite cities across the country. You will enjoy entertainment, even movie films, and Vaudeville acts. I applaud you for your forward thinking."

The room erupted in applause, though the judge frowned his disapproval. Beatrice stared sadly at her hands. Had she been gone that long? She had hoped the structure remained a skeleton and the people had lost interest in the theater.

They could die in his firetrap, and it would be her fault for not stopping it.

"Miss Walsh?" Judge Graves was watching her in duty-bound concern. The jury and the onlookers also gawked at her. She reached for her neck and labored to breathe.

Luke stood, but the judge motioned for him to wait. The entire room watched her, as if she was a side-show at a circus.

The doors opened. Evan came through, tall and strong and so

wonderfully out of his true character in that silly suit and bowler hat. He pulled the hat off as he stopped short, staring at her. The crowd turned to watch him, but he didn't seem to notice. His eyes sought hers with an unspoken question. The invisible hand around her heart eased its cruel grip, if only slightly.

He sat down in the front row, nodding at her in encouragement. She heard his silent message.

Whatever happens, we'll get through it together.

Thirty-Six

Evan could see as plain as day Beatrice wasn't doing well. He wished he could help her, but judging from the somber-faced group of men on the jury and the stern expression of Judge Graves, he was powerless. All he could do was pray she'd have the strength to withstand it.

Throughout the morning, it became clear Jacob had one key piece of evidence, his eyewitness. Elvira was brought back to the witness stand to repeat her testimony. Jacob must have bribed her. Her eyes darted to his face often, as if she was afraid she wouldn't get the story straight. Couldn't the judge and jury see the shifty behavior?

Overton didn't call Beatrice to the witness stand. Evan could only guess why not, but he was relieved. The prosecuting attorney would only press her about her involvement and Evan was afraid for her condition.

Mid-afternoon, Evan was called again to the witness stand. It had been his request of Overton, because the first time around had been so rushed and incomplete. He had given Overton specific questions to ask, and he prayed the man would comply.

"Evan Masters, please state your relationship with the defendant," Overton said in a bored tone. Evan was tempted to pick up the lazy little man and knock him around until he took care with his job.

"We are friends. We have been for twelve years."

"A friend might cover up the wrong done by the defendant. Your affection for Miss Walsh is no secret, is it?"

"It's the truth. I've always held an interest in her. But Miss Walsh has never returned that affection. She insisted we remain acquaintances for reasons she wouldn't reveal. I am not testifying because I'm her friend or because there's no one else. I'm here because I was with her that evening and I can assure this court she did not commit this crime."

Overton waved his hand for Evan to explain.

Beatrice's fierce expression caught his eye. She wouldn't like him telling the whole story. But Joshua had encouraged him to speak the whole truth, even if it revealed her mistake.

"The night in question, I couldn't sleep. I took a walk and ended up passing by the theater site. I noticed someone in the midst of it, and I found it to be Beatrice Walsh."

Evan had the attention of everyone in the room. Beatrice watched him, breathing quickly and holding the armrests of her chair with white knuckles.

The lawyer even seemed a little nervous to let him continue. At least Overton was actually showing some interest in winning his case. Wylie smirked, confident that Evan's story would seal the guilty verdict. He probably assumed Evan was doing his job for him.

"Well, go on," Overton said. "What was she doing?"

"She was setting a fire."

The room erupted in murmurs. Beatrice's eyes flashed with a sense of betrayal.

He spoke firmly and loudly over the voices. "I'm not finished."

The judge pounded his gavel against the podium. "Order in the court." They quieted. "Go on, Mr. Masters."

"I asked her what she was doing and she said she was trying to protect the citizens of Dempsey. She didn't want them to experience the same devastating loss she had."

He avoided Beatrice's gaze. He was partially guessing as to her motive. He could only assume her family's deaths were connected to her worries about the theater. He wanted them to know exactly what had happened to her, but he didn't know, and even if she'd told him, it wouldn't have been his story to tell.

He pressed on. "I told her it wasn't the way, that I would help her. We put out the fire. I made sure it was completely extinguished, and then I saw her back to her apartment.

Overton didn't belabor the point. "As you said before. No further questions."

Jacob Wylie's lawyer stood and adjusted his designer suit. "Mr. Masters, do you believe that two wrongs make a right?"

Evan narrowed his eyes. "Of course not."

"And yet, you have not presented all of this evidence before now. You have been protecting her. It's almost as if you believe you are above the law."

"I'm not. I only believed that she had the right to tell her story herself."

"And yet you have told it." The lawyer stepped into the aisle and approached him. "What did you believe would happen as a result? That we would all become sympathetic to Miss Walsh's reasoning for her wrongdoing?"

"She didn't do anything wrong." Evan rolled his fist into a tight ball, wishing he could slam it into the man's jaw. "Neither one of us said it before because we were afraid it would be used against her. But I'm speaking the truth now because I believe in the people of this town. I believe they are capable of being reasonable and seeing facts for what they are. They can be trusted to see there is a lack of evidence against her, and they are probably already doubting Jacob Wylie's concocted story. His crimes of paying off a witness and setting the fire himself exceed Beatrice's momentary lack of judgment."

"You forget you have no evidence to back your claims, Mr. Masters," the lawyer said. "No further questions, your honor."

The judge was quiet for a long moment. His brow furrowed as he absently tapped the gavel against the desk. Finally, he heaved a sigh and looked at Beatrice.

"We've heard most of these testimonies before. Is there anything new to add?" He looked straight at Beatrice. "Miss Walsh, are you willing to tell us why you set the fire that Mr. Masters says he put out?"

Jacob Wylie stood up. "Objection! This is not how a trial is supposed to be carried out."

The judge glared at him. "Sit down, Wylie. This is my courtroom and I'll ask all the questions I want before a decision is made."

Jacob huffed, but he didn't reply.

The judge nodded at Beatrice.

Evan watched her survey the room with distrust. She wasn't going to say a word. He knew her well enough to know it. Her silence might well cost her the case.

As he suspected, she refused to speak.

The judge seemed pensive. "If you've nothing to say for yourself, we'll recess for the jury to deliberate on their ruling."

Beatrice shrugged.

Evan watched the sheriff lead her out of the room. He pressed his lips together and rubbed his temples. He needed evidence. Something to prove Jacob Wylie and his witness were lying.

He went to the hotel and found the woman who had testified. She was sweeping the long porch that wrapped around the front of the hotel.

"You have to tell them the truth," he said, standing in front of her and blocking her path. He hated to use his size to intimidate her, but he didn't have the luxury of time and she had lied to the court, after all. He saw her eyes widen and dart to either side, looking for an escape.

"I already said what I saw," she said in a shaky voice.

"You told the court a lie because Jacob Wylie paid you. Can you really let her go off to jail for something he did? Have some decency. That woman has been through so much, and it's not fair for you to do this in the name of greed. If she is sent away, she will die. Her very life is in your hands."

"What do you mean?" the woman asked suddenly. "Is she sick?"

He noticed her face had paled. Had he misjudged her?

"She has a heart condition."

The woman shook her head and held a hand to her forehead. "How did I get in the middle of this?"

"Did you see something that night?" Evan prodded, trying to keep his voice gentle.

She slowly nodded.

"What?" He took a step toward her. She backed up until she met the brick wall behind her. She seemed afraid of him.

"You saw Beatrice?" he asked.

She shook her head. "I saw Jacob Wylie." Her voice was a whisper. He had to lean in to hear what she was saying. "He set the fire. And then he saw me looking in the window watching him. He came in and threatened me. Said he'd hurt my babies. I have five kids and a husband who ran off. They'd be sitting ducks while I'm at work. I couldn't let anything happen to them. He told me I had to say I saw Miss Walsh setting the fire."

Evan felt pity as well as hope. "What he's done is a crime. If you tell the truth to the court, he won't be able to do anything to you or your family. He'll be in prison."

"What about me? Won't I get in trouble for lying?"

"Not if he threatened your children. Listen, this is his lie, not yours. No one is going to blame you."

She considered his words. "Do you promise we'll be okay? I sure don't like sending that woman to jail, especially if she's sick, but I have to put my kids first."

"Come with me. We'll talk to the sheriff. He can protect you."

The woman hesitated. For a long moment, he thought she might not agree to it. But to his relief, her features softened and she set the broom against the wall.

"Lead the way," she said.

Thirty-Seven

Joshua Whitley came to her cell to take her back to the courtroom. Beatrice knew the verdict. She was sure she was about to be convicted as he led her back down the aisle to the defendant's chair.

"You doing okay?" Joshua asked with genuine concern. She wished she could tell him. Tell someone. Anyone. The truth was a burden she wished she could unload. But who could she trust? Who wouldn't use her pain against her? It was better to remain quiet. After all, her pain belonged to her alone. It was her story. Her tragic song of a life gone horribly wrong.

No one would want to hear such a sad song, anyway.

The men in the jury box avoided eye contact, so she could guess what they had decided. And given the story they'd been told, she could hardly blame them.

She was guilty, after all. There was no getting around it. She *had* set a fire. If Evan hadn't found her and stopped her, she would have done exactly the crime she was accused of committing.

"Jury, I assume you've reached a verdict in this case?"

The foreman stood.

Before he could utter a word, the door burst open. Evan hurried through the doors, followed closely by the sheriff and the woman who had testified.

"Judge, we have new evidence to present," Evan said, out of

breath from exertion or excitement or both. "And you're going to want to put Jacob Wylie under arrest before he bolts right on out of here."

Jacob's face changed, reddening with anger. Joshua Whitley stepped up behind him and grabbed him by the arm.

"What is it, Masters?" the judge asked tentatively.

"Your honor, this woman was threatened by Jacob Wylie. She was made to do what he told her. He threatened the safety of her children."

"Your testimony was a lie?" Judge Graves asked.

Tears were in her eyes. "He made me do it!" She looked at Beatrice. "I'm so sorry."

"So you did not see anything that night?" the judge continued.

"I saw plenty," she replied. "I saw Jacob Wylie setting fire to his own theater."

♫

Beatrice went to the church from the courthouse. She didn't know what else to do. The jury had found her not guilty. She was free, but she sensed no release from bonds chaining her to the past.

Jacob had sworn the woman was lying, so the sheriff had gone to search the room he was staying in at the hotel and found a half empty glass bottle of kerosene and a store of large amounts of cash, which meant he had stolen some of the money given to him to build the theater. Beatrice assumed her missing money was probably included. Mavis arrested him immediately and promised he would escort him to Columbus the next morning for a criminal trial.

She hadn't even looked Evan in the eye on her way out. She knew he would hope if she did. He'd think they could be together. But being with him would take too much of her. More than she had. It would require the part of her she'd lost along the way.

The church was quiet when she entered. She went to the piano and touched the keys with trembling fingers. A longing went so deep her chest ached. What would it be like to really play? To expose all the hurting corners of her heart?

But she couldn't play a single note.

Amelia Morehouse came rushing from the back of the auditorium. "Beatrice! I just heard the news. I couldn't be happier for you."

Beatrice became enveloped in a warm hug that twisted her aching heart further.

"God be praised for truth claiming the victory," Amelia said, enraptured.

Beatrice tried to smile, but her eyes fell back to the keys. Wistfulness overwhelmed her. She saw no victory. She was still behind bars.

"Why don't you play?" Amelia asked. Beatrice could tell the woman was sizing her up. Trying to understand her. Next, she'd try to fix her. It was really too bad for Amelia that Beatrice was a hopeless undertaking.

"I can't."

"I've heard you play many times." Amelia sat down at the piano and her fingers casually met the keys. She started to play a melody Beatrice didn't recognize. The notes danced together in seamless harmony, evoking a peaceful feeling. Beatrice heard a minor chord, followed by a more hopeful major comrade.

Beatrice remembered Amelia telling her how she played the piano by feelings rather than by musical notation. Now she found herself intensely curious how it worked.

"Tell me how you do that."

Amelia stopped playing and patted the bench next to her. She nodded toward the keys.

"I have no music," Beatrice said.

"You don't need music."

Beatrice shrugged helplessly. Amelia considered her for a long moment before she rose and disappeared into the office. She came back within a minute, holding a white handkerchief.

"May I?" Amelia held the handkerchief in front of Beatrice's eyes.

Beatrice didn't want to be blindfolded, but stubbornness and curiosity got the best of her. She nodded.

Amelia tied the blindfold loosely around Beatrice's head and lifted her fingers to the keys. "What do you feel?"

"The keys."

"Tell me more. How do they feel?"

"Cold." Beatrice sighed, thinking of the way the cool ivory felt beneath her fingers. A strange thought occurred to her. "Sad. They make me feel sad."

"Why?" There was no judgment in Amelia's voice, only interest.

"Because I want to play them as if I know them. I want them to tell my story. I can hear yours as you play... how you have lost so much, but you still have hope."

Beatrice was surprised she had revealed so much. It was as if the words had escaped without her permission.

"You can play your song, Beatrice. You don't have to be afraid of it any longer," Amelia said softly.

Beatrice forced a laugh. "I can only play if I read the notes. I'm not like you."

"You can play by heart," Amelia insisted. "Play your song. Let everyone know what has happened. Let everyone know where your hope comes from."

Beatrice swallowed back the lump in her throat. "I don't have any hope left."

She felt Amelia's hands on her shoulders. "That's okay. Hope doesn't come from within you. Just be honest and admit where you are and watch how God shows himself to you."

Beatrice pulled the handkerchief off and shook her head. "It's no use. I can't feel him as you do. I think he left me when I lost everyone. He knew I'd never be able to trust him again."

Amelia was quiet as she ran compassionate fingers lightly over the length of Beatrice's hair. "You know Jesus suffered too, don't you?"

Beatrice considered it. "I guess I'd never thought about it."

"I don't even think the worst of his pain was his torture and death. I believe it was when his Father left him. God had to look away from all our sin Jesus was bearing. That moment, when Jesus watched the sky turn dark and knew he was without his father, that is when it seemed his world fell apart."

The silence of the church surrounded Beatrice like a comforting blanket. The tender cadence of Amelia's musical voice, so hushed and reverent, touched Beatrice as much as the song Amelia had been playing.

"Jesus knows how it feels to lose everything. He cares so much about your losses. He's cared every moment your song has been playing, from before the moment you gasped your first breath of air. He'll care just as deeply until the day you breathe your last, and then he'll hold you for eternity. Only trust him, Beatrice. He's big enough and strong enough to take on the pain that has been louder than your song." Amelia looked at her hands, blinking back tears. "I told my Kathleen the same. Jesus can be trusted with your hurts and your sin."

"*My* sin? I never did anything. I was the victim."

Amelia smiled and squeezed her arm. "We don't mind our sin as much as God does. He sees it from a different perspective. It helps to think of the choices you've been making from other perspectives. What have you done to God and to others by the choices you've made?"

Beatrice didn't expect to feel any differently, but she did as Amelia suggested. She thought of the Merchants and of Evan, trying so many times to provide for her needs.

"Was it sin to refuse to let people help me? Take care of me?"

Amelia didn't answer, but tears gathered in her eyes.

"And blaming God for the evils of this world... I guess that was wrong as well."

"If you could but see things from his perspective. How he loves you, Beatrice. How he loves."

Beatrice said nothing in response. She hardly dared to breathe lest the words find her and melt the ice around her heart. She couldn't afford trust. She didn't want to feel again. It was too painful, and it never ended well.

Amelia stood suddenly and moved away. Beatrice lifted her eyes to see what had caused her to leave so abruptly. She understood when she saw him.

Long moments passed. They had heard the soft click of the door as Amelia left, but neither of them spoke.

Finally, Beatrice sighed. "Go away, Evan. Leave me. You deserve to find your happiness. You deserve someone who isn't broken."

Evan shook his head, tossing his hands in the air in a gesture of frustration. "Why are you giving up? You've been given a second chance."

Beatrice shook her head and looked down at the piano.

His voice broke as he softly said the words. "Can't you see how hard I'm fighting for you?"

♫

Beatrice stared at him. She just sat there and stared at him with that maddening passive look on her face. Couldn't she at least look conflicted if she was going to reject him once again?

"I deserve it. You know, more than anyone else, that I deserve to be punished for what I fully intended to do that night with the fire."

He shook his head. "I don't accept that. I was there to stop you. You realized it was a bad idea and you didn't go back. I couldn't have just stood by and let that man run over your reputation and the rest of your life just as he might with that silly car if you were standing in his way in the road. Now he's the one who's going to jail for a long time. That's a victory, Beatrice. Can't you see it?"

She sighed and stood up. She went to the window and pressed her fingers against the pane of rolled glass. The texture distorted the view.

"Why are you doing this?" Evan's words echoed in the church building. He took two large steps and stood behind her. Close enough that he felt her body heat. Breathed in her lovely, delicate scent that had nothing to do with perfumes or lotions, but only her.

"I'm a danger to you, Evan."

He chuckled. "A danger? Have you noticed I'm a foot and a half taller than you are? Not to mention it would probably take about four of your arms to make one of mine. I feel safe enough."

A small smile played with the edges of her mouth, delighting him.

"That's not what I mean," she said, turning around. She probably hadn't realized he was standing so close. His chest was inches from her face. She looked up, startled, but she brought her hand to his chest and placed it over his heart. "I'm dangerous for your heart."

"Beatrice, that doesn't make any sense." He covered her hand with his.

"It does!" Tears appeared in her eyes and her hands turned to fists against his chest. "I didn't ask for this! I didn't ask for any of it!"

"Ask for what?" He grabbed her fists and bent closer to her face. "Tell me. Tell me why you're such a danger to me. Is it because you don't love me? You never did? I'm a grown man. I've been through the unimaginable. I've proven I can handle your rejection. So tell me. You owe me the truth."

She sniffed and shook her head. "If only it were that simple."

He hesitated. He'd expected a quick rejection. His eyes must have filled with hope because she shook her head.

"Don't even think it," she hissed. "You don't understand the whole story."

"Then tell me! Tell me why you would turn your back on everyone in this town. Why you would give up on God and accept a punishment you don't deserve."

A tear slipped from the corner of her eye. She attacked it with the back of her hand. "I had to give up on God. He asked too much."

Evan shook his head. "That's not his nature, Beatrice. He only asks us to face what he already knows we can get through with his help. His heart is for us. He is trustworthy."

"How can you say that?" She backed away from him, her features twisted in agony. "How can I ever trust a God who would tear me away from everyone I loved in the span of ten minutes and give me a lifetime of nightmares for my trouble?"

Evan felt a rush of emotion at the memories her words evoked. He'd been through hell, too. He knew what that felt like. "God didn't make those things happen, Beatrice. Not in the least. He was crying right along with us when we walked through our dark valleys."

"He could have stopped it. He's *God*! I trusted him enough to love my family, and he took them away. I won't let him do that to me again."

Evan understood then. "You're trying to protect yourself from love?"

She shook her head. "I'm not protecting myself. I'm protecting *you*."

Thirty-Eight

Evan felt his head spinning. "What in the world do you need to protect me from?"

She stared at him with flashing dark eyes, so even and calm though they were misty with tears. "You want the truth? Fine. I don't want you to have to watch me die. I don't want you to suffer because of me, and if you continue to pursue me, if we were to marry, you *would* suffer and it would be my fault. That is why I must protect you. We've both already had enough sorrow. More than any one heart should have to endure. Let it be. Leave me be."

He chuckled softly, more a sound of disbelief than mirth. She turned and sat down in the first row, prim and reserved. Her silence told him she'd shut down again.

"I'm sorry," he said, working to subdue his voice. "Your logic is fault-proof, I'll give you that. But to anyone else listening to it? It's hogwash."

"I don't care if it makes sense to you or not," she said with a certain air of superiority that infuriated him as much as it made him want to grab her and kiss her senseless. "It's *my* choice, Evan Masters."

"So let me get this straight. You lost your family and your fiancé, and you were injured badly. A doc gave you the idea you weren't going to live to see your thirtieth birthday, so you decided that instead of living every moment you had left to its fullest, you'd just retreat and wait to die? That doesn't fit your personality, Beatrice. I don't buy it."

He saw the flicker of interest in her expression. She glanced at him.

He continued. "You're smart. Really smart. You have thoughts that boggle my mind. You are funny and sharp and the most talented musician I've ever heard. All these gifts God gave you… he never meant for them to be packed away."

"How do you know that?" She lifted a cool gaze to his. He was amazed at her ability to withdraw from her emotions so suddenly.

"If you don't believe me, what about that story Jesus told? Pastor Merchant preached about it a while back." Evan went to the large display Bible on the communion table in front of the pulpit. He flipped to the gospels.

After hunting around for a moment, he found it. "Here it is. Matthew 25. *Then he which had received the one talent came and said, Lord, I knew thee that thou art a hard man, reaping where thou hast not sown and gathering where thou hast not strawed. And I was afraid, and went and hid thy talent in the earth: lo, there thou hast that is thine.*"

Beatrice calm disdain didn't soften. "What does that have to do with anything?"

Evan slapped his hand on the page. "Don't you see it? You're that servant, Beatrice! You're afraid of the one who gave your life to you. He wanted you to use it for his glory, not hide it away until it was time to face him. He expects us to do something with what he gave us, even if we lose everyone and everything and have to start over from scratch."

Suddenly she was standing, and her fists curled into tight balls. Her cheeks went pink and her breathing was labored. "You have no idea what I lived through. Don't speak to me about loss."

He almost reminded her of his losses. He could tell her the story of how a twelve-year-old boy violently lost his whole family in one day. He could tell her how it felt to set out on his own and have to work for everything he had. How hard it was to learn to trust again, and how many times he wished he'd died with everyone else. He knew it would prove his point. But he could see her wounds were deep and they'd healed poorly. She needed tenderness. She needed someone to stay by her side and love her out of the place where she hid from the pain. She didn't need a lecture.

"I'm sorry, Beatrice," he said, taking a step toward her. He reached for her hand. "I know you've been hurt. I don't mean to trivialize it."

There it was. He saw the moment a crack opened in Beatrice's wall of protection. A flash of vulnerability passed over her features and she bit her lip to keep it in check. He didn't intend to waste the opportunity. He took a big step toward her and let his arms do what they wanted, to slip around her waist and pull her to his chest. He didn't care that they were standing in church where anyone might walk in and see them. He figured he'd earned one embrace.

At first, he felt her body resist him. She pulled away, but as he gently pressed the back of her head toward him, she suddenly stopped fighting. She buried her face in his shirt and grabbed the seams with her fists.

And then Beatrice Walsh began to sob. "It's not fair," she cried. "It was all so pointless."

Evan's fingers tangled in her hair, as soft and inviting as he'd always imagined it to be. "Will you tell me about it?"

She hesitated. But soon she sighed against him, and more fight bled out of her. "Okay."

He took her hand and led her back to the first pew. They sat, and he pulled her small fingers to his lips. "I'm listening."

"I've seen the worst of people," she said sadly. "I've seen the vilest side of humanity and it makes me loathe the idea of trusting another human being. I suppose that sounds like nonsense."

He breathed a mirthless laugh. "You might be surprised."

She met his gaze and slowly nodded. Knowing that he could

relate seemed to give her courage.

"I gather your family died in a theater fire?" He prompted.

She slowly shook her head. "No. There *was* a fire when my family died. But my mother was trampled to death by a panicking mass of people pressed up against a theater door that was locked from the outside. Locked from the outside – so people wouldn't try to sit in better seats than they paid for. Was that really worth all those lives? Someone knocked my little brother over the balcony to be trampled below. My father and fiancé died trying to save others dealt the same fate."

Evan squeezed her hand. "I can't imagine. I had no idea. When did it happen?"

"It was the Iroquois Theatre Fire of 1903. In Chicago, just a few days after Christmas."

Understanding dawned. "I remember reading about it in the papers. So many died. Oh, Beatrice. Why didn't you tell me?"

She took a labored breath, covering her chest with her free hand. As he watched the motion, he realized exactly how her heart had been injured. It wasn't smoke or fire. She'd been trampled, too.

He squeezed her other hand in support, reaching to hold it with both of his hands, his arm resting across her leg as he leaned toward her. When she spoke, her voice was small and fearful.

"The worst was what happened to the children. They were crying… calling for someone to help them. Either they had been separated from their parents or their parents were trampled or died in the initial explosion. I remember… two little girls. They were probably sisters. They were holding each other and crying, when this large man ran past them, headed for the exit. He pushed them over and didn't even look back as the crowd trampled the girls to death."

Evan felt a hitch in his throat. "Beatrice, I'm so sorry," he whispered.

"A little boy reached for me and cried for my help. He was so scared. I tried to get to him, but before I got there the crowd pulled him under as he screamed for his mother. And then there was the baby…"

Beatrice's voice broke and Evan reached for her, holding her up as silent sobs shook her body. She trembled.

"It's okay," he said quietly. "Don't say it if it's too hard."

But as soon as he spoke the words, he felt her body tense. She steeled herself, pulling away to stare into his eyes. She was fierce, as if determined not to let the memories win this fight. He watched the tiny little woman in his arms become a warrior, and he thought he'd never seen a more lovely sight in all of his thirty-three years.

"The baby was dead, lying on the floor. His clothes had been ripped off." Her voice took on a high, shaky cadence as she drew a ragged breath. "His eyes were open, still in the expression of terror and suffering. His little body was battered and bloody." She shook her head in disbelief. "A *baby*, Evan."

His own eyes filled with tears as he tried to push away the memory of his dead baby sister. "I don't know what to say," he confessed. Now he understood the haunted expression she'd worn when Kathleen asked her to hold one of the twins. "Nothing is enough to tell you how sorry I am you had to see that. That those little ones had to suffer alongside your loved ones."

They were silent as they shared the burden of the memories for long moments.

"Was that when your heart was injured, then?" He finally asked.

She nodded. After swallowing hard, she opened her mouth, but it took a few seconds for the words to find a voice. "When I tried to grab the boy, I was carried up in the crowd, and then thrown to the floor on the other side of the door. People crawled or walked on top of me trying to get out of the burning theater. There… there were hardly any unlocked exits and all the ushers must have left. My chest became their floor. I remember lying there underneath all the shoes and feeling the constant pounding. I wasn't able to breathe. But someone pulled me up. I don't know who it was or how they got me out of the theater. I didn't wake up again until I was in the makeshift hospital fighting for my life."

The air in the auditorium of the church was still. Peaceful. As if all the violence of their pasts had made way to the surface and bled over, and all that remained was resignation.

"I know who saved you." Evan knew he must choose his words carefully, or her wounds would never heal. She would reject both God and him, and only darkness would remain for her future. He hesitated at the responsibility.

Jesus, help me speak the truth in a way she can accept.

He looked full into her reticent expression and took a deep breath. Her life depended on what he said next, and he felt the weight of it.

"I know who saved you in the theater, because it's the same person who saved me."

She met his eyes.

He steeled himself against the memories. "Pure evil took over my town that day. I knew it wasn't true, but it felt like God turned his eyes away and let the devil have his way for a few hours. My ma…"

He stopped and took a bolstering breath. It was too late to stop the barrage of recollections. He had thought about them so infrequently, the events had become like a locked chest in the corner of his mind. The images shocked him, as clearly as they had the day it happened. He steeled his jaw against the rage he felt.

"They… raped my ma and my older sister. They tied up my pa, put him along the wall with the other men in town and made them watch. The Barry Gang was convinced one of us knew where a box of gold had been buried, and they used the womenfolk to get someone to talk. It didn't work because none of us knew anything. That's when they started shooting folks."

Beatrice stared at him in horrified surprise, which gave him some measure of comfort. At least someone understood no one should have to die that way.

"They kept killing until every soul in that town was dead.

Thirty-seven people. Everyone except me."

"Why did they leave you alive?" she asked in a quiet voice.

"They didn't know they did," he answered. "They shot me same as everyone else." Evan stood up and pulled out his shirt, lifting it up so she could see the scar from the bullet that had pierced his abdomen. "I still remember the face of the boy who did it."

"A boy?" Beatrice gasped.

"He was about the same age as me. So nervous he was as white as a sheet. His old man forced him to look me in the eye and pull the trigger. I figure that's how outlaws are born. In moments like that."

"If only you could tell him he didn't kill you."

"He's mostly likely dead by now." Evan sat back down and folded his hands, leaning forward and resting his elbows on his knees.

They were quiet again. Evan tried to back away from the memories before he ended up thinking about how they'd killed his baby sister, still clinging to his dead mother.

"What in the world would give you hope after that?" Her tone was sharp, as if she challenged him to find any reason to live after such evil and devastation.

He sighed as he considered his answer. "My ma taught me from the time I was itty bitty that God was the boss. No amount of evil that happens in this broken world is big enough to take away his control. And she said that one day he'd make everything right. So really, there's nothing to fear. All evil is temporary. It can't stand against grace."

"*In the world ye shall have tribulation: but be of good cheer; I have overcome the world.*" Beatrice quoted the verse from the gospel of John in a hushed tone.

He nodded. "Where did you learn that?"

"My mother," she said, her voice distant. "I guess I put those things aside because they reminded me of her. Thinking about her makes me sad."

"When I first came to Dempsey, Pastor made me angry at every mention of the Lord. Which, as you know, was nearly constantly." Evan smiled at the memory.

She nodded and made a face expressing her agreement.

He chuckled. "Thing is, after a while I got used to it. I learned to associate God's words with my new life, and it lost the sting and gave me courage and power to go forward. That's the thing about Jesus. It's hard to stay away from him when he keeps reaching for you so hard. Letting you know you aren't alone."

Beatrice frowned. "Jesus never did that for me."

Evan tried not to laugh. How could she not see it? "Never?"

She caught his smile and her eyes narrowed. "I think I would know if God was speaking to me."

He nodded. "Thing is, most of the time his voice sounds like someone else's."

She pondered the thought as he watched her and waited for the truth to sink in. Finally, she looked up at him in surprise. "You."

He took her hands in his. How could he help it? She was so small and vulnerable yet so beautiful and fierce. He loved her. He'd always loved her. "If the only reason for me sticking so close all these years was so you could know God was reaching to you, I don't regret a single moment of it."

Thirty-Nine

Evan figured the rest would be easy. Of course, Beatrice would immediately let go of the sorrows of the past and live happily ever after with him in their new life together. Nothing was standing in their way now.

But he'd come to see people rarely cooperated with his dreams. And by people, he meant Beatrice.

She retreated into her apartment and stayed as summer overtook Dempsey in an array of hopeful, sunny days. If she came out, he saw her from his desk at the office, since he'd reluctantly asked for his old job back.

Since Evan had lost his home, Joshua invited him to live with them at the farm until he figured out what to do. The Whitleys had plenty he could do to help. It was too far to travel every day, though, so Doctor Luke invited him to stay at his apartment above the clinic during the week. He went to the Whitleys on weekends.

A month passed by, though it felt more like a year. The Merchant's house was quiet, and Evan couldn't help but listen for any sign of life from the apartment upstairs. He worried about her heart, and set a jar of lily water on the stairs every week, along with hearty casseroles from Mrs. Merchant. Beatrice took the offerings. It was the only way they knew she was still alive.

Being at the farm made it clear that Joshua and Kathleen were still struggling. They'd grown apart. The kids felt the strain and ran wild as Amelia tried to keep them entertained. She never complained, but Evan could see the stress of the environment wearing on her sensitive spirit. She was pale, and when he asked, she admitted she hadn't taken any time for writing lately.

Evan wondered why Kathleen was no longer tending her massive garden. In years past, it had been her pride and joy. But Joshua didn't question his wife's disinterest. It began to weigh on Evan. Kathleen was in the same place as Beatrice. She knew what needed to happen, but she wouldn't do it. She remained in limbo, and so everyone around her did as well.

Evan couldn't do or say much. So he prayed and tried to stay out of the way. God knew what needed to happen in each woman's heart to make them willing to look their sorrow in the face and accept it as part of their story.

"It's not easy, Lord," he prayed on his knees in the church early one June morning. "I know it first-hand. I still struggle some days to make sense of the pain. But you didn't put us here to be paralyzed by our wounds. You're stronger than anything we've faced. You're stronger than our stubbornness. Have your way, Lord. Whatever it takes, God, only be gentle with their hearts."

♫

Beatrice opened her eyes not long after she went to bed. She felt herself breathing fast, and her heart raced. What had pulled her from sleep?

She sat up. Voices. Panic.

At first, she planned to stay where she was. It was not her concern. She couldn't do anything, and no one expected her to, anyway. But she heard the door close down below and the sound of footsteps running along the sidewalk. Then the emergency bell sounded.

"Evan," she whispered into the darkness. What if he rushed off to some crisis and gave his life? Could she handle any more sorrow?

She rose and dressed in a hurry before descending the stairs with heavy, stumbling feet that wanted to return to the safety of the apartment. By the time she turned the corner by Wilson's drugstore, billows of gray smoke were wafting into the night sky, illuminated by the telltale light of flames.

The alarm continued. Beatrice panicked, her knees locking together and sending her careening to the blue slate stone sidewalk. She wanted to run away as far as she could to escape the horror.

The new theater was on fire.

Her fear of fire caused her to stop short and fight for breath. She was about to turn and run back home, but one sound kept her from fleeing. A child cried out, a haunting, pitiful sound nearly lost to the sounds of panic in the street and alarms blaring. She wondered if she had imagined it.

"I'm coming," she mumbled, pushing herself up and rising to her feet. She was before the theater in seconds, and the problem became obvious.

Jacob Wylie had promised the small-town theater would be built with every safety function in place. No one would die in his theater. He said he was concerned for public good, and he wouldn't cut corners to make more money.

He'd been a liar. She could see from a quick survey of the scene the large building had only one exit. Two doors, which swung inward, were impossible to open because of the mass of bodies on the other side of the thick glass. She stared at their faces and felt their terror. Smoke wafted from the windows just above them. They were coughing. Trying to breathe. Trying to escape.

She saw the sign above the theater. A film was advertised for that night. "*A Favorite Fool*, featuring Eddie Foy and the Seven Little Foys," she mumbled as she read the grand marquee above the doors. Eddie Foy? She knew that name.

She closed her eyes and saw his face. The panicked star Eddie Foy had stood on the stage of the Iroquois, trying to calm the crowd and keep them in their seats. She remembered feeling his indecision as he told them to stay seated and not to worry. He'd been worried. Enough to unsettle her and make her think it would be best for them to dash from their seats. Which is just what everyone eventually did.

Whoever had taken over the theater after Jacob Wylie had been sent to jail must have possessed as little integrity as their predecessor. She could easily see by the mass of people clamoring on the other side of the ineffective doors that far too many people had been allowed inside. Standing room only.

A full house, and now they would all die.

A man climbing a ladder to the second-floor window caught her attention. Was it Evan?

"No!" she screamed, running forward. "Evan, no!"

Her voice was swallowed up in smoke and noise. She saw him break the window with an ax and climb inside. She ran after him, lunging for the ladder and climbing up before anyone could stop her. She reached the top and crawled through the window, raking her palms over jagged glass and feeling the sticky warmth of blood.

"Evan!" she cried again, seeing him just ahead, proceeding undaunted through a thick haze of smoke. She coughed, recognizing the sensation of smoke filling her lungs.

He turned around, shocked. "Beatrice?" He hurried back to her. "What are you doing in here? Do you realize how dangerous this is?"

"*You're* here!" she snapped.

"I'm a volunteer fireman. It's my duty!"

"And I almost died in a theater fire. I know what to do. So I'd say it's my duty, too."

He only hesitated a few moments. Then he grabbed her hand and they ran.

They came through the office and into the auditorium so filled with smoke it was hard to see more than a foot in any direction. He stumbled along the aisle, holding her up. They found the entrance to the grand hallway where the people struggled, pressed up against the exit. Evan pushed through, determined to free the crowd. He held her hand tightly as they stumbled into the hallway.

Beatrice could think of only one way to attempt to subdue the panic. "Remain calm!" She yelled when they reached the doorway. "You must remain calm, or everyone will die!"

To her amazement, several around her stopped struggling and stood still to watch her. Others followed suit, though the majority of the crowd ignored her.

"We need all of you to take several steps back. Give Evan room so he can open the doors and free you. We'll all die here if you don't back up and give him enough space to open these doors."

At first, no one made a move to comply. They were screaming, crying the dreadful cries of the doomed. But she didn't give up. She yelled louder, aided by Evan's booming voice, and they pulled at the arms of the closest people, begging them to follow instructions. Finally, one by one, the people stopped wailing and took awkward steps back. They coughed and fought for air, carrying little ones or the injured in their arms.

Evan worked for a few tense moments to open the heavy glass doors surrounded by gold plated steel. He used the limited space he had to hack away at the thick glass until it finally broke, then he cleared the door of jagged edges so people could safely pass through. He was able to pull the other door open enough that people could begin to file out.

The two of them remained at their post and encouraged the people to make their exit in an orderly manner. Evan and Beatrice helped them through and made sure every man, woman and child was out of the foyer before they thought of leaving themselves.

Beatrice watched with satisfaction as children passed through the exit unharmed, their hands securely held by their parents. Maybe it didn't always have to end badly. Maybe people could learn to do things in a better way. Maybe the people of Dempsey didn't have to receive the same fate as those in Chicago that afternoon so many years before.

Maybe there had been a reason for the pain.

The room became darker, and she wondered if the smoke was

getting thicker. Her heart slowed, causing a warm, sleepy feeling to creep over her consciousness and steal it away.

She fell to the ground in a heap.

Forty

Beatrice tried to open her eyes. Her eyelids felt like cement blocks, her brain sluggish and foggy. She could not have been prepared for what she saw when she finally convinced them to open.

She sat up, staring around her in astonishment. She was lying on the stage of the Iroquois Theatre. It was untouched by the fire. Thick asbestos curtains lined either side of the polished planks that made up the stage floor. Lights illuminated the empty space with all of the thousands of chairs eerily vacant.

"Looks different than you remember, I suppose."

Beatrice whirled around and cried out in shock. "Edward?"

He stood across the stage, his hands stuck in his pockets, his white vest peeking out from under his gray pinstripe suit jacket. He wore the very same white straw hat with the black felt stripe she had seen him wear the last time she saw him. No soot marred the crisp white handkerchief in his pocket, and his face was as smooth and clean-shaven as ever. He wore his typical lopsided grin.

"I'm dead," she said.

"You aren't. This is just a visit."

She shook her head, confused. He came and helped her stand up. His hands were as cool and soft as she remembered.

"Why is this happening?" she asked, searching his dear

features for answers.

He smiled. "Because we have a message for you. Something you need to hear."

"We?" She peered around him.

"Your parents and brother are here," Edward said in confirmation.

Her heart felt like it swelled inside her chest. "I don't see them. There's no one here but us."

He raised an eyebrow. "Look again."

She did and suddenly the room was full. Children stood everywhere, their hands folded in front of them, smiles on their faces. Mothers held babies. Fathers stood in the background with easy grins. Her parents and brother stood in the front. Her heart clenched when she saw them.

"Can I talk to them?" she asked around a sob stuck in her throat.

"I speak for all of us."

Her eyes found Edward's again. He watched her in the tender way he once had. She smelled the aftershave she hadn't recalled in so many years, but now it seemed so familiar she could hardly believe she'd forgotten. She reached to him and felt his smooth face.

"You have something to say, Edward?"

He smiled. "You know me, darling. A man of few words."

"Who, then?"

He considered her, his smile never wavering. "I think you know."

She did. God was speaking to her.

"Thing is, most times God's voice sounds like someone else's."

She closed her eyes. "Evan said that."

"You've been avoiding him far too long. God never meant this for you. He has better things in store. But he won't force you to let him work in your life. You have to move aside and let him."

"But I don't know how to let you go, Edward. Or them. All I

ever see is your faces as you were dying." She nodded toward her family members, standing silently, watching her.

He chuckled softly and tweaked her chin. "We are just fine, Beatrice. Your parents and your brother and all those little children you wish you could have saved – we're at peace. Not one of us have wished for even a moment that our lives could have continued longer. We're where we are supposed to be. And someday, you'll be with us. But your song isn't over yet. There are still verses to be sung."

"I don't know how," she whispered.

"I know, beautiful girl, I know. But Jesus knows your song, backwards and forwards. You must trust him, and put your fingers down on those keys, and play. Just play, Bea. Play whatever song comes from your heart. That's what he wants for you."

Suddenly, Edward vanished, along with the rest. She was alone in the Iroquois theater. Fire had scorched every inch of it. It smelled of singed wood and damp earth and the unmistakable scent of suffering and death.

The door on the highest balcony was open. Light spread from it and reached all the way down to where she stood on the smoldering remnants of the stage.

"Come on, Beatrice." She heard Evan's voice, faint, but insistent. "Come to me."

For a long moment, Beatrice toyed with the idea of staying. Maybe Edward and her family would come back and take her to the happy place where they rested. She would like that.

But a greater part of her wanted Evan. Her heart clamored for him. He was worth the awful task of climbing out of the ruins. Maybe if she could make it out of the destroyed theater, just maybe... she could have a life with him. Maybe it would all make sense if she climbed out.

She opened her eyes, sat up and started toward his voice.

Forty-One

Most of the people had escaped before Evan was able to catch sight of Beatrice again. He didn't know if she'd already gotten out or if she'd retreated further into the burning building. He'd heard her shout directions to the crowd. She'd saved their lives. Every one of them owed their existence to her careful instructions.

But where was she now?

When the last person had passed through the exit safely, he went back, trying to shield his face from the smoke and heat from the fire that raged around him. The theater would be a pile of ashes in minutes.

He saw her then, and his heart lurched. She was lying in a crumpled heap on the floor, her arms at awkward angles. Was she dead?

"Beatrice!" He grabbed her and pulled her into his arms, making a mad dash for the exit. Behind him, an explosion rocked the building, and a ball of heat rose up so close he could feel it singe the back of his neck.

He took a flying leap through the broken window of the door and landed outside, gasping for air. He took Beatrice's limp head tenderly beneath his hand and used his other to check for a pulse in her neck.

Nothing. Neither did her chest rise or fall with breath.

"Breathe, Beatrice!" He stared at her, desperate. What should he do? Would anything bring her back?

As he called, frantic, Luke pushed his way through the crowd of gawkers.

"She's not breathing," Evan cried. "Please do something!"

Luke listened near her mouth and felt for a pulse. "Get them back," he said to Evan before he covered Beatrice's nose and put his mouth on top of hers.

Evan pushed back the crowd. "Give him room. This woman just saved your lives. Get back!"

He turned to see Luke breathe into Beatrice's mouth again. Hope flared as he saw her chest rise. But several moments later, Luke looked up at him with a stricken expression. He shook his head slightly.

"No." Evan fell to his knees beside Beatrice and grabbed her hand. "Please, God! Don't take her."

The crowd had gone so silent the only noise was the crackling of fire and the steady spray of water as the firemen tried to put out the blaze. Evan watched Beatrice's soot-covered and beautiful features, still and vacant.

"She's gone." Luke's tone was hushed.

Evan didn't believe it. His heart went numb, unwilling to accept that the love of his life had breathed her last and gone on to that mysterious other side where his parents and sisters dwelled.

"No," he whispered again.

But he saw a sudden tremor. Then her body went rigid and she heaved a violent cough.

"Sit her up," Luke commanded as he brought his stethoscope to her chest. "Her heart is beating again," he said in wonder.

She opened her eyes, watery and red from the smoke and the fit of coughing. She looked straight into Evan's eyes. "I'm alive?"

He laughed through his tears. "You're alive. You've lived through two fires, Beatrice. You're still here."

She didn't wake up again for several days. Luke had her

transferred to Mount Carmel Hospital in Columbus, where they could treat her burns and her heart. Evan stayed at the hospital, sitting beside her and holding her hand.

Finally, her eyes opened and met his. He saw the familiar flash of her stubborn will. "What are you doing here?" she mumbled with a raspy voice that delighted his soul.

"I'm waiting for you to wake up," he answered, feigning irritation. "It's about time."

♫

Beatrice fought the fog of her brain until she felt more clarity. She licked dry lips as Evan helped her sit up. He held a cup of water to her lips.

"Do you remember what happened?" He asked gently, the cadence of his deep voice resounding in her chest and through the bed beneath her. The room was quiet and nearly empty. A nurse moved nearby, checking a patient. The pure white of her uniform showed no hint of wrinkle or stain. The room smelled of carbolic lotion. She remembered the odor from the weeks she spent in the downtown Chicago Passavant Hospital so many years before.

"I didn't die," she said. He chuckled, and the sound vibrated on the invisible strings of her heart. She smiled. "I wish you'd been there the first time I woke up. After my family died. I was all alone."

"You've been alone for far too long, Beatrice," he admonished. The tenor of his tone surrounded her as a warm blanket, thawing the icy places of her heart that remained.

"I have," she admitted. His hand slipped into hers, his thumb creating a comforting passage across the back of her hand.

"You didn't have to face your demons alone," he said softly, in a low voice meant only for her. "I would have shared them with you."

She nodded. "I know it now. But then all I knew was pain."

"Pain, and an annoying man who wouldn't leave you be," he joked, but she saw the worry in his expression. Worry that it was still the truth.

"No. Never annoying."

He was quiet for a long time. "Why did you resist me for so long?"

Beatrice battled the honesty. It was difficult to tell the truth when she'd hid the real story from him for so long. "I have always been drawn to you, Evan."

His eyes widened in surprise at her calm admission. He sat up taller. "So then... why did you pretend I was the low-life scum of the earth?"

She felt an unexpected giggle rise up from her chest and release without her permission. It sounded rusty with disuse. Awkward. A grin broke out across his face, and he tentatively offered his other hand. She slipped her small fingers between his large ones.

"First of all, because the memories of what I went through are still very strong. When I am close to you, though you look nothing like him and have a completely different personality, it reminds me of Edward. It makes me feel like he died all over again. But I'm starting to wonder... well, perhaps it would get easier with time."

He nodded in silent agreement. He waited for her to go on. They both realized there was a question yet unspoken.

"But...?" he prompted.

"Beyond that is the more difficult problem," she said, tugging her hand back. He refused to release it. She gave up and let him hold her and give her strength to speak the truth. She opened her mouth, but she couldn't form the words.

He was resolute. "This is only between you and me. It's a discussion we need to have. You can say anything."

She gave a short nod and stared at their intertwined fingers. She hesitated, clearing her throat. He waited patiently.

"The doctor who told me I would likely not live to see the age of thirty also warned me it would be dangerous for me to marry and have children. I didn't want to start a life with you, knowing I could die in your arms the first day. Not to mention the desire you have for a family. You haven't made that a secret."

"I remember you hinting at that when we were out in the woods." He sat back, exhaling.

She continued. "If I was to be with child, the pregnancy or labor would probably kill me. And your unborn child."

After a hesitation, he nodded. "I understand what you're saying. I've had occasion to consider it."

She waited, watching him.

He leaned forward, holding her hands against his chest. "What did God say when you prayed about it?"

She had no answer. She felt the familiar pull toward the divine. Why did she keep rejecting Christ's love? Fear? She no longer had any idea why she resisted him. "I guess I never really asked his opinion."

"You never asked mine, either."

She faltered as she tried to speak. "I don't know why… it just seemed like there was only one choice that would keep you safe. I didn't believe God would want us to be married when it posed such great risk to you. It wasn't fair."

"You made a decision for both of us without having all the facts. You only considered your own opinion. Beatrice, I don't believe God gives us life so we can always be safe and never know loss. That is our risk as fragile human beings. I could walk out of the building and be run over by one of those Roadsters and never breathe another breath. We are all really just one heartbeat away from heaven. That can't be why we do or don't do things. It *can't*."

"Maybe it's like my mother used to say," she mused. "If you're scared of something, you don't run away from it. You go toward it. And you realize it isn't as frightening as you supposed it was at first."

He nodded. "I'm no stranger to loss. I'm not afraid of it, either. Since God has extended your life – and mine – this long, and kept you safe through not one, but two theater fires, maybe he's got a different plan for you than what that doctor told you. Is it possible you might die? Maybe. But until we're dead, we have to find a way to make it work."

He refocused his gaze on her face, and smiled tenderly. "I love you, Beatrice. I'd never do anything to hurt you. If something caused you stress, I wouldn't do it. I'd wait as long as you needed to make sure you were relaxed and comfortable. And then what if you came to be expecting? We'd get through that the same way. One day at a time. We'd beg God to be merciful and heal your heart so you and the baby could survive."

He smiled with such affection, she thought her injured heart might twist right out of her chest, it ached so.

"Wouldn't you like to live every day God has for you to the fullest? He already has the span of your life counted, to the very day and hour. The Bible says that. And I'd like to spend every moment you or I have left on this earth – together."

She didn't know what to say. He was opening a door she'd assumed was impossible to unlock. Now that it was standing open, it seemed so easy to step through it. To take that leap of faith and trust. But would he regret it?

"I want to trust God," she admitted. "I want to trust you."

He brought her fingers once more to his warm lips and his face took on an almost pained expression as he tenderly kissed her knuckles. "Then marry me."

She decided to answer before she could think better of it. *Lord Jesus, if this is a mistake, stop us. Don't let us go down a road you haven't planned for us. For him. But if it's what you want, I surrender. Completely. Both to you and to him.*

"I suppose," was all she said aloud.

He scooted closer to her on the hospital bed and brought his lips near hers. He paused, searching her eyes for permission. She slowly nodded.

His lips closed over hers in the sweetest sensation she'd ever felt. It was not her first kiss, but this was different from Edward's youthful expressions of young love. Evan's kiss told her he would love her in her weakness and vulnerability. Protect her by his gentleness and kindness. She was cherished, and he would see that every last day she survived meant something. As he brought his hand to her neck and pulled her closer, tilting his face in order to kiss her again, she felt her heart speed up and a warmth settle in her middle.

Before the kiss became overly passionate, he leaned back and smiled. He reached a gentle hand to the space on her chest just below her collarbone and waited to feel her heartbeat.

"A little fast," he decided. Then he brought her hand to his chest, where she felt a wild thumping. "But not as fast as mine."

Forty-Two

Evan heaved a sigh and stared at himself in the mirror. It seemed surreal. The day he'd longed for nearly half his life had come. Today he would make Beatrice Walsh his wife.

Now that he was looking marriage in the face, he could see he'd been looking at it through a rosy hue.

"What if she dies on me?" he breathed the words meant only for his Savior. "Or… what if she gets mad at me for something and won't talk to me for ten years?"

Beatrice wouldn't be the easiest woman to love. He had to be reconciled to that. He had to be willing to go the distance she might not go. It was his responsibility. He was taking on the role of the husband. He had to act like Jesus.

Act like Jesus. How did a sinner go about such a task? It seemed too big.

He came out of his room and down the stairs and saw Luke writing notes at his desk in the clinic. His friend looked up.

"Beautiful day for a wedding." Luke gestured to the window where sun streamed in with subtle promises. "How do you feel?"

"A little nervous," Evan admitted. "What if she doesn't show up?"

Luke laughed. He stood and adjusted his tie as he crossed the room to Evan. He held out his hand. "She'd be crazy to run away now, Evan. One step in front of the other."

Evan shook his hand, and they left the clinic. "Any last words about how I can keep her well?" He asked as they crossed the busy Saturday morning street and headed toward the spires with the ringing church bells.

"Love her. Be gentle with her. Your tonic seems to have made improvements, so keep making it for her. Make sure she eats the foods God made, gets regular exercise and plenty of sleep. That's all you can do, Evan. Beyond that, pray for her healing."

Evan was nodding at Luke and didn't see a man headed his way. They collided and Evan fell hard.

"Sorry, sir." Daniel Barrington, Wylie's foreman for the theater and the man who unsettled Evan with a sense of familiarity, offered a hand to Evan. Evan started to reach out, but he saw something that stopped him. He stared at the hand with a sudden recollection. Barrington's right palm bore a small white scar in the shape of a B.

"You." Evan scrambled to his feet without help.

Daniel looked at his palm and at Evan. He took a step back. "Pardon?"

"You were with the Barry gang."

Daniel held out his hands in front of him. "Look, mister, if you're mad about the theater fire, I don't know what to tell you. It was Wylie who took the short cuts. It wasn't my call."

"I'm not talking about the theater. You were a member of the Barry gang in Wyoming territory twenty years ago, weren't you?"

Daniel chuckled, nervous. "I was just a kid."

Evan felt like a ton of bricks was pressing on his chest. "Am I wrong?"

"How do you know about that?" Daniel took another step back, his eyes darting to the side as if he was planning a swift getaway.

"Every soul in my town was murdered that day. I think I'd remember a tattoo like that. You all had them." Evan stared at the man's features. He had piercing blue eyes and black hair. Just like the kid who had pulled that trigger. "You were the one who shot me. Daniel Barrington is really Dan Barry, isn't he?"

Daniel went pale. His face showed fear, but mingled with a strange shade of hope. "You mean I didn't kill you?"

Evan's fists clenched at his sides. His breathing got faster and his face felt hot. Nothing would have felt better in that moment then slamming the man to the ground. His voice sounded tight when he spoke. "Your gang killed my entire town over a stupid box of gold we didn't have. Your people raped and killed my mother and sister. Murdered my pa and baby sister."

A look of despair came over Dan Barry. "I didn't want to!" He stepped back again, probably seeing the rage looming in Evan's stormy expression.

Evan breathed in and out of his nose, trying to control the urge to pummel him. He seethed, imagining what he could do to the scum standing there as if he deserved to live. He should die. He deserved to know as much mercy as he'd shown to Evan's family.

"I knew my past would catch up with me," Dan admitted, taking his hat off his head and wringing it in his hands.

"Oh, it has." Evan took a step toward him.

But a gentle voice spoke over the rage buzzing in his mind. He saw the man with different eyes he knew weren't his own. He saw brokenness. He could tell Dan hadn't recovered from that day any more than he had. Barry gulped and looked down at his hat like he was embarrassed to look him in the eye.

Barry abruptly pulled a gun from the holster at his side, causing Luke and everyone standing close enough to see it to gasp and jump back. Evan stopped short, putting his hands in the air. He was transported back to that moment twenty years before when he thought his life was over.

But Dan handed him the gun, handle first. "You all are my witnesses. I tried to kill this man. I thought I *had* killed him. The guilt's been eating away at me half my life. He's within his rights to shoot me dead."

The onlookers murmured to each other, but nobody tried to stop him.

Evan raised the gun.

He wanted to pull the trigger. He ached for revenge. He peered over the sight, finding the same perspective Barry had on him when they were kids. The thought of Barry lying in a puddle of his own blood gave him a feeling of satisfaction. He wanted it more than he'd wanted nearly anything else in his life.

Nearly anything.

Beatrice came flying down the apartment stairs of the parsonage, holding the hem of a white lacy dress with one hand and a bouquet of daisies with the other. She raced to the edge of the group and pushed her way through the onlookers.

"Evan, what are you doing?" She labored as she struggled to breathe.

"Beatrice," he faltered, staring at her. "You're… you're so beautiful."

She shook her head, her expression terrified. "Evan, what are you doing with that gun?"

Evan's gaze returned to Barry, who stood contritely, almost as if he wanted Evan to pull the trigger. As if it was the only thing that would release him from the guilt.

"This is him, Beatrice." Evan's finger played with the trigger. "The guy who shot me. Remember I told you what they did to my parents? My sisters?"

He could see her shaking her head out of the corner of his eye. "Lord, help him," she murmured.

Barry shifted and stared hard at the ground when he spoke. "My pa… he was a bad man. I was scared of him. He said he'd kill me too if I didn't shoot you." Barry still didn't look him in the eye as he spoke. "If it makes a difference – I didn't kill anyone else. I promise you. I didn't hurt anybody, either."

"Evan," Beatrice said. "Please put the gun down."

"I been living with this guilt so long. I just want to be free of it," Barry said.

Evan shook his head. He knew the way for a man to lay down the burden of sin. And it didn't involve getting shot with his own gun. *Lord, help me. What am I doing?*

He dropped the gun to his side. "I don't have any more right to kill you than you did me."

"I don't blame you. Neither will anyone else. No one cares whether I live or die," Barry said quietly.

"You have nothing to fear from me. I killed someone's son once, too. He forgave me that offense and took me on as his own family."

He looked up at Beatrice and saw the edges of her mouth curl upward in a small smile as she understood his words. Barry, on the other hand, registered shock.

Evan stepped forward and handed the gun back to Barry. "I forgive you."

He started to move toward Beatrice as the crowd around them began to disperse. Dan caught his arm. "But why? And who did you kill?"

"Jesus. My sin killed Jesus. When I didn't care about his love, when I wanted my way, that's when he died for me. In my place."

Evan turned away from Barry's stunned face and took Beatrice's hand. "I believe we're expected at the altar."

She squeezed his hand and they started to walk away. Dan Barry's voice stopped them a moment later.

"Do you believe that he died for everyone's sins?"

Evan turned around, and as he laid eyes on the man who had once attempted to take his life, he felt a rush of divine affection. He went back and clapped the man on the arm, feeling tears sting his eyes. "I don't just think it, Dan. I know he did."

Beatrice came forward and took Evan's hand again, looking at Dan. "You're welcome to attend our wedding. You could talk to our pastor afterward."

A smile threatened to break out in Dan's stormy face. "That'd be nice. Thanks."

And so, that sunny summer afternoon on the most perfect of days, two miracles occurred. First, Evan Masters actually lived his dream and stood up next to Beatrice Walsh and said his marriage vows. The true surprise came when – everyone held their breath to see if she'd actually go through with it – she said them back.

Then during the celebration of a union no one ever thought would come to be reality, a man broken by his past and by the burden of his wrongdoing laid it down at the cross and bent his knee to appeal to the Savior.

Lives changed forever that day. And in that wonderful, mysterious way that the good Lord leads his children, joy was found in the midst of sorrow. In the hollow, aching minor chords of a song that had been played too long, God wrote a new melody. The dark sounds were not erased, but they were redeemed as they found companionship in hope that comes from surrender and trust.

Epilogue

"I can hear that no good guitar-picking all the way back in Dempsey some nights. You ever going to learn how to play that thing?"

Joshua's teasing voice caused Evan's fingers to fall away from the strings of his guitar. "You come all the way out here to harass me in my own home?" he called.

Joshua came out of the brush carrying a sack over his shoulder. He climbed the stairs of the log cabin Evan and Beatrice had built themselves, deep in the woods. He shook Evan's hand with an affectionate crinkling around his eyes. "That what you're calling this? Home?"

"Home, sweet home," Evan said. "You can have your fancy farm with land to spare. I'll take this any day."

Joshua laughed and pounded Evan on the back. "Good to see you, brother."

"And you. Did you bring the kids?"

"Oh, yeah. They've already run down to the creek looking for your young'uns. Kathleen sent plenty of supplies as well, just to warn you. I have no idea where you'll put it all but the woman insisted and I haven't found a way to say no to her."

"You always were a pushover when it came to one woman." Evan smirked.

"Huh. That's a little funny coming from you."

Evan smiled. "How are things, Josh? How's Kathleen?"

Joshua nodded. He sniffed and set the heavy sack down on the porch. "You know how it goes, Evan. Life is hard. Marriage is hard. But Kathleen and I are doing okay. Much better these days. She's come back to me."

"You don't know how glad I am to hear that," Evan said, truly relieved.

"Hi, Uncle Evan." A redheaded girl with shiny curls and the biggest bluest eyes Evan had ever seen came up behind Joshua. Her cheeks were pink and freckled. She regarded him with a shy smile.

"Well, hello, Ellen McClellan." Evan smiled, using his pet name for the child. "Look at you, looking just as pretty as your mama."

"And my sister who lives with Jesus," she added.

"That's right." He put a hand on her shoulder. She waved and ran down the side of the yard toward the creek.

Joshua turned back to him. "Kathleen stayed home this time because she's feeling poorly." He chuckled sheepishly. "Actually, she's expecting."

Evan laughed. "That's great news, Josh. Congratulations."

"Kathleen ain't so sure. She told me if it's twins again, I'm to take my own bedroom."

"Can't really blame her."

Joshua's smile softened and he cleared his throat. "How are you doing, Evan? Really?"

Evan sighed as he felt a wave of emotion pass over him. "I have a home full of folk I love more than life. How could I not be well?"

Joshua nodded as a wail pierced the cabin's calm. "Sounds like nap time is over."

Evan motioned Joshua inside. He climbed the stairs and stepped into the little room with the crib he'd built when Beatrice was expecting their first child, a boy they'd named James Edward. They'd had another boy, Charlie, two years later.

He'd worried about her during both her pregnancies, and she'd had a scare or two, but she'd come through them feistier than ever. Four years had passed and they'd figured they were done having kids, but then she had surprised him with the news she was expecting again.

Evan picked up the wailing toddler, who quieted immediately. "Let's go see Uncle Josh."

Joshua grinned as Evan came down the stairs with his daughter. "Lily Sue! You're getting so big, ain't you, though?"

"Starting to look just like her ma," Evan said of her dark hair and chocolate eyes. "I think she's got her stubbornness, too."

"Lord, be merciful," Joshua said with a low whistle.

Evan put the toddler down and she went for Joshua's sack. Joshua pulled out a little teddy bear Kathleen had sewn for her. "What are you going to do, Evan? Any plans yet?"

Evan paused. He stared at his daughter. "I might go west. Start a cattle ranch. Raise this passel of Masters out on the open prairie as God intended."

Looking at Lily made his eyes sting with tears. He walked to the big window in the front of the house and looked out, trying to get control of his emotions. "I always said I was prepared to lose her. But I never thought I'd lose her like that."

Joshua didn't speak until he crossed to Evan and stood next to him. "I know, Evan. None of us did. It was just one of those things that happens to women after childbirth sometimes."

Evan nodded. "When she died after Lily's birth, and not from a weak heart, I thought I wanted to die too. It nearly did me in, even though I'd always promised her I'd be strong if I lost her. I couldn't imagine going on without her, even though it had always been the risk. But I made a promise to her and I will keep it. I will raise this family and not give in to the sorrow. I owe her that."

"And you will, brother."

Evan sighed and looked out the window again, where children danced up from the creek bed with screams of laughter. "They're good teachers. Children, I mean. They go on. They live. Even when their mama dies."

"One of the blessings of God, to be sure," Joshua agreed.

"It helps that I can still hear her song. It's faint, but I hear her playing on. So, I will, too. No matter where the road takes us. As long as it ends with me seeing her again."

Joshua nodded and spoke in a soft voice. "They're all waiting. All the folks we've lost. Singing us home."

"Oh, to be where they are." Evan sighed.

Joshua grabbed his shoulder and squeezed hard. "We will. Someday soon enough. Until then, we'll live."

Lily cried and reached for him to pick her up, which he did.

"I guess we better get on with it, then."

The End

A Note from the Author

To the mothers of those two little girls, that young boy, and that baby, who really did live and breathe and die an unimaginable death in a burning theater full of panicking people, I feel it is necessary to assure them someone has paid attention to their story. I have shed tears on their behalf as I imagined the terror they experienced in their final moments. It is my attempt to honor them by telling this story.

Though the world seems to want to forget the travesty and tragedy that happened on a cold afternoon in December of 1903, it will be remembered here, for whatever it is worth. Through Beatrice, I have expressed the pain I felt over what happened to those children, and so many other beautiful little lives that were cut short that day.

To the parents of these little ones: I can't imagine what it was like for you to lose grasp of your children in that crowded, burning theater. Did you succumb to the fire? Were you trampled? Is that why they were left alone? Did the mass of humanity press in and move you away from them? Were you screaming and reaching in desperation as you watched them slip away to their senseless deaths?

I can only pray to God, who is still present there in those moments with you, that he breathed his peace into your heart. That you found his salvation and comfort. That Jesus gathered your babies into his gentle arms and loved all the darkness away.

Now to you, my readers: I must tell you this was a heavy book to write. But I knew if I was going to tell the story of what happened to these children and over six hundred other souls, all in the space of a few minutes one cold Wednesday afternoon, I would have to be honest.

I wondered if the subject matter might be too disturbing to frame a story such as this, but in the end, I could not turn my back on it. There is a time for remembering the forgotten and pausing for a moment of reflection.

It is up to you what you do with this consideration. Whether you walk away and never think of it again, or you let the reality of the message of this story sink in and become a part of you, it is your choice.

You and I may never have to face the horrors they experienced in that theater, but none of us escapes seasons of sorrow, seasons of fear or seasons of loss. May we give our hurts to Jesus. May we surrender our lives to whatever lies before us with the joy of knowing no matter what this life can possibly throw at us, it can never take away his love. He is our constant. He is our sure, strong Rock.

Trust him with your wounds, friend. Have courage, walk forward in faith, and give him all.

For more information on the Iroquois Theatre fire, please visit my Pinterest page: www.pinterest.com/mirandashisler/this-is-my-song/

Acknowledgments

Thank you to Erin. Your friendship has meant so much to me over the past two years. Thank you for inspiring this book in the way you know you did even though you won't admit it. Thank you for being willing to embody Beatrice and take on a little bit of her sorrow as you posed for the cover art. Thanks for being my cheerleader on the dark days when I would rather hide and deny God ever called me to this ministry of writing. God knew I needed someone to believe in me.

Thank you to Angela, for being my proof that people who say they don't like reading fiction or don't have time for it can become one of the best reading buddies a girl could have. You deserve an award for how many books you've read in the past year. But then again, they are their own reward, aren't they?

Thank you to my mom. You're my inspiration. I'll never possess half the strength and poise you carry with you, especially after every valley God has asked you to walk through, but I'm proud to be your daughter. I love you. As you can tell, I've also found the advice about pursuing things that scare you until they don't scare you anymore helpful. So, thanks for passing that on.

Thank you to my pastor who presented a thought-provoking study on the life of Joseph that spurred Pastor Merchant's sermon.

Thank you to the best editor in the world, Tanya Dennis. (Learn more about her at tanyadennisbooks.com.) I trust you because you are honest. You're a woman of integrity. And you're really, really smart. Thanks for being emotionally and intelligently involved in every story and telling me exactly what I need to hear. I would have a hard time doing this without you. (And not nearly as much fun!)

Thank you, Jesus. I'm in awe of you. What a Savior, what a Friend! All for you.

About The Author

Miranda Shisler started writing stories when she learned to read. From that point on, she could usually be found either reading or writing.

She pursued music education and vocal performance at Cornerstone University, but after marrying the love of her life and starting a family, she clearly felt God's call to a writing ministry.

These days, she is busy homeschooling her four children, serving in the music ministry of her church, reading all the quality fiction she can get her hands on, and spending her evenings quite literally writing her heart out.

Connect with her online!

mirandashisler.blogspot.com
facebook.com/authormirandashisler
pinterest.com/mirandashisler/ (See the *This is my Song* board!)
goodreads.com/mirandashisler

Please remember this series is an Indie project so you can have the best reading experience. You can help Miranda (far more than you might think) by doing a review for *This is my Song* on Amazon and Goodreads today!

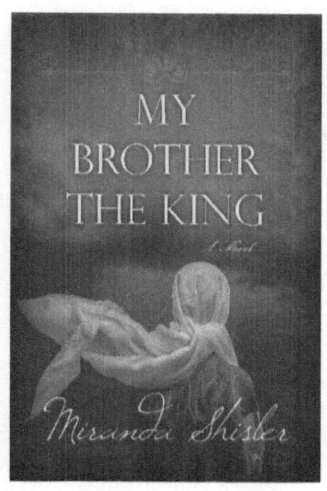

Unstable times. Oppression. The family of a carpenter, troubled by conflict.

This humble Nazareth home kept a secret. A king had been promised. And he would set their people free. But none of them expected their older brother to be that redeemer.

Take a journey into the stories of the brothers and sisters of Jesus. Ponder what it might have been like to grow up in the same house as God… and see him give his life as a ransom for many.

A ransom for them.

MY BROTHER THE KING
May 2018

www.ingramcontent.com/pod-product-compliance
Lightning Source LLC
Chambersburg PA
CBHW030319200626
46816CB00006BA/1846